Within Golden Bands

A Home for My Heart

By Norma Gail

GLOSSARY

A beannachd - Gaelic, a farewell blessing

Aga cooker - a heat storage stove and cooker, which works on the principle that a heavy rame made of cast iron can absorb heat from a relatively low-intensity but continuously burning source, and the accumulated heat can then be used for cooking.

aff my heid - Scots, I'm crazy

bairn - Gaelic, a baby or small child

bampot - trouble maker

bangers and mash - a traditional dish of Great Britain made up of sausages served with *mashed* potatoes. The sausages used to burst or "bang" while cooking because of rusk (dried bread) being added to the meat.

bannocks - a usually unleavened flat bread or biscuit made with oatmeal or barley meal and cooked in a skillet.

biscochitos - Spanish, a cookie made with lard and seasoned with anise and cinnamon developed in New Mexico from recipes from the Spanish colonists

bonnie - Gaelic, pleasing to the eye, pretty, attractive

bothy - A small shepherd's hut or rough holiday cottage

braw - Scots, fine, grand, superb

Brighde - (BREE-da) Gaelic, female name, equivalent to Bridget

burn - Gaelic, stream

caber - a pole, especially: a young tree trunk used for tossing as a trial of strength in a Scottish sport

cairngorms - Gaelic, are a mountain range in the eastern Highlands of Scotland closely associated with the mountain of the Cairn Gorm; a light-colored, usually yellowish smoky quartz that is used as a gemstone.

ceilidh - (KAY-lee) Gaelic, a social event at which there is Scottish or Irish folk to: music and singing, traditional dancing, and storytelling.

Cock a'leekie - a traditional Scottish soup of chicken, leeks, and either potatoes or barley.

coos - Scots, cows

Culloden - the final confrontation of the Jacobite Uprising of 1745. On 16 April 1746 the Jacobite forces of Charles Edward Stuart were decisively defeated by Hanoverian forces commanded by William Augustus, Duke of Cumberland near Inverness in the Scottish Highlands.

cuzzle - cuddle + nuzzle, to hold close in one's arms as a way of showing love or affection

Dinna fash yerself - Scots, don't worry or stress yourself, calm down

dreich - Scots, dull and rainy

drookit - Scots, soaking wet

eijit - Scots, fool, idiot

Eilidh - (AY-lee) Gaelic, a girl's name of Scottish origin meaning "sun, radiant one." Long popular in Scotland, this attractive name is widely considered to be the Gaelic version of Helen.

fair wabbit - Scots, exhausted, out of breath, unable to function due to extreme tiredness *feileadh mor* - is a long piece of cloth, which is hand pleated and wrapped around the user.

Garb Eilean - the name of an island at the east end of Loch Garry

guid – Gaelic, good

haggis - Gaelic, a savory pudding containing sheep's pluck (oatmeal, suet, spices, and salt, mixed with stock, and cooked while traditionally encased in the animal's stomach, though now often in an artificial casing instead.)

hen - Scots, a term of affection for a woman you have a close relationship with.

Hogmanay - (HOG-mə-NAY) Scots, the last day of the year and is synonymous with the celebration of the New Year (Gregorian calendar) in the Scottish manner.

hyperemesis gravidarum - is a pregnancy complication that is characterized by severe nausea, vomiting, weight loss, and possibly dehydration. Feeling faint may also occur.

Isla - (EYE-la) a feminine given name traditionally of primarily Scottish usage, derived from "Islay," which is the name of an island off the west coast of Scotland.

kirkyard - church yard

kyloe - Scots, a breed of small Highland cattle

loch - Gaelic, a body of water either a lake or a bay, literally "arm of the sea"

Madainn mhath - Gaelic, Good morning

mathair - Gaelic, mother

midges - a type of biting insect often referred to as "no see ums" in North America. The bite of the female causes a histamine response similar to mosquito bites.

mo bhrathair - Gaelic, my brother

mo chridhe - Gaelic, my heart's desire

mo gràdh - Gaelic, my love

mo mhac - Gaelic, my son

mo nighean - Gaelic, my daughter

mo phiuthar - Gaelic, my sister

Moran taing – Gaelic, much, or very great thanks or gratitude

nick - British slang for police station

peely-wally - Slang, pale and unwell

reivers - Scots, raiders along the Anglo-Scottish border from the late 13th century to the beginning of the 17th century.

Saltire - the Flag of Scotland is a white X-shaped cross, which represents the cross of the Patron Saint of Scotland, Saint Andrew on a blue sky. The flag is called the Saltire or the Saint Andrew's Cross.

sgian dubh - (skee-un DOO) Gaelic, a small, single-edged knife worn as part of traditional Scottish Highland dress along with the kilt.

skelped - Scots, to be smacked or slapped, usually about the face or buttocks.

stramash - Gaelic, a disturbance, racket, or crash

Seumas - (SHAY- mus) Gaelic, is a masculine given name in Scottish Gaelic and Scots, equivalent to the English James.

Shelagh - (SHEE-lə) Irish, a female name meaning heaven

Tha gaol agam ort - (Ha GOOL Akam orsht) Gaelic, my love is forever

wheesht - Scots, quiet

WITHIN GOLDEN BANDS

(For Kieran)
Such was my trust
That I gave you to hold
My fragile heart in your hands.
God blessed us so much
He placed us within
A circle of golden bands.
I ever will thank
My dear God above,
So carefully He watched over me.
He gave me to love
Such a precious heart,
No other will ever complete.
Through all of our years
I will have no regret,
If I searched a thousand lands.
So gently you keep
My own tender heart
Within our golden bands.

CHAPTER ONE

FORT WILLIAM, INVERNESS-SHIRE, SCOTLAND

The incessant beep of a heart monitor drew Bonny MacDonell out of the blackness, forcing her to look around. In the dim light of the yellow-curtained cubicle, her eyes traveled up the dark red length of tubing to where blood dripped from a plastic bag. The unpleasant odor of sickness and antiseptics only added to her panic.

Albuquerque?

Scotland?

Hazy images floated through her mind. Stabbing pain. Red spots on the carpet. Eleanor kneeling. What was their housekeeper doing?

"My baby!" Bonny's left hand slid to her abdomen, cupping the imperceptible swell of her tiny, unborn baby. The fear of losing this baby was a horrific monster ready to snatch their miracle. Why was she here?

Surgery failed. Pregnancy impossible. The voice sounded familiar, and Bonny lifted her eyelids, squinting in the half-lit room. "Dr. Carson?"

The old dream had come again, leaving brokenness in its wake. Stars flickered against a background of darkness. When a wave of nausea hit, she squeezed her eyes tight.

Morning sickness. Blue eyes filled with joy. Our baby. Hope-filled dreams made her want to laugh, dance, and sing. "Kieran?"

Icy rivers of disappointment flowed through her veins. Why was she alone?

A warm hand touched her arm, and she startled.

"Mrs. MacDonell, you're awake." A tall, slender woman with dark brown hair knotted on top of her head and soft brown eyes stood beside her.

"Y … yes." Her new name still sounded strange.

"I'm Sister Isla, your nurse."

Bonny's insides shriveled, curling into themselves. "Where am I? Where's Kieran?"

"You're in Belford Hospital in Fort William. You arrived by helicopter. I'll find out about your husband." Isla switched on the light and slid a paper from the pocket of her blue scrubs. "American. From Loch Garry. On holiday?"

The bright light hurt Bonny's eyes for the moment they took to adjust. "American, yes. But my husband … we have a sheep farm on Loch Garry." *Helicopter?* Fear fluttered, millions of moths trapped in her stomach, attempting to escape. The monitor beeped faster. "My baby?"

"Dr. Moncrieffe will want to know you're awake. I'll tell him." Isla slipped through the curtain and pulled it closed.

Tears brimmed, memories of the morning forming a knot that rose from her stomach to her chest. It lodged in her throat and pricked, pinecone-sharp. *Kieran went to the Laddie Wood after stray sheep. Cell phone service there was patchy at best.*

Their honeymoon began in the emergency room in her hometown of Albuquerque, delayed three weeks after the wedding, while they waited for Kieran to recover from a gunshot wound. Bonny grasped the edge of the sheet in her left hand and swiped her eyes, remembering his joy when they discovered she had become pregnant in those joyous first days of their marriage. She tried to warn him the risk was high. Her failed surgeries for endometriosis, the scar tissue, all made pregnancy risky for her and the baby. Were they to lose their miracle child at two and a half months?

"I heard you were awake." Dr. Moncrieffe's calm, deep voice pulled her from the memory of Kieran's sky-blue eyes dancing with sheer delight. The tall, white-haired man in green surgical scrubs who slid open the curtain was the epitome of kindness. They first met two weeks ago when her severe nausea, *hyperemesis gravidarum,* required a new prescription after their return to Scotland. The ultrasound was scheduled for the next day, twelve weeks after discovering her pregnancy.

She straightened the sheet, twisted into a knot in her hand. "Kieran went to the woods south of the loch searching for missing sheep. I'm certain he'll be here soon."

Eleanor would have sent Angus to find him. He'd challenge anyone who threatened to slow him, speeding to her side in his green Land Rover. "Is our housekeeper here, Eleanor Hume? She must have called the helicopter."

"Isla said there's a Janet MacIntosh. Do you want her with you?"

The thought of her best and first friend from when she arrived to teach in Scotland slowed her heart rate. "Yes, please. I'm a little confused."

"It's the pain medication." Dr. Moncrieffe nodded and stepped just outside the cubicle. "Isla, send in Mrs. MacDonell's friend, please." He turned back and moved closer to the gurney. "Tell me what you remember."

"I was dressing when I felt a sharp pain, down low, and saw blood. I don't remember anything more. I've fainted a few times." If the baby were all right, wouldn't he have said so right away?

Janet, blonde hair swept into a French twist, lavender-blue eyes wide, walked in, and Dr. Moncrieffe slid the curtain closed behind her. "Are you okay, love?" She moved to the other side of the gurney and reached under the sheet to grasp Bonny's hand.

The doctor's hand rested on her shoulder. "We did an ultrasound while you were groggy with pain medication. Do you know what an ectopic pregnancy is? When the embryo implants outside the womb?"

A lump grew in Bonny's throat, pricked, and exploded. Unable to speak, she nodded. *You'll do nothing but rest and care for yourself and our wee bairn.*

Kieran's absolute joy at the news of a child tromped through her muddled brain like an elephant. There would be no miracle.

"You have the most dangerous kind due to the internal bleeding. You've lost the baby, Bonny. It can't wait." His voice gentled, but his words came slow and deliberate, as one would deliver a death sentence. "I suspect scar tissue from your previous surgery made it impossible for the embryo to reach the womb. Remember, I said in the office, the report from your doctor in New Mexico indicates it's a miracle you conceived at all."

Hope strangled, and fear bloomed, weeds on the grave of her dreams. Warm tears trickled down the sides of her face and into her ears. Their *wee bairn*. Why would God grant them this unexpected gift only to snatch it away in a cruel hoax?

You may have conceived on our wedding night, mo gràdh. My darling. How Bonny longed to hear one of Kieran's Gaelic endearments. Instead, she must tell him they would never hold the answer to his prayers, the embodiment of their love. No MacDonell heir to inherit Stonehaven Farm. No red-haired child with eyes blue as the Scottish flag would fill their days with joy and laughter. Pain, sharper than any surgeon's scalpel could inflict, knifed through Bonny's heart.

"We have to operate. You're losing far too much blood." Dr. Moncrieffe's voice returned her to stark reality. "I'm sorry your husband can't be here, but you must sign the permission form." The bedside table squeaked when he rolled it over, paper and pen on top, and raised the head of the bed.

"Is this related to how sick I've been?"

"No. It can happen to anyone, but with your history …"

With a shaky hand and blurred eyes, she scrawled an unrecognizable signature before the pen slipped through her fingers and clattered to the floor. *Dear God, how can I bear to disappoint him? If only I'd told him about Dr. Carson's warning that having a child could take my life.*

A wave of nauseating pain swept over her when the doctor walked out. Bonny heaved a slow, deep breath and tried to listen for God's voice, but he remained silent. When Adam Lawson broke their engagement. When her parents died. When Brennan Grant shot Kieran only six weeks before their wedding. In the past, her heart felt God's comfort only after the crisis ended. Why in the midst of tragedy, must she trust through the Lord's silence? "Why?"

Janet dabbed her cheeks with a tissue. Her cool hand smoothed a curl from Bonny's forehead. "Some things are impossible to understand."

Metal rings clinked. The curtain slid open and a nurse dressed in green—only a little taller than the gurney—stepped in. "I've come to take you to the operating room. Am I interrupting?"

"Please," Janet said, "can I pray with her first?"

"Of course. I'll be right outside." She backed up and closed the curtain behind her.

With difficulty, Bonny strained to hear Janet's words over the thump of her heart against her ribs. But it didn't matter. All she desired were Kieran's arms around her.

Once again, she faced a painful trial alone.

೫ ೪

Bonny closed her eyes and took shallow breaths to avoid aggravating the deep, burning pain in her lower abdomen. An insistent voice repeated her name, and someone rubbed her shoulder. She moved hesitant hands to her abdomen and met bandages. "The surgery's over?"

"Aye, you're in recovery. I'm Fionna. You have company if you're up to it." The nurse raised the head of the bed and held out a cup with a straw. "Take a sip for me first, pet. I'll give you more pain medication."

Cool water soothed her parched throat but not her heart. "Thank you. Where's my husband?"

"There's a gentleman out there. One more sip, lass." She set the cup within reach and walked away.

Bonny closed her eyes and took shallow breaths to avoid aggravating her incision. She dreaded Kieran's pain more than her own but craved the comfort of his arms.

The curtain opened and their pastor, Graeme MacDholl, stepped aside, allowing Janet to precede him. A waterfall of fear gushed from her eyes, and

Janet stooped to kiss her cheek, wiping her face with a tissue. "Oh, love, I'm so sorry."

"Where's Kieran?"

Deep brown eyes met her own. Her husband's best friend rested his hand on her arm. "We don't know. The farmhands are searching, Bonny. He wasn't where Angus expected. They'll find him soon. His parents are on their way."

"What do you mean you don't know? He always checks in if he's out longer than he expects. He should have been back by now." Her stomach turned upside-down—fear born of loss and disappointment. Janet reached for the basin and cradled Bonny's head when her abdomen clenched and burned.

The pastor went for Fionna, who brought water to rinse Bonny's mouth, placed a cool, damp cloth on her head, and wrapped a warm blanket around her.

Janet's hand squeezed her icy fingers, while the chills from anesthesia chattered her teeth. "You know there's a reasonable explanation. He probably had to go farther than he expected. Remember there's terrible mobile service in the Laddie Wood."

Reasonable? Didn't anyone else realize an earthquake rocked the entire world? Bonny splinted her abdomen with her hands as sobs thrust upward. "How do I tell him?"

Fionna returned. "Your in-laws are here. I can't allow four at once."

"We'll be right outside." Janet kissed her forehead and stepped out.

A black curtain descended around her. Two statements screamed in her head.

Kieran.

Our baby.

Kieran.

Our baby.

Metal rings clinked again. Her in-laws stepped through the peach-colored curtain and Hamish MacDonell bent to kiss her cheek, grey hair tousled from running his fingers through it, the same way Kieran did. "We hurried to get here, lass. We're a poor substitute, but we won't leave you alone."

Maggie, blue eyes rimmed in red, placed a cool hand on her other cheek and kissed her forehead. "I'm so sorry, love. Dr. Moncrieffe explained everything. I know how it hurts to lose a child but to hear there will never be another … I have no words. I don't understand God's purposes, but we love you. We're here for you."

White-hot anger coursed through Bonny. Why did people always say there was a divine purpose? Yes, she believed in a God of love, but at times life appeared contrary to his nature when he allowed circumstances to take their natural course without intervening. How else could one explain her father's cancer diagnosis seven months after her mother's death from a brain tumor, or two broken engagements? "Why would God steal our miracle baby? Why delay Kieran when I need him? Must I lose everyone? Nothing makes sense. Nothing."

Her father-in-law's hands rested gently on her shoulders. "There, there, *mo nighean*. You're the daughter we never had, and I'd take this away if I could. We love you and will stay with you. *Wheesht*, cryin' will only make you hurt worse. Kieran will show up soon. Remember when we paced the hospital halls after the poacher shot him. God never leaves you with nothing or no one. Though we may not feel him, the Lord is with us."

"I know." Bonny's voice sounded so weak she barely heard herself. She was fragile and broken inside as her mother's fine crystal vase when she shattered it at age seven. It had been so difficult to work up the nerve to tell Kieran she couldn't have children. When she did, he became so angry. Given time, he returned, but how would he handle another disappointment after already losing both a wife and child?

"He kissed me goodbye and left to find the sheep with a promise to return in a few hours. What if his disappearance is somehow related to the poaching?"

"We won't borrow trouble, lass. Stay calm while Angus and the others search. You concentrate on getting better."

She turned her face to the wall and closed her eyes.

No matter what they say, I don't see God in this. Kieran will be a pastor soon, but God has deserted us, and no one understands.

Fionna returned to wheel her into a private room with a partial view of Ben Nevis. What irony to look out at the "mountain of heaven" and feel the same as the day she arrived in Scotland.

Separated from God.

Bereft of hope.

☙❧

There is loss too deep for tears. Bonny awakened when a new nurse hung another unit of blood. Sun peeked around the blinds. Morning. And still no Kieran. On his visit the previous evening, Dr. Moncrieffe said she had lost almost half her blood volume. What if she died without one last glimpse of his beloved face?

One more touch.

One more kiss.

So alone.

She had twisted the sheet into knots in her worry. Hamish and Maggie, in exhausted sleep a few feet away, only made the lack of his presence more palpable. How could he disappear on their own farm?

Angus MacTeague had been the farm manager since Kieran's childhood, almost family. He spoke to him last and knew where the sheep should be. Even in the wildness of Stonehaven Farm, someone should be able to find him. Hamish, Angus, and Kieran wore their knowledge of the land comfortably as their kilts, a lifelong familiarity. What weren't they telling her? Bonny grabbed the side rail and tried to roll over but fell back breathing hard, the room twirling from even that small motion. She was helpless. Dear God, please lead them to Kieran. Don't let him die.

Only five months ago, she searched alone when Kieran failed to return from tracking a poacher. She found him bleeding in the snow from a bullet to the abdomen. His horse had spooked with highland temperatures plummeting when a fast-paced blizzard approached. He would have died if she'd waited for the police. Maybe he waited somewhere now, alone and in need of help.

The farm covered vast acres of thick woods and steep terrain alongside Loch Garry. High mountains and shaded canyons still lay robed in snow, while sunlit trails dissolved into thick, soupy mud from run-offs. Impromptu waterfalls and hillsides littered with trees felled by snow slides made for treacherous travel in the backcountry.

How far had he gone in his search for the missing sheep? Kieran was a shepherd after the heart of the Good Shepherd, who left the ninety-nine to search for one. He would not give up until he found them all.

Struggling for a deep breath against a weight of weakness on her chest, Bonny stared into the darkness and breathed a feeble prayer. "Lord, you say you'll never leave or forsake us. I believe you offer comfort and answer prayer. Please bring him back. You've already taken his child. Don't take the man I love too."

Her pain increased each time she roused, expecting Kieran at her side like he'd been in the past when she awakened from a coma following a car accident. Once, in a dream, he carried a laughing little boy high on his shoulders as he strode across the lawn, Loch Garry sparkling in the sunshine. Now, that child who would never draw a breath would live only in her dreams. When the pain reached its worst, Bonny was transported to her father's graveside once again, lost and alone, with no one to call her own.

How cruel to keep her on the maternity ward. Baby cries filtered through the closed door. Mothers stirred in hushed tones, their exclamations of joy and awe seeping into Bonny's heart the way tears soak a handkerchief. Sadness born from the death of hope, newly raised and crushed too soon, clogged her throat and knotted her insides. She should never have allowed herself to share Kieran's joy of anticipation.

Sunlit clouds cloaked Ben Nevis with the pink light of dawn, evoking memories of the sunset reflected in the calm waters of Loch Linnhe the first time she and Kieran talked, kindred hearts that budded into love. Wouldn't she sense if he were gone?

Her father-in-law's cell phone rang, startling him awake. He fumbled in his pocket and held the phone to his ear. "Hamish here."

Bonny raised the head of the bed when Maggie awakened, straightened in her chair, then rose to turn on the light.

"Tell everyone thank you. Yes, I'll call later." Hamish hung up and took a deep breath. "Angus found Kieran near the Bolinn Wood, in a ravine. God be praised, lass, he'll be here soon. Someone hit him over the head a good one. He escaped but passed out at the wheel. The Land Rover hit a rock and stopped on the edge of a fast-flowing *burn*."

"Thank God. My prayers are answered." Her love was coming. Sadness almost crushed the joy when a sharp pain stabbed deep. "Does he know?"

"Aye, he asked to go home to you first. Angus told him." Hamish stood and walked to her side. "They think he suffered a concussion. You'll heal together now."

Sun shone from Maggie's eyes with the certainty her only son was safe. "Hamish and I will stay at the farm until you two regain your strength. Kieran won't rest unless we're there."

A forlorn waif stared at Bonny out of the mirrored tray in the bedside table. Her pallid skin contrasted against dark circles under her green eyes, making them appear even larger. A frizzle of tangled red curls framed her wan face. "Can you brush my hair and bring me a washcloth, Maggie? I don't want to look too awful. He'll be worried enough."

"Aye, you're a wee bit *peely-wally*, but with good reason, dear. Let's see what we can do." Maggie took a makeup bag from her purse, rose, and wet a cloth at the sink.

Bonny sipped some cold tea for energy. Memories of the rainbow she and Kieran once marveled at from atop Urquhart Castle on Loch Ness danced through her heart. She longed for his kiss now more than the first time. The band of pain around her heart eased a little. Her love would be with her soon.

Maggie worked a brush through the stubborn knots, then applied blush for Bonny's cheeks and pink for her lips. It seemed pointless to darken her colorless lashes only to create mascara streaks down her cheeks when Kieran appeared.

Her heart lurched when the door creaked open and a pale, disheveled Kieran entered. Broad shoulders sagged. With mouth taut and his face framed in a fiery display of tousled red-gold hair, red, swollen eyes met hers. He limped to her bedside, bent his six-foot-five frame, and brushed her lips with his. Tears mingled as his mouth claimed hers, then pressed harder, pouring his love into the passion of his kiss. When it ended, they were alone, their pounding hearts and sighs the only sound. She would treasure this embrace for a lifetime.

The bed groaned under his weight and solid arms eased her close. Their heads rested on each other's shoulders while he shook with grief and disappointment. Their oneness anchored her, took hold deep in her soul, and held on with a shared bond stronger than she believed possible.

Kieran reminded her of the mighty Ponderosa pines surrounding her house in New Mexico. His legs and back strong to withstand storms, arms like sturdy branches offered shelter and protection, roots sunk deep into the soil of faith. This man dwarfed her in the physical and spiritual, yet his touch caressed her skin with the gentleness of snowflakes.

"My poor love. I'm sorry I wasn't here." He cradled her against him and smoothed the hair that tumbled down her back. Big hands spread from shoulder to shoulder, a solid shield of comfort. His love breathed life into her weak and shattered spirit.

Bonny moved her hand to the springy curls at the back of his neck and encountered a sticky substance. Her fingertips came away tinged with blood and mud. "Kieran, what happened?"

"I never found the sheep. I sat on a rock the slopes of Beinn Tee for a drink when someone hit me on the back of the head. A big man with dark hair and a face filled with rage. I turned, and my fist connected with his jaw. When he staggered, I rushed for the Land Rover, but the *eijit* grabbed my foot and threw me to the ground. I kicked him in the side, pulled myself up with a tree, and ran. He caught me as I climbed in. My shirt tore, and when he stumbled, I shoved him with my foot, slammed the door, and locked it. The keys were in the ignition. I gunned the engine and headed down the mountain, but lost consciousness. If the truck hadn't hit a rock, it would have rolled into the chasm of a *burn*, running deep with snowmelt."

"Have you seen a doctor?" She cupped his rough, unshaven cheek, auburn whiskers contrasting with the lighter color of his hair. Her finger traced a purple lump along his jawline. The knuckles of the hand grasping hers were swollen and bruised.

"They said you could have bled to death. I had to see you first, *mo chridhe*, to hold you in my arms. Now, I'll go downstairs and see to my own injuries." His lips quirked into a grimace. With a sob, he buried his face in her hair. "I was so frightened."

My heart's desire. Her sore heart swelled at the sweet sentiment of his Gaelic. "Kieran, I'm so sorry. Dr. Moncrieffe blames it on the scar tissue from before. If only …"

He lifted his head and cupped her face with calloused hands. "It's not your fault, love. Children would be a blessing. But I need only you."

"God gave us hope and then took our child."

Rough but tender fingers brushed the tears from her cheeks. Eyes, bloodshot with fatigue and sorrow, met her own. "We'll walk this road together. Every step."

A light rain slipped in gentle cascades down the windowpanes and crept through her heart. "You shouldn't have gone alone."

"Shh, I'm not the enemy. It's your grief talking." He stroked Bonny's hair, but she pulled away.

"I could have lost you. Kieran, you prayed for a child. How can God allow this?"

He pressed a tender kiss on top of her head. "God is loving, but we're too blind to understand. We've both grieved before and healed. Loss hurts, but we're neither one alone this time. I'm content with only you. I made my peace before we married."

Perhaps it was pain medication and weakness, but every struggle of her life combined into one crushing burden. His swollen jaw burned hot beneath her fingers. "I can't help my anger. First, Brennan Grant shoots you, and now you're attacked out of nowhere. Did this man say anything?"

"Get off my land." Kieran lowered his eyes and shook his head. "I have no idea what he meant."

 C3 80

Bonny snuggled deeper under the blankets, chilled as the transfusion trickled into her arm. The flash in her husband's eyes didn't promise a pleasant conversation when Hamish and Maggie returned to the room.

"How could anyone claim part of Stonehaven Farm?" Kieran raised the head of his hospital bed. The gracious staff had allowed them to share a room while they observed him for a severe concussion. The pitch of his voice rose with every word, eyes focused on Hamish. "You inherited it and your father before you."

"Lad, I should have told you—"

"What?" Kieran's pale face flushed with anger, his eyes narrowed and wary. "You're sayin' this maniac makes sense?"

"Let your father explain." Maggie stood and patted her husband's hand. "I'll try and find us some tea."

Red spots of anger bloomed in Kieran's pale cheeks. The combination of a blow to the back of his head and his forehead meeting the steering wheel triggered blinding headaches. With Bonny's blood count near normal, the doctors agreed to release them into the care of his parents the next day.

Chair legs scraped across the floor as Hamish scooted between the beds. "It happened before you were born, *mo mhac*."

My son. Bonny was beginning to understand the Gaelic endearments used by her new family. It erased the sense of being an outsider.

"It was wrong—my not telling you. I'm sorry, lad. The years went by, and nothing happened, so I didn't think it mattered."

"How could you withhold important family information? What if a legal matter came up after your death and I didn't know?" Kieran's face reddened. His voice grew louder. One fist pounded the bed. A pillow flew to the floor.

Her father-in-law cleared his throat and turned to face her. "Lass, you know about my great grandfather, Euan MacDonell, who bought back the land we lost in the Highland Clearances of the late 1700s. A distant cousin, Cormag MacDonell, bought the Greenfield land. The families were never close, but we owned the Laddie Wood to the east, which required permission to drive our flocks across their land."

Bonny shifted a glance toward Kieran.

His bruised hands balled into fists. "Why not tell me someone had prior claim to the land?"

"Keep your kilt on, man. I'm gettin' to it." Hamish leaned toward his son, one hand on the bedside rail. "Not long before I inherited Stonehaven Farm, Cormag's great-grandson, Diarmid inherited the Greenfield land. A ne'er do well if ever I saw one, drinkin', gamblin', leavin' his wife and *bairns* with precious little to survive on. Your mother and grandmother were always givin' them handouts."

Kieran ruffled his hair until it stood on end. "What year, Da?"

"After they dammed the loch about 1960. One day, Diarmid knocked at our door, disheveled and drunk, sayin' the government was takin' his land for taxes. He begged for a loan, and we worked out a deal where I obtained the deed to Greenfield in exchange for payment of the taxes. When he saved enough to buy it back, I would return it to him. We wrote the agreement on the back of the deed, and both signed."

"He never paid you?" Impatience coarsened Kieran's voice. Only God, Bonny, and his parents came before his love and devotion to the mountainous, wooded glen of loch and verdant pastures they called home.

"Will you be patient, *mo mhac*?" Hamish's voice raised half an octave, eyes flashed, and he gulped from his water bottle. "The last I heard, Diarmid lived and worked on a sheep farm in Caithness. The deal was for ten years. He never returned." A choking sound gurgled from his throat. "Bear with me. It's difficult after all these years. I had a baby sister, Brighde, the bonniest lass in all of Lochaber. Your Bonny reminds me of her, a wee lassie with red curls and bright eyes, though Brighde's were blue, not green—"

"Da!" Kieran interrupted. "You're sayin' I had an aunt I never heard of until today? Granny and Granda never mentioned their own daughter?"

Despite the tension, Bonny stifled a smile. Their accents grew much more pronounced when emotions ran high. The endearing trait provided a helpful cue to their feelings. Kieran clenched his bristled jaw, blue eyes gone gray.

Maggie stepped through the door bearing a tray with four cups of tea, set it on Bonny's bedside table, and handed around the cups. She sniffed the hearty aroma. Her eyes roved from her son to her husband and back again.

"There were painful circumstances. I'll get around to it all. If Diarmid wasn't bad enough, his older brother Taran was worse, and a more black-hearted seducer I never met, angered by his father's decision to disinherit him. Ach, I hate the name." Hamish's anguished voice roughened, like a truck on a graveled road. "My wee Brighde, at seventeen, and eight years younger than me, loved him from the day they met by the bridge over the loch. Your grandparents forbade her to see him, but there's many a hidin' place in those hills. Before long, they arrested Taran for killin' a man in Tomdoun and jailed him in Fort William."

"Drink your tea, Hamish," Maggie said. "I put extra sugar to ease your throat."

"Thank you, love." He savored the warm drink, closed his eyes, and sat back. "With Taran gone, Brighde confessed she was carryin' his child. They'd planned to elope, but with her startin' to show, my parents had to know. I've never been so furious or seen my father angrier. He swore no child of Taran MacDonell would ever enter his house. Told wee Brighde to find a home for the *bairn*."

"Oh, how awful." Bonny wiped her arm across her eyes. The tubing from the blood transfusion snagged on the sheet, and she untangled it with care. A tide of sorrow threatened to drag her under a sea of grief at the idea of giving up a child. "The poor thing."

Kieran eased himself out of bed, took the few steps to hers, sat, and hugged her close.

"Things were different then, lass. Having a child without a husband meant scandal. Brighde threatened to leave before givin' up her *bairn* and packed her bags."

"A true MacDonell, hardheaded as rocks on the Ben." Maggie nodded toward the window, where Ben Nevis raised its snowy head.

"My mother pleaded and cried, and Brighde agreed to stay for a while. A few months later, they gave Taran the death sentence for stabbin' the man in the heart. Ach, my poor sister—inconsolable. A terrible storm came up during the night, and in the mornin' she was gone. The note on her pillow said she wouldn't give up the child."

Kieran's strong hand caressed her barren abdomen the way he'd once cradled their child. "Go on."

"We reported her disappearance to police all the way to Inverness, Aberdeen, and Glasgow, advertised in newspapers, checked with hospitals, without a trace. My mother decided Brighde must have drowned herself in the loch. Bein' full of trees and razed homes after they dammed the loch, a body might never surface. Your grandfather insisted no one speak my wee sister's name again." A sob wrenched from his throat. "I didn't intend to hide it, lad." Hamish rubbed his hand over his face, and leaned back, eyes closed. His down-turned mouth and sunken eyes made him look old and tired.

"What year did she disappear?" Kieran's voice softened, and he turned his gaze to the window.

"About four years before you were born. Shortly after, Diarmid's entire family vanished without a word."

"Kieran, love." Maggie walked to his side, placing a hand on his back. "I'm sorry. We couldn't go against your grandparents. If this man is related to Diarmid and Taran, we'd expect brutality."

"Have you told the police?" Kieran wiped the tears from Bonny's cheek with the back of his hand.

Hamish shook his head. "No, lad. We needed to explain first. The police can wait until tomorrow or the next day, after you're home."

Bonny shivered, and Kieran pulled her to him. First, the shooting and now this.

Chapter Two

Stonehaven Farm, Loch Garry, Scotland

If only Detective Sergeant Alasdair Kavanaugh wouldn't drum his fingers on the table. Weak and on edge, Bonny found it difficult enough to appear composed without him driving her to distraction. The exhaustion the doctor warned of, coupled with grief and disturbed sleep, made her a shaky, fragile mess. To take one breath after another was hard work.

A tall, thin man in his mid-thirties with a complexion once ravaged by acne, Kieran had known Alasdair for years. Her eyes slid across the table to the head of the investigation, Detective Chief Inspector Bruce McLeod. Perhaps in his mid-fifties, he impressed her as a friendly, personable sort of man—under different circumstances. Both reached for the Buchan Thistle cups and saucers Maggie handed around when they accepted her offer of tea.

Warmth trickled through Bonny's veins at the sight of the homey, hand-painted pottery in spite of the uncomfortable conversation. With both she and Kieran weak from blood loss and grief, Maggie and Eleanor waited on them hand and foot. Headaches from the blow Kieran received consigned him to bed in a dark room several times a day.

"I've started an investigation into deeds on the property," Alasdair announced. "Disputes aren't unusual when land holdings this extensive have passed down through the generations."

"Do you want the original copy of the deed, Detective?" Hamish tugged the yellowed paper from an age-worn envelope.

"Let me look it over. It will be invaluable if the case goes to court after we catch this bloke. Keep it locked in the safe and mention it to no one." DCI McLeod's eyes skimmed the paper front and back before he returned it.

With all the talk about Kieran's secret aunt, deeds, and damming the loch, Bonny realized she had much more to learn than tending sheep.

"Investigators made casts of the footprints from where you were attacked. We'll be out from time to time to check and recheck details, but I'll never send anyone unannounced." McLeod's business demeanor vanished when he nodded toward her, his lips curving into a kind smile.

"I remembered more about my attacker in the shower this morning." Kieran accepted a warm, fresh scone from his mother and slathered it with clotted cream. "A wild man, hair to the middle of his back with feathers braided into it. A long beard and a *feileadh mor.*" He glanced toward Bonny. "An old-fashioned great kilt, longer in the back than the front, and no shirt. He spoke the Gaelic. His eyes darted around. Never met mine. Unhinged. A *bampot,* ready for a good *stramash.*"

Cold fingers of horror crept up Bonny's spine. Wasn't it enough to deal with the death of their child without a crazy man creating trouble?

After a few more questions, which Kieran couldn't answer, the detectives rose. "Please don't hesitate to call, day or night." DCI McLeod's voice gentled, and he clasped Bonny's cold hand in his. "I'm sorry for your loss. We'll do everything possible to ensure your safety."

When Hamish walked them to the door, Kieran pulled her into a bear hug. With the solid warmth of his chest beneath her cheek, Bonny melted into him. Her overstimulated nerves settled. "Can you trust me to be careful and take care of you, love? Angus and Seumas, and the rest of the farmhands know to be on the alert. This will be all right."

If only she felt the assurance Kieran expressed.

∛∞

Grabbing the phone, Kieran vaulted from his chair and stepped into the hall. Bonny napped on the couch, a warm blanket up to her chin, honeyed lashes shadowing her cheek.

"Hello."

"Kieran, it's Dan. Are you all right?"

Outside the window, mist lifted from the water as shafts of sun streamed through the clouds dappling the loch with light. "Ach, Dan, sorry if I sounded abrupt. Why did you call my mobile?"

"Bonny didn't answer."

"She's asleep." Kieran padded to the kitchen. Her best friend Kari, in New Mexico, must have had her twins. He would tell them Bonny lost the baby before giving her the phone, but no amount of explanation would ease the painful situation.

Dan laughed. "Yeah, Kari napped a lot too. Pregnancy takes a lot out of them. I suspect twins will make it worse."

Kieran closed his eyes against the pummeling headache and sank into a chair, head in his hand. "Kari had the babies then?"

"A couple of hours ago. Can you wake Bonny up to hear our news?"

"Aye, but we need to talk first. Can Kari listen too?"

"I'm here," Kari spoke up. "What's wrong?"

"We've had a rough time of it. They airlifted Bonny to the hospital when she hemorrhaged and they performed emergency surgery to remove a tubal pregnancy. You know the baby was a miracle to begin with and now she'll never have another. She almost bled to death. She went through it all alone because I was attacked and hit over the head while I searched for stray sheep. I escaped but passed out. It's a long story." He choked and cleared his throat.

"Oh, Kieran, no." Kari sniffled. "Should we wait to tell her?"

He scrubbed his hand over his face. "We're struggling, but she'll want to know. Hold on while I wake her."

"Sure," Dan said.

"Thanks. I'll take her the phone."

Bonny lay staring out the window when Kieran entered the bedroom. "It's Kari and Dan calling. I have the phone on speaker."

She grabbed a tissue from the box beside her and sat upright. "Dan, did Kari have the babies? It's four weeks early. Tell me all about it."

"Resting well and more beautiful than you can imagine. They were born about two hours ago. Two babies without anesthetic. Six hours of labor. Isn't my wife amazing?"

Bonny smiled. Kieran sat and slipped his arm around her shoulders, swallowing hard at the unexpected joy in her voice. "How big are they? And what are those names you've kept such a secret?"

"Apparently twins often come early because they run out of room. William Wallace MacDowell weighed in at five pounds. His younger sister, by two minutes, Annie Laurie, weighs four pounds and eight ounces. She's on oxygen, but they don't expect she'll need it for long." Dan's happiness reached across the miles.

"They're big for twins." Bonny squeezed Kieran's hand. Her smile belied envy or pain. His heart ached to watch her share the happiness of her friends, ignoring her own loss. "I love the names."

"We'll call them Willie and Annie." Dan's buoyant mood carried across the miles. "I emailed photos. Gosh, I wish you were here, Bon."

Kieran remembered his exaltation, a sense of pride, in Bonny's pregnancy. He held her closer, prepared for the breakdown.

"Honey, Kieran told us what happened. I'm so sorry." The love behind Kari's words created the expected flood of emotion. "Airlifted. Are you all right?"

Bonny wiped her face and gripped Kieran's hand. "I lost such a large amount of blood. It will take a while to regain my strength. He experiences cruel headaches, and his parents are running the farm. But we're excited for you. A boy and girl both. The perfect family. I'm proud of you."

Kari sighed. "I'm grateful. What the delivery lacked in length it made up for in intensity. I couldn't have managed much longer. They're beautiful. But I hate to talk about our happiness after what you've been through."

"Aunt Bonny and Uncle Kieran are excited, in spite of our loss." She quivered and laid her head against Kieran's shoulder.

Her tiny frame hid a heart of iron. He rested his forehead against hers. To realize he might have lost this incredible woman sent a current of ice through his veins. He'd lost one wife. How could he survive a second time? She twisted her hair when nervous, and the firm set of her lips indicated a thinning of her cheerful veneer. "Kari, we need to go. We'll talk again soon."

Bonny nodded her thanks. "I'll get into my email and look at the pictures right away. I love you."

"Bye, we love you," Kari and Dan answered together, then hung up.

She wept to the accompaniment of the old clock. Kieran joined in, heart aching, speechless. Time and God's strength would dull the hurt and perhaps fill the emptiness with new purpose. Words alone lacked the power to ease pain, and scars never completely healed.

♋♎

Stifled sobs shook the bed and roused Kieran from sleep. He scooted across the cold sheets and wrapped his arms around Bonny. The bathroom night light didn't provide sufficient light to see her face. "Why did God give us a baby only to take it away? I don't understand."

"There are no answers, love." He pressed a kiss on her forehead. What an incredible yet powerless feeling to have her seek comfort in his arms. "All I can do is mourn with you."

"I'm a terrible person to feel jealous over Kari's two babies. We'll never experience the birth of a child created from our love." Angry words spewed forth the way steam escapes a boiling kettle. "When Dan said she went through the entire labor without drugs, I wanted to scream. I sound ungrateful. You're home safe. I'm alive. Niall Moncrieffe offered to help us adopt."

"You're not terrible, just human, but it's too soon to discuss adoption. Concentrate on healing first." The best friends had lost their dream of children born close together. How could he comfort her and not reveal his own confusion?

"I want children, Kieran." Bonny nestled underneath his chin, a warm, sweet weight. "I felt so sick but I knew a part of you grew inside me. For years, I believed my family would be formed through adoption, now it's true, and it hurts."

"*Wheesht*, God will reveal his plan. For now, we'll leave it with him." She began to relax in his arms, but he remembered his shock and anger the day she told him children weren't possible. "I have all I need." Was he being completely honest with her … and with himself?

"To work on the farm and share your life means everything. We're blessed, but …" Her words drifted off and her breathing slowed.

Kieran closed his eyes, running his fingers through the thick mass of her curls, imagining their silken, red beauty, the emerald of her magnificent eyes. "Da used to share a verse with me from Deuteronomy. 'Your castles and strongholds shall have bars of iron and bronze, and as your day, so shall your strength, your rest, and security be.' Go to sleep, love. We will survive."

She stiffened. "Where were those bars of protection when our baby died and you were attacked?"

"I don't know, except that we're both alive, and I trust God's love. Our marriage proves God's faithfulness in a world where nothing makes sense. I almost lost you, to the car accident, and to another man. When I struggled with depression, you gave me strength. Let me be yours now." He stroked her brow with his fingers, something his mother did when he was a child. She drifted off to sleep while he stared into the darkness, her head heavy against his chest. Rain pelted the window, a fit accompaniment for the ache in his heart.

Rumbles of thunder echoed with memories of the day another red-haired beauty, his first wife, Bronwyn, bled to death on the kitchen floor from a premature separation of the placenta. Their full-term son Liam, stillborn. Neither of his children ever saw the light of day. The loss went deeper than Bonny would ever know.

His parents and grandparents passed down great pride through their clan history and the growth of Stonehaven Farm into a nationally renowned producer of prime wool and mutton. Could he or his parents accept and love a child not of their blood?

Father God, I always believed I would hand the family lands down to a son. To know I'll never have an heir, never feel the tug of little arms around my neck, or see Bonny hold a baby to her breast, stings like a horde of angry bees.

Bonny sighed and rolled over in her sleep. His heart yearned for her from the moment she walked into the faculty meeting so long ago. Small, delicate, with eyes and a smile capable of driving a man mad. Their similar thinking and ease of conversation made him love her before the end of their first evening together.

Lord, help me relinquish the dream and show Bonny she's all I need. No matter how soon after their loss, she could already consider adoption. Head throbbing, he reached to the nightstand for pain medication. If only it could ease a broken heart. When they grew strong enough, the farm and chapel would take their minds off strange attackers and irreplaceable losses. Adoption was an option he wasn't ready for. He'd deal with Bonny's certainty when an aching head didn't scramble his brains.

ঙ৪৪৪

One glimpse out the window revealed a *dreich* morning. The mountain stood shrouded in dark clouds, and Kieran had dressed without awakening her. Days of rain turned the yard into a swamp. The air smelled wet. Bonny's skin felt wet. Her eyes were never dry. Her empty arms ached more when the heavens cried with her, and rain seldom ceased on Loch Garry.

Kieran walked through the bedroom door as she stepped out of the shower. He smiled and crossed the room to embrace her. "You were sound asleep, and I didn't want to wake you. Graeme and Janet are here."

"I forgot they were coming. Why are they together?" Those two hadn't been alone together since a long-ago ski weekend in Aviemore when Janet told Graeme about her divorce and her certainty that people wouldn't accept her as a pastor's wife. "They were in the same car together for almost an hour?"

"Hurry and we can find out, *hen.*" Kieran dropped a warm kiss at the nape of her neck before she pulled away and walked to the closet.

He headed for the door and she blew a kiss in his direction.

Driving rain pelted the windows, and the farmhouse juddered in the winter wind. Thunder reverberated off the mountainsides and rumbled through the glen. The history professor in her imagined cannon fire from a siege against the ancient castles that dotted the landscape. She offered a prayer of thanks for the solid, old stone house.

The warm comfort of her favorite sweatshirt with its flag of Scotland and a pair of loose, gray sweat pants were perfect for the day. Leaving her hair in wet ringlets down her back, she rubbed blush into her cheeks, applied mascara to pale lashes, and headed downstairs.

Janet's laughter and the deep voices of the men directed her to the library. The fragrance of her favorite balsam-scented candles greeted her at the door. In spite of the violent storm, the room glowed with light, love, and laughter.

"Good morning. Sorry, I forgot you were coming. I overslept."

"Don't be." Janet and Graeme rose from the couch, faces animated, eyes bright. Something was up.

Bonny hugged them and seated herself next to Kieran.

"Do you feel any better?" Graeme's tone held concern.

"They say I'll be tired for months. Healing is a journey filled with hills and valleys. One minute you think you'll survive, and the next you're positive you can't go on."

"Call me when you feel down." Janet's warmth and friendship remained constant as the rain. "Maybe I can listen in a way Kari can't right now. When you're up to it, we'll have lunch in Fort William and shop like we used to when you were teaching. Fort William Christian College isn't the same since you two left. I miss you."

"Girlfriend time would be a real treat." Janet's warm invitation soothed Bonny's heart, a true friend in her new country.

Kieran stood to sweep stray embers from the hearth. "What brings you out all this way in a storm?"

"We have a surprise." Graeme beamed at Janet, her face reddening under his gaze. "That's obvious." Kieran stood still, hearth brush in hand. "Janet, I've known you since we were what, five? Something's up."

"I'll resign from Faith Chapel next month to become Chairman of the Department of Apologetics at Fort William Christian College when Phil MacKenzie retires," Graeme said. Apples in autumn couldn't glow brighter than Janet's cheeks. "Dùghlas Cameron offered me the position while you were on your honeymoon. My doctorate is in apologetics, you know. I always planned to teach one day."

"Congratulations." Kieran hung up the hearth brush and sat next to Bonny again. "We appreciate your visit, but you could have told us over the phone instead of driving out here in such a storm. The single-track becomes such a mess in this weather. There must be something else."

Graeme glanced at Janet. "Since I'll be a professor, not a pastor, Janet's agreed her divorce doesn't disqualify her from a happy life. We started to see each other right after you left on your honey—"

Bonny leaped off the couch, laughing and crying, to pull Janet into a hug before he finished. Kieran followed and pumped Graeme's hand with enthusiasm. "Congratulations."

"No one but my mum knows for now." Janet's face shone with joy.

Kieran wrapped her in a hug and kissed her cheek. "I don't know what I would have done without you these last few years. I wish you all the best."

"You were there for me after my divorce. I guess knocking some sense into you about Bonny makes us even." Janet laughed.

Graeme sat close to her this time and reached for her hand, his brown eyes sparkling like *cairngorms,* the lovely jewels found only in the Scottish mountains bearing their name. "I called Dùghlas the day I found out about Phil's retirement. He never interviewed anyone else. When I knew for certain, I told Janet. I've never been more sure in my life."

Janet's head tipped toward his dark one, shoulders and thighs touching. It was obvious how new and exciting their world had become. "I can't imagine

Faith Chapel with another pastor. All things are possible with God, but I'll admit, I didn't pray like I believed it."

Graeme smiled at her with complete adoration. "We're telling you in strict confidence. Janet insists we not appear in public together until I step down as pastor."

"I'll bet your mother's thrilled. Agnes has prayed to see you happily married." Bonny sighed in gratitude for a moment of unexpected joy.

"Mum's ecstatic. You know she loves Graeme. And Kieran, you can pay me back." Janet's voice lowered. "We hope you'll perform our ceremony when the time comes."

He threw his head back and laughed. "What a turnabout. The prodigal performing the pastor's wedding. Bonny, did you ever think you'd see the day?"

"*Reformed* prodigal." She kissed his cheek. "You'll be wonderful."

He nudged her and flicked his head toward Janet, who wiggled her fingers to loosen Graeme's never-let-you-go grip.

"Counsel us like you would any other couple. You've taken the classes, and have the life experience," Graeme said.

"He can do it." A gust of wind shook the house, and Bonny burrowed deeper under Kieran's shoulder, glancing around the warm room. Wood paneling, walls lined with books, green carpet, and blue-and-green MacDonell plaid furniture. Such a homey room with the roaring fire and good news almost chased away the dampness.

"You three have a lot more confidence in me than I do." He shook his head.

"I hate to rush off, but we need to get back to Fort William." Janet stood and crossed the room to kiss his cheek. "I can't think of anyone I would rather have perform our wedding than my oldest and dearest friend."

"Thank you." He flushed red and stood. "I appreciate your confidence. We'll stay home from church until the doctors clear us to drive. I still have headaches, and Bonny's much too weak."

She rose and walked toward the door with one arm around Janet. "Thank you for braving the storm to share your news. It will be great to spend time with the two of you again."

Kieran rested his hand on Janet's shoulder. "It's about time you came to your senses. Be careful on your way back." Closing the door against the rain, he drew Bonny into his warm, solid arms to watch Graeme's car splash down the puddled drive. "They'll be good together."

"Yes, but no one can top us."

His eyes were two bottomless pools, and Bonny read them well. "You're thinking how close we came to losing each other when I refused your marriage proposal."

"Aye, only by God's grace."

"If he could work that miracle, he can take us through whatever comes." She stood on tiptoe to kiss his cheek.

"I'm sure of it."

"We just acquired a Scottish Kari and Dan, friends we can count on. I appreciate Janet's offer to talk when I feel down."

Kieran reached for her hand and turned from the window. "Come on. I'll rest with you for a while. Upstairs or the library couch?"

"The library. Stairs wear me out. But I don't need to lie in bed all the time."

He steered her across the hall. She settled with a book while he tucked a blanket around her legs and drew close. "Patience, Mrs. MacDonell. My head clears a little more every day. Your appetite's better. We'll be back on top in no time. The best cure for grief is patience and the routines of daily life."

CHAPTER THREE

An all-unbearable darkness of spirit overwhelmed Bonny again. Worsened by Kari and Dan's twins and Kieran's hesitance about adoption, her lethargy created limbs of lead and the will of a slug. Each day she slipped further into despair. In sleepless hours of the night, grief muted her attempts to pray.

Rain poured down for the third straight day, swamped the yard, cascaded down windowpanes, and hid from view all but the trees closest to the house. Janet and Kieran had warned her how the rainiest part of Scotland affected moods. Accustomed to New Mexico sunshine, the damp and cold seeped into her bones. Her boat took on water faster than she could bail.

Her nine months at Fort William Christian College and the few months before she married Kieran were full of excitement, new love, and dreams come true. Nothing penetrated the fog of depression that now descended over her.

Voices drifted up from the kitchen where Kieran, Hamish, and Angus discussed farm duties for the week. Anxious to get back to running the farm, the doctor still refused to clear Kieran for work until the next visit. Bonny had no such desire. The breakfast tray, deposited beside the bed by Maggie, lay untouched, and a shower required too much effort.

The steady rush of rain through a downspout outside the window was a mere trickle compared to the flood of longing for her child who would never experience rain or sun. Dan received prosthetic legs after an IED explosion in Iraq. She had a piece of her heart amputated in Belford Hospital, but no prosthesis could make her a whole woman.

Pain pills on the nightstand offered the oblivion of sleep, a refuge from the kindness of Maggie, Hamish, Eleanor, and the haunted echoes of impossibility. Unscrewing the cap, Bonny took two, swallowed them with water from the half-empty glass, and drew the blankets over her head to block out the light. One day, she must face the world. Not today.

Sometime later, a hand shook her shoulder, dragging her up from the depths of a drugged slumber. "It's noon, *mo gràdh*. You must eat to heal." Kieran knelt beside the bed, his deep voice tender.

"Leave me alone."

His firm grip on the blankets made it impossible to hide her face. "You'll feel better if you dress and come downstairs. I'll read to you or play the piano, but you must get out of bed." He extracted the blankets from her grasp. "Sometimes we have to be forced to live in order to survive." With one swift movement, he sat Bonny on the bedside then lifted her to stand.

"Kieran … no."

"Eleanor made potato soup and fresh bread for lunch." His strong hold prevented her from turning back to the bed. "You'll join us at the table, and you will eat. You needn't carry the sadness alone. It was *our* baby—*our* hope. I need you."

"Dr. Moncrieffe said to rest." She stamped her foot for emphasis and tried to turn away. "Let me go!"

In answer, he propelled her toward the bathroom with gentle but firm hands. "Do I stand you under the shower in your nightgown, or will you cooperate?"

Bonny acquiesced with reluctance. It would do no good to resist.

The warm water flowed over her head and back, relaxed her, and her stomach growled in hunger. When she stepped out, Kieran wrapped her in a plush, red towel. The rub of terrycloth against her skin further increased her circulation. After she dressed in the soft, pink lounging pajamas he laid out and coiled her hair into a knot, Kieran drew her close. "We'll do better together than when you're miserable in bed and me miserable downstairs."

He followed her down the back stairs to the kitchen, the heartbeat of the old house. The old, white Aga cooker, a cast-iron monstrosity of ovens and cook plates in its alcove of blue and white Dutch tiles, radiated heat throughout the room. Bonny accepted the chair he offered. Maggie set hot soup and bread in front of her and caressed her shoulder before returning to her own meal. "Kieran promised us a piano recital. I haven't heard him play in ages."

As the soup spread warmth through her, Bonny relaxed. No smiles, but family was a blessing. If she thanked God for one thing each day, perhaps she could begin to heal.

Snuggled on the living room couch near the fireplace, Maggie beside her, peaceful strains of hymns and Scottish folk songs eased her hopelessness. The most loving man she knew set aside his own grief and chose her favorite tunes to lift her spirits. How his big fingers skimmed over the keys with such delicacy caused her to marvel.

When he finished, Kieran moved to her other side. "I plan to drive down to the chapel tomorrow and check the progress. Come along. We'll pray, looking out at the loch and forward to the day people worship there for the first time. We need to focus on the positive, love. I'll offer encouragement faithfully the way you did for me during my depression."

Infertility posed no new challenge, but this time Kieran shared her sadness. Janet's offer of lunch might do her good. Maybe a woman, who wasn't her mother-in-law, could speak light into her darkness. Perhaps Kieran's old friend would suggest a way to engage him in a serious discussion about adoption.

୧୨

Cheerful laughter, the homey clatter of dishes, and Angus heading out the door to set the farm in motion met Bonny when she descended the stairs the next morning. In her desire to please Kieran, she realized how much she needed the people she loved. Time alone took her mind to places better avoided.

Next to the library, the big farm kitchen with its dark wood floors, wainscoting, and huge, rectangular table was her favorite place in the house. This morning, the wide windows framed by blue and white curtains, blue placemats, and bright sunflowers grated on her frayed nerves. Everything about this kitchen screamed Bronwyn, as did most of the house. Kieran agreed to redecorate before the wedding and morning sickness followed by grief interrupted her plans. Conversation around the kitchen table hushed when Bonny stepped into the room.

"What's wrong?" Maggie and Eleanor dished up more eggs, *haggis*, black sausage, and *bannocks* than she could eat while her sweet husband pulled out her chair.

"When Mother sits down, we'll tell you." He scooted her chair toward the table.

Hamish nodded his greeting and scooped a forkful of *haggis*. "It's good to see you up and dressed, lass. Your cheeks gain color every day."

"I'm trying." She'd never manage the breakfast Maggie placed before her, but she joined hands for grace. "Now, why do you all look so serious?"

"We received a letter from a solicitor in Inverness," Kieran said. "Someone called Gavin Gunn claims the Greenfield area belongs to him. He sent a copy of the same deed Da mentioned, without the handwritten agreement. We're driving to Fort William to our solicitor later. If Janet is free for lunch, you can ride along." His warm hands kneaded the knots in her neck.

"Sounds like a great idea. But who is Gavin Gunn?" At least something besides her caused the hush this time, and she longed for a talk with Janet.

"We don't know. I'll call for a late morning appointment when the office opens." In spite of the new concern, the brightness of Kieran's eyes mirrored the sky outside, free of rain for the first time in a week. He patted her knee, making her glad she came downstairs.

"Maggie, do you want to come? Agnes would love to see you." The little food she ate to satisfy them already formed a lump in her stomach.

"No, dear, I have mounds of reservation requests for the Heather Hill Inn. Bridget can't manage everything without me. You have fun." Maggie pushed back her chair and reached for the men's plates. "Keep your plate, Bonny."

"Not hungry. Maybe lunch will spark my appetite." She handed over her plate, turned from the wrinkled brow and grim turn of Maggie's lips, and sighed in relief. She could bare her heart to Janet in safety.

The inn Maggie and Hamish started after they turned the farm over to Kieran had been a dream of Maggie's for years. Inherited from her MacKenzie ancestors, the lovely old Dickens-era house in Beauly enjoyed increasing popularity as one of the loveliest bed-and-breakfast establishments in the Highlands. Her sacrifice to leave seasonal preparations to Eleanor's daughter Bridget did not come without cost.

"I'll come with you, love." Kieran stood and pulled out her chair.

The hand he settled in the middle of her back on their way upstairs drew her into an embrace when he closed the door to their room. "It will be good to have you along. We can go shopping when we're finished. Today's sunshine might put the pink back in your cheeks."

The scent of his cologne and nearness of his lips invited her closer. She gazed up at his rugged, handsome face. "I don't need new clothes, but we can walk around if I have the energy after lunch."

"We'll have time alone while Da places orders for Angus." His lips brushed hers. Poor man, so eager to see her mood improve.

"It's my first time out other than to the doctor. Let's wait and see if I have the energy."

"Of course. What's wrong, *hen*? You're too quiet." His forehead rested on hers and their eyes met while her emotions roiled and churned.

"I … I think Janet can help. I'll call her." She disentangled herself from his arms and walked to the nightstand for her cell phone. "I'll be fine."

"Come down when you're ready." His frown revealed how much he longed for the wife he knew. Her sadness left him at a loss.

Janet suggested The Stables Restaurant in the center of town. Time with Kieran's lifelong friend and her best friend in Scotland always lifted her spirits and provided insight into his mind. And it offered a chance to find out the latest on the wedding plans.

If only Hamish and Kieran would receive good news from the attorney.

ᘓ ᘔ

Fort William, lovely town of sparkling water and mountain beauty, edged the shores of Loch Linnhe and Loch Eil in the shadow of Ben Nevis, the places she and Kieran first met and fell in love. Bonny gazed up the hill toward the fairytale cottage provided for her during the nine months she taught at FWCC.

Poignant memories of arriving alone after the cancer deaths of both parents and a broken engagement nipped at her like *midges*. Here, she came back to life, in part due to the friendship and patience of Janet, her mother Agnes, and Graeme.

Bonny hopped out when Hamish pulled to a stop in Janet's driveway and leaned in Kieran's lowered window for a kiss.

"Enjoy yourself, love. No hurry, but save enough energy for me."

"Call when you finish at the lawyer … uh, solicitor's. We'll plan where to meet."

Janet waited at the open door and waved. "Such adorable newlyweds. Hello Kieran, Hamish. I'll take good care of her. I promise."

"We'll always be newlyweds." Kieran waved while Hamish backed out and headed down the street.

Her friend's warm hug started the deluge of emotions again. "Are you certain you want to go out? I can make lunch here."

Bonny wiped her face, pasted on a smile, and headed for Janet's little blue car. "You said The Stables, and I'll hold you to it. Girlfriend time and your wedding plans are all I need. What's the latest?"

"We do things simply." She unlocked the car doors. "Kieran told Graeme we'll be your first event at the chapel, even before your opening service. Graeme only has his sister and her husband, with their kids at school in London. My lot will be the majority of guests. Of course, we'll invite faculty members from FWCC, old friends from Faith Chapel, and Kieran's parents, about fifty or sixty in all. I plan to wear my sister *Shelagh's* wedding dress. And there you have it." Janet's joyful smile was a delight after watching her suffer for over a year.

"What about flowers and reception?"

"White roses and purple heather. We'll clear away the chairs and hold the reception in the chapel. You'll be my matron of honor, of course."

"Not one of your sisters? If I had family, I'd want them in my wedding. My feelings won't be hurt."

"You and Kieran are our best friends. I'm closer to you than to my sisters, with them all in Glasgow. Please say yes."

Fingers of warmth wrapped around Bonny's heart. "Yes, but let us host your reception in the house. Since Kieran enlarged the living room for church fellowships, we have more than enough room."

"I'd be crazy to turn down such a generous offer. Thank you."

They parked down the street and walked, giggling like teenagers about the men they loved. Janet held open the heavy door of the stylish restaurant. The waiter showed them to a comfortable booth with artistic renderings of Highland cattle on the walls.

"*Still* water," Bonny said to the waiter. The term brought back memories of her first restaurant experience in Scotland when asked her preference for *still* or *sparkling*. In America, they assumed plain water.

"Kieran wants a *ceilidh* next month. You can see what a perfect place the new living room would be for your reception. I need help anyway," Bonny confessed. "I have no idea how to plan one."

"You can count on Mom and me. How do you feel?" Janet's eyebrows narrowed with concern. "You're too thin."

She sucked in a deep breath, determined not to cry. "I … I have nightmares and can't eat. Janet, I grieved my infertility a long time ago, but renewed hope revived the pain. The hardest part is Kieran's disappointment."

Janet laid her fork down and clasped Bonny's hand between her own. "You're both upset, pet. It's natural, but you were in such danger. He's thankful to have you alive."

"I know, and I believe God will heal us. I want to adopt, but he insists we're not ready. It's a huge shift from single college professor to a sheep farmer's wife and soon-to-be pastor's wife. One of my biggest frustrations is Bronwyn's touch in every room. You remember how Kieran made a shrine of their bedroom before he created ours from two others and turned theirs into a guest room. I live in another woman's home. Of course, I love the MacDonell memorabilia. They're my family now too. But …"

"A woman wants her own home. What changes would you make?"

Bonny relaxed against the back of the booth with her friend's patient understanding. "Simple things. I wouldn't change the library or foyer. They make Stonehaven Farm the MacDonell family home. I appreciate Bronnie's talent, and keeping some of her art would honor her memory, but I want to replace her blues with my own reds, golds, and browns. We brought back some paintings of New Mexico scenery from our honeymoon. They'd make me feel more at home."

"You settled the concerns over the house in your premarital counseling."

"We did. He even set aside the money. First, Kieran needed to recover, and then I got pregnant and sick. My forced inactivity makes the rainy-day depression worse. I miss dry, sunny, New Mexico weather, and sitting around makes me think about unfinished projects. A lonely farm is a lot different than teaching in town, enjoying the newness of Scotland, and falling in love."

Janet's lips curved in a smile. "I warned you there were big changes ahead. Kieran's love for New Mexico doesn't surprise me. Dry, sunny weather is as much a novelty to us as rain is to you. You say you're a desert rat, and it takes time to grow webs between your toes like a duck."

Bonny's phone vibrated, and she slid it from her purse. "Yes, love, we're finished. Meet us at The Stables. We'll walk around a little."

"Look at you, the entire salad eaten and bread too." Janet laid her napkin on the table and signaled the waiter. "Talk to him. Kieran will do anything, even redecorate the house, to make you happy. Let's get together again soon. The four of us can meet in Spean Bridge for dinner now and then. Give him time to get used to the idea of adoption. He'll come around."

"I'm more relaxed after lunch with you than at any time in weeks. I didn't plan to walk around with Kieran, but you lifted a huge burden from my shoulders. Keep us in your prayers. We still have a long recovery ahead, and we haven't learned how to be Mr. and Mrs. MacDonell yet. It's not easy to let go of the past. You'll find out for yourself."

They paid the bill and Janet held the door. "I'm sure we will. Graeme doesn't realize the baggage Sean's infidelity and verbal abuse left behind. There's no one more patient and loving than Kieran, unless it's Graeme. Now go enjoy the sunshine and your husband."

಴ ಏ

One look in the mirror revealed new color in Bonny's cheeks and a renewed sparkle in her eyes, in spite of feeling tired and sore from their outing. Two hours of alone time had relaxed them both. If only it would last.

She changed clothes, still savoring the sweetness of the afternoon when Hamish summoned them into the library. He and Kieran refused to discuss their appointment with the solicitor until they could talk to everyone together.

"Sheep in a thunderstorm aren't more nervous than we've been waiting to hear about your appointment. Why must you explain in person?" Maggie glared at Kieran and Hamish as Eleanor handed around the ever-necessary tea.

"It's him." Kieran met Bonny's eyes, jaw muscles working, hands fisted tight. She pried his fingers apart and took his hand. "Gavin Gunn not only wants our land, he kept me from the hospital when you needed me."

"How can you be certain, lad? You only caught a glimpse before he *skelped* you." Bonny laughed at the Angus' use of the Scot's word for the blow to Kieran's head. She loved the tall, sinewy man, who reminded her of the weather-beaten and twisted cedars and piñons of New Mexico.

"Ach, I wouldn't forget such a *bampot*. Lachlan Menzies called Gunn's solicitor in Inverness, Rory McDuffie, who believes Gunn has a legitimate claim to the land. He has no doubt he'd cause a *stramash* if crossed. I'd sooner strangle the man than deal with him." Kieran's face grew redder with every word. "There's more, and it will hurt you, Bonny. He went on a rant, says my American wife doesn't belong here, and our children will be mongrels, unfit to inherit. Of course, he doesn't know we can't have children. But I'm concerned about you."

Heart pounding, she pulled her hand away and met his stormy eyes. "You mean he'd try to hurt me?"

"We're all in danger. You must stop thinking about adoption until it's safe."

"That's an excuse, Kieran. You don't want to adopt. And it's not only me who needs to think." Her throat tightened with emotion, giving her voice a strangled quality. "Did he describe this man?"

"Adoption?" Maggie's brows knitted together over stormy blue eyes.

Kieran glared at his mother and reached for Bonny's hand but she tucked it under her leg. "Love, you're not strong enough yet, and now's not the time to discuss it. Gunn doesn't have a phone and gave McDuffie no clue when he'd return. Apparently, he lives off the grid, in the far north of Caithness. His description fits what I remember. He speaks English but prefers the Gaelic. Claimed he'd be back when he returns to Inverness but didn't indicate when. This could be more complicated than it first appeared."

Hamish swallowed half a scone covered with blackberry jam and nodded his approval toward Eleanor. "Mr. Menzies looked the deed over and assured us it's legal."

"They'll set a court date, but with no way to notify Gunn, he might not show up." Kieran gulped the last drop of tea, his cup clattering on the saucer. "Ach, he might not accept a rulin' of the court. We won't borrow trouble, but it's best to prepare for anythin'. Angus, describe him to the farmhands and tell them to watch for suspicious people or activity, especially near Greenfield."

Bonny looked around, emotions roiling like storm clouds over the loch. The lovely room, a serene haven of fine woodwork, floor-to-ceiling bookshelves, and latticed windows of ancient glass provided a scenic view of the loch and pastures. Had the long-ago conversations about the deed and Brighde taken place beneath the carved clan crest above the great fireplace? "Kieran, if Gunn claims Greenfield, how did he find you in the Laddie Wood?"

"He either followed me or hid there since it's wooded. He knew who I was." He chewed the last bite of his scone with such gusto, it might have been Gunn himself.

"Calm down. You'll have a headache." Maggie stood.

"She's right, love. Don't let your anger consume you." Kieran's tone disturbed Bonny. He still suffered severe headaches and her concern outweighed her frustration. She moved her hand to his cheek, savoring the rough whiskers and strong, square jaw, thankful for his determination and strength. "You'll make yourself worse. He won't blend in if he shows up on the farm."

"True." Kieran's laugh sounded forced. "Sorry, I'll try to remain calm. We can only trust God and wait."

"I'll gather the men before they leave." Angus glanced toward the late afternoon sun, which slanted through the windows and headed for the door. "Maybe we'll catch him. Caithness could be a lie to throw us off the track."

Hamish rose to shake the hand of his old friend. "Aye, you're right. The more watchful eyes, the better."

"Kieran, I don't think you should go out alone for a while. A crazy man stalking you to make good his failed attack scares me." Bonny's heart hammered against her ribs. "Please be careful."

"I agree," Maggie spoke up. "You can't risk it."

"We won't live in fear." Kieran pounded his fist on his knee. "He won't control us."

"It's not cowardice to take common-sense precautions." Maggie crossed the room and began to gather cups and plates. "Be considerate of your wife, *mo mhac*. The entire situation is far from ordinary."

Hamish rose, put his arm around Maggie, and motioned Bonny to his side. They crossed the room to where the map of Stonehaven Farm and Glen Garry hung above an ancient writing desk. "Your great, great granda gave all he had for this land. We won't lose it by your blood, Kieran. Keep one of the farmhands with you at all times. And watch your back."

CHAPTER FOUR

The girl looked about fifteen, huddled in the corner of the couch with head tucked. Dark blonde hair partially covered her freckled face and heavy eye makeup. He cringed inwardly at the noticeable bulge under her blue shirt.

Really, Lord, now? And on my first day?

"Emily? I'm Pastor Kieran MacDonell. You can come back now."

Shyness, hopelessness perhaps, appeared to drag the girl down when she stood. With a pretty but blemish-marked face and guarded eyes far too old for her years, she shuffled across the small lobby and offered a limp handshake. Once seated in the office, she stared at child-size hands clenched tight in her lap.

Kieran took the chair across from her, unwilling to place a desk between them. "What can I help you with, Emily?"

"I … I'm pregnant. My mum's raising my sister's three kids. Can you find a family for my baby?" Mascara streaked down her cheeks and dropped onto her jeans.

"We'll do our best. How old are you, and when is your baby due?" Why did young girls, still in school, have babies when he and Bonny couldn't?

She accepted a tissue and scrubbed her face. "I'm seventeen. The baby's due in three months. Mum raised me right. My boyfriend and I used precautions. We didn't mean it to happen, but I won't have an abortion."

"You came to the right place but it's an area where I have little experience. Can you give me a few days to look into the possibilities?" Bonny would want this baby.

She stared at her hands. "How long?"

If only he could offer a family now and send her off with the knowledge her child had a home. Helplessness and long-held objections weighed him down like the 175-pound *cabers* he used to toss in the Highland Games. "I'll have options for you on Friday afternoon. Can you come back then?"

"Yeah, sure." She stood. "If you don't, my boyfriend will make me have an abortion. I can't …" The streams of mascara began again.

Kieran stood and opened the door. "Next Friday then. Same time."

Her feet dragged across the waiting room.

"There are answers. I won't let you down."

She stepped into the hall. Kieran closed the door and sank into his chair, head in his hands. *Lord, why send her to me now? Others are much better equipped.*

But who? The interim pastor at Faith Chapel was from Edinburgh and unfamiliar with resources in the Highlands. Graeme wasn't familiar with options either. The research was up to him, and Bonny would sense his weighty concern when he walked through the door. Whether he wanted to or not, mentioning Emily would force an adoption discussion.

Rival emotions battled all the way home, but he needed Bonny's help. She was researching adoption agencies. The brochures covered her desk.

I'm not ready.

Young, pretty, her whole life in front of her, Emily tugged at his heart.

Too young to be a parent.

Too heartrending to keep to himself.

He swiped at his face, unable to erase the anger, frustration, helplessness, and longing.

Bonny would read the expression in his eyes.

The answer would hurt her.

☙❧

Dreich and *drookit.* Days of dark, damp clouds when rain dripped from the gutters and slid down the windows seeped into her soul. Would she ever get used to weeks of wet and fog? Too much time alone allowed Bonny to dwell on the small stone Kieran placed in the Fort William *kirkyard* with *Baby MacDonell* engraved above a lamb.

Hearing the Land Rover splash through puddles in the drive, her spirits lifted like New Mexico clouds. At the creak of the garage door springs, she ran for the comfort of his arms—anxious thoughts distracted with him home. When he dragged his briefcase from the car, it appeared to weigh two tons. Steps lagging, he forced a smile and crushed her against him with a hug that muffled his hello in a sob.

"What's wrong?" She drew back, staring into eyes grayer than the clouds.

He followed her into the kitchen in silence. "You're a much better counselor than I am." He sank into a chair and reached for the teapot. "Hot?"

"Yes. What happened?" He waved away the biscuits she offered. Pouring her own cup, she sat down, hand on his shoulder.

"A young girl came in today. She needs help fast." The story poured forth like water over a broken dam. "You're researching adoption agencies. I need your help. Where can I send her?"

Bonny's breath caught. *Don't cry. It's ministry work. God will open his eyes when the time is right.* She climbed the stairs to the office for the information. *Thank you for bringing Emily to the office on Kieran's day, Lord.*

When she reentered the kitchen, he sipped his tea and stared out at the rain. She laid the information in front of him. "There's one called Forever Family. It's London-based, but there are churches in Aberdeen, Perth, and Glasgow who collaborate with them. It's a growing movement to find foster and adoptive homes for children in the UK. It might be what Emily needs. Maybe Faith Chapel and Hope Chapel could become involved."

"Glasgow's not bad. What's closest?"

"There's not much in the Highlands, though Inverness and Aberdeen have agencies offering foster care and adoption. Inverness is closest for appointments."

"First thing in the morning, I'll call." He continued to stare out the window.

"Emily wanted help from a church. We could—"

"No."

She scooted her chair out, picked up the dishes, and headed for the sink. His hands came to rest on her shoulders, insistent, begging. She turned, unwilling to meet his eyes.

"Come sit with me in the library. I can't discuss us now. Can you understand?"

Bonny accepted the handkerchief he offered but refused to look up. "No, I don't. Emily could have gone to another church any day of the week, but a pregnant girl came to our church today when you were there. If God wants us to adopt a baby, he'll show us. Will you at least pray about it?"

Kieran walked to the cold fireplace and rested his hand on the mantle, staring at the ashes. "You had your mind made up long before we met."

"I believed you were ready to have a family the only way I could give you one."

"Why think about it until we married and knew for certain? It's not the only way. There are fertility clinics. Significant scarring doesn't mean your womb can't carry a child." The raised tone of his voice, so uncharacteristic, surprised her.

"It would be *our* child, conceived in our hearts rather than in my womb. Bonny moved closer to him and cupped his face in her hands. "I have one ovary covered in scar tissue, stage IV endometriosis, and the surgeries failed. Dr. Moncrieffe wasn't encouraging about other methods."

"A small-town doctor. If we go to Edinburgh, Glasgow, or London, they can do more. We could try." He gripped her arms, eyes bright, hope and determination in his voice.

"I'm afraid, Kieran. We live so far from help. What if I had problems again? Is it so important for a child to have MacDonell genes? Children are children, and God puts families together in many different ways. Kari is adopted, and few people we know are more well-adjusted and happier."

"When Bronwyn and I lived in Glasgow, we had some friends who adopted a little boy. Months later, when they felt like a real family and the adoption was almost final, the birthmother changed her mind and took the baby back. They were heartbroken—gave up on their dreams—never tried again. I've lost two children. I can't lose another. You talk like adoption's a sure thing, but it's not."

"Fertility treatments aren't either. We just lost a child and you almost lost me. Kieran, there are no guarantees. Why didn't you tell me about your friends before?"

"I hoped you'd wait to discuss it until you were stronger. Bonny, I don't want to adopt for a lot of reasons. I'm not certain I could love someone else's child as my own." Kieran drew her tight against him, fingers tangled in her hair. "Please, visit the fertility specialist for me. If you can't get pregnant or it's too risky, we'll discuss adoption."

"No more surgery. I can't take it physically or emotionally." Bonny disentangled herself from his arms and headed back to the kitchen. "I'll call you when dinner's ready. Genetics don't matter to me. Motherhood does. Pregnancy and birth are short-term experiences. Parenting lasts a lifetime. What's more important?"

She didn't wait for his answer.

C3 80

Emily—pretty, pitiful, and more heartrending than Kieran described. This baby might be for them, but God, not her, must convince him.

When Kieran asked Bonny to sit in on the Friday appointment, she brought in pictures for the walls, a small table, a lamp, and a couple of plants to make the counseling office at Faith Chapel warm and homey. It still felt cold since they were not going to offer to take the girl's baby.

"They'll give you profiles of adoptive parents to choose from, people who have passed all their training and background checks. Loving people who want children desperately." Bonny bit her tongue until it stung.

"Mum and I agree they need to be Christians. If I can't raise the baby, we want parents who will teach him right." Puddles formed in Emily's dark blue eyes. "I shouldn't have slept with my boyfriend, but he's older, twenty-one. I thought he'd marry me."

"An agency in Inverness works with Christian families. We'll start with them and make the phone calls for you." She hoped to secure a social worker who would travel to Fort William. How would she ever remain objective?

Neither spoke on the ride home. Bonny bit her tongue and fought a tug-o-war between anger and sadness, staring out the window rather than facing Kieran.

"I'm going to *Torr na Carriach* early in the morning to check on the *kyloe*. I'll prepare for Sunday's Bible study tonight and eat dinner in the office while I work." He announced it when they pulled into the garage. Clearer than the clouds mirrored in the loch, she recognized his determination to avoid discussing the cry of her heart.

"You weren't supposed to go off alone." Anyone could check on the Highland cattle.

"I refuse to allow a maniac control over our lives."

"You make an adoption discussion taboo but you can endanger yourself. What kind of sense does that make?"

"When I asked for help, I knew you'd want Emily's child. You'll counsel her better but I can't adopt now, Bonny. Accept it." The chill in his voice withered her hopes like leaves at the first frost.

"Fine." She climbed out and slammed her door. "I'll save the chicken for tomorrow and make sandwiches. Go ahead and do what you want without regard for anyone else. This isn't the man I thought I married. I can't believe you'd be narrow-minded enough to insist on a MacDonell pedigree. A child in need of a loving home isn't good enough. I'm going to bed early and read until I fall asleep."

"I'll get busy then." Without stopping, Kieran headed upstairs the minute they walked inside, leaving her alone in the kitchen.

Oh, I could shove him into the cold loch if I had the chance. Lord, if you want us to adopt, you have to convince him, because I can't be objective at all.

Kieran slid into bed after midnight. Bonny remained on her side, feigning sleep. Instead of drawing closer together through the first trials of their marriage, he seemed to pull away.

The next morning, he informed her they had an appointment with a Glasgow fertility specialist in one month. Everything he hoped for frightened her.

⊳⊴

Kieran left before Bonny awakened the next morning. She scrambled eggs and warmed up leftover patties of black sausage to boost the iron in her blood. A day spent alone in the house would only feed her still-simmering anger and insidious rebellion lurking like the Loch Ness Monster. If Kieran could go off alone, she would too.

With a full stomach, she headed upstairs for her riding clothes, pulled on boots, and walked across the lawn to the barn, lunch in hand.

"Mornin', lass." Angus walked out of the barn office. "Are you taking Misty out? She's feeling her oats without your wild rides."

"It may not be wild yet, but we both need the exercise." She headed for the tack room.

The gentle old man brushed past and blocked the door to the tack room. "Kieran would think I'd gone *aff my heid* if I let you saddle her yourself. You look *fair wabbit* before noon every day. I'll do the work. You enjoy the ride."

"If you're testing my Scots, I understood every word. You're not crazy and I am tired. Thank you." She sat on a bale of hay while he groomed and saddled the little mare, keeping the conversation to farm matters.

He led her saddled horse into the sun and gave Bonny a hand up. "If you'll pardon me, I noticed the chill in Kieran's voice when he left. Make your differences right before the day's end, lassie. It does no good to let resentment build between the two of you. My missus and I never let the sun go down on our anger. If it's to do with your longing for a *bairn*, give him time. The MacDonells are a proud lot when it comes to their heritage."

"How did you know?"

"He told me about the lass at the church, and I pieced it together. I know him well."

"Thank you, Angus. I'm headed to the point near *Garb Eilean*. You don't need to worry about where I've gone." She nudged Misty into motion and headed out. The islands at the east end of the loch offered the privacy she craved. Better to remain on the north side of the bridge with Kieran south at *Torr na Carriach*. They both needed space.

"Don't stay out too long, Bonny. You'll worry him. The Lord be with you."

 CB & BO

Garb Eilean

The ghost of Emily walked alongside her. Bonny headed off the single-track road into the grass along the shore. She needed solitude, and if Kieran took chances, she would too.

She settled her Stetson lower to shade her from the warm sun. With her western saddle and boots—along with a MacDonell tartan scarf around her neck—she'd make a rare sight for anyone who happened along. Today, she needed the comfort of familiar things. Her lunch held a turkey sandwich with green chile and *biscochitos* from the freezer.

Homey foods turned her thoughts to Albuquerque and their honeymoon visit to Old Town for the Christmas Stroll and tree lighting. The warm glow of the luminarias enveloped the sidewalks, rooftops, and porch rails with a golden radiance the way their new marriage and the unexpected gift of her pregnancy illuminated their lives. Flickering lights bestowed a simple beauty on ancient adobe buildings. Everything had been peaceful and serene. Where had their closeness gone? They were really still honeymooners.

Aside from the new environment, nothing prepared her to be a wife under such strange and trying circumstances. Their delayed honeymoon that began with a visit to an Albuquerque emergency room, where they discovered her pregnancy, had taken an even more bizarre direction.

Enough. She came away from the house to avoid morbid thoughts. The sparkling loch, lined with tall trees and green grass carpeted with yellow gorse, mirrored green mountains fading to blue. She drank in the lovely view and breathed deep of the fresh, sweet-scented air. Here and there, a few early sprigs of bright-pink, cross-leaved heath heather waved in the breeze, a cheerful banner, and one of her favorite Scottish flowers. A pair of broad-winged hawks soared on the breeze, and in the trees above, a blue-winged warbler sang its song.

The isolated shores of the islands near the east end of the loch beckoned her. Without a boat, she imagined her trouble and confusion floating downriver in the clear, rippling water.

Marriage wasn't supposed to be this hard, especially when her husband was the most selfless, generous man she'd ever known, except for her father. Her mind connected the dots between the loss of the baby and Emily's appearance with no detours between.

Before she and Kieran were married, they seemed to agree on everything. Now, they disagreed about both challenges they faced. How could they argue when a child needed parents and a young girl begged for help they could provide?

At a flat, grassy spot with a clear view of the islands, Bonny halted Misty and dismounted. The blanket in her saddlebag provided protection from the damp ground, while the gray mare cropped tender new shoots of grass near her side. She led the horse to the shore for a drink and sat on a sun-warmed rock while a woodpecker tapped on a tree the way questions needled her mind.

The sandwich filled the empty spot in her stomach, but failed to satisfy her heart. A wee bit of homesickness niggled from the combination of anise, sugar, and cinnamon in the cookies.

Her mother once said men's brains organized everything in tidy boxes with no connection to each other, while women's brains were a tangle of electrical wires. Each sparked the one next to it, all linked, never at rest. Kieran had pigeonholed adoption in a box he refused to open.

Bonny grew up knowing a lot of adopted kids, and because of them, believed adoption answered her desire for a family. When Kieran accepted her infertility and proposed, she assumed he agreed with her need to adopt. The loss of their unexpected miracle, and the appearance of Emily made a neat little package of God's intervention. Her mother would say to give him space, the same way Angus and Janet warned her to let his heart follow its own path to the answers.

Living with a man wasn't easy, especially a proud one. Though he did everything to please her before marriage, now differences appeared on an almost daily basis.

The sun had passed its midpoint. Misty's eyes were closed, her back to the rising wind. Bonny stood, stretched out the kinks, and picked up the remains of her lunch. Angus would worry if she didn't return soon, and Kieran shouldn't come home to an empty house.

"Thanks for filling in the blanks, Mom. I miss you." She turned for one last look at the islands.

Snap!

She stood. Eyes scanning the woods and down to the loch's edge where something moved in the shadow of a tree. A tidal wave of fear rushed through her veins when a man stepped into the sunlight. She was looking at a character out of *Braveheart*. He fit the description of Gavin Gunn. He lunged toward her, mouth twisted in an evil grin of yellowed teeth and tangled beard.

Instinct propelled her into the saddle. "Giddup, Misty! Fly!" She kicked the little mare into a gallop.

Her hat flew away. Her ponytail loosened, hair streaming free. Bonny laid over the horse's neck. Urged her faster.

Halfway home, where the road curved away from the loch, she slowed the horse to a trot and looked back. No one followed. Perhaps he was on foot?

Prodding Misty back into a gallop, she headed for the farm. Neither of them should be out alone. How could they consider bringing a child into such a dangerous situation?

☙❧

Torr Na Carriach

The lowing of his Highland cattle always soothed Kieran. The sheep ignored his presence, but the small, shaggy *kyloe* allowed him to rub between their ears. The *wee beasties* listened without judgment. *Coos* were a way to preserve

Highland heritage and also a source of excellent beef and a good income. He saw them as friends.

Bonny wasn't pleased when he came alone after she and his mother urged him to avoid it, but today called for solitude. Her wide-eyed fear, the disbelief in her voice when he insisted on a fertility specialist replayed again, a horror movie stuck in a loop. It seemed logical. Why hadn't her beloved Dr. Carson suggested it? Yes, the severity of her endometriosis made pregnancy more risky than normal, but he hadn't said it was impossible.

When he fell in love with a thirty-year-old woman, Kieran expected the large family he'd craved as an only child. After fifteen years with Bronwyn, he assumed he had marriage figured out, but Bonny presented a new challenge every day. Both were fiery redheads with minds of their own, but the resemblance ended there. The opposite of quiet Bronwyn, content with her painting, Bonny involved herself in every aspect of farm life, and never gave up without a fight. Strong opinions were etched in her mind like a stone tablet.

Irresistible from the moment he spotted her across the room at the faculty meeting, their love was an unexpected gift. Emotional and tenacious, her ideas on adoption weren't going away.

He developed a fascination with his ancestor's portraits in early childhood. Stern, stoic, in colorful tartans, and crackled with age, they survived *Culloden*, the outlawing of the clans, and confiscation of their homes. His second great grandfather achieved an extraordinary feat when he bought back the sacred trust of family lands generations later. Throughout his years in Glasgow, as a math professor and bagpipe master, Kieran never doubted he would return to the farm out of love, not duty.

A cold meat pie in the shade of a gnarled old tree he climbed in as a child served for lunch. Laid back in the grass, he watched puffy, white clouds float across a cerulean sky, lulled by the susurrus through the trees. He would die for Bonny, but raising a stranger's child sent chills through him.

She had a point. Kari was nothing like her adoptive family, and it appeared to bother no one. To spend a few minutes around them was to sense their family love and unity. He selected the number from his phone and waited for her to pick up while he sniffed the sweet scent of new clover and a red squirrel chattered in the tree above.

"Kieran? What's wrong?" Kari sounded frightened and out of breath while a baby wailed in the background.

"I didn't mean to scare you. We're fine. From the baby noises, it's not a good time to ask difficult questions."

"Ooof. There, I have him. Hush, Willie. Give me a second, Kieran." The phone clattered against a hard surface, and the crying ceased. "I'm back. Sorry, they're persistent when it's mealtime. I already fed Annie. Is Bonny alright?"

He couldn't help laughing. "Better every day. Are you getting the hang of the twin thing?"

"Sometimes. Today's a good one."

"I won't keep you long. We're at a stalemate, and I need wisdom from someone who knows adoption and my wife. Please don't say I called. I need time to work through this."

Kari laughed. "Her mind's been made up for years. What can I tell you?"

"How does your family do it? I've lost track of the number of adopted and biological, but it works in spite of the differences. Have your siblings always blended in the natural and easy way they appear to?" Of course, they didn't. What a dumb thing to say. "Sorry. I guess the question should be, how did you work through the adjustments?"

"Prayer and commitment, the same as in marriage, Kieran. My parents determined to make it work. They were honest with their birth and adoptive kids about the difficulties and handled it with prayer, firm discipline, family meetings, and occasional counseling. It's not always easy, but they believed God put our family together the way he wanted it. Hard work and unconditional love make a family, Kieran, not blood.

"We're not all the best of friends, but we respect and accept our differences. My parents looked for strengths and helped us build on them. They never allowed us to put one another down. We learned to be cheerleaders for each other, the strong helping the weak. Am I answering your question?"

Fireworks exploded in his overloaded brain. "I suspect there's a lot more behind it."

"Yeah, I guess so. My parents believed adoption was a Christian duty. They wanted a huge family, and after my mom went through a difficult delivery, they chose adoption. One of my brothers spent time in jail. They visited and loved him. He created an example for the rest of us of how not to live, but he remained part of the family, and we supported him."

Kieran took a long swallow from his water bottle and tried to formulate a question. "Would they do it again? Would you?"

"Hold on while I settle Willy." After more shuffling and a baby burp, she picked up the phone again. "I believe they would. Dan and I discussed it before we married. We'd adopt in a minute. Consider this. God adopted us and loves each one for who we are, the same way we love the variety of wildflowers. He said all people are our brothers, so why not our children?"

The fireworks went wild.

"Kieran?"

"I … I'm here. Just overwhelmed."

He heard a loud burp, and Kari giggled. "I think I've filled my little guy's tummy and your brain. If I said too much at once, I'm sorry. You can call me again, anytime."

"You've given this a lot of thought. I'll never remember it all."

"Because I was adopted out of a bad situation at fifteen, I understand it differently than children adopted at birth. Once I had a real family, I felt like other kids. To me, adoption is a gift, a natural outgrowth of someone caring enough to give a child in need a home and love."

"Ach, what a lot to think about. Maybe in time, I'll feel different."

"Dad always asked both biological and adopted children three questions at bedtime. He'd tuck us in and ask, 'Who gave you to me to love?' We'd answer, 'God.' Then he'd say, 'How long will I love you?' We'd answer, 'Forever.' Last, he'd ask, 'Is there anything you could ever do to make me stop loving you?' Our answer was 'no,' and we believed it."

"What a lovely way to help any child understand love."

"I went to sleep certain of their love from the time I joined the family. I had never known real love or parents who didn't force me to be the adult. I learned about fathers and God at the same time. I never felt less important or loved than their biological kids. God created our family, and we never questioned it."

Kieran stood and paced across the pasture, emotions roiling. "I'm amazed. From my end, the differences look insurmountable."

"Differences make life interesting. How mundane the world would be without them. I hope I've helped. No one can decide for you. Dan and I suspected Bonny would be ready sooner than you."

"I appreciate your prayers. I may call again."

"Anytime. I need to change Willie's diaper. And thanks for being such a wonderful husband to my friend."

"Bye, Kari. Thanks." Kieran hung up the phone, climbed into the Land Rover, and headed home. She offered a new perspective. He couldn't have the dialogue Bonny wanted, but maybe a dinner date was in order. A little romance might distract from the stress and remind them they were still honeymooners.

When he started across the bridge, Bonny raced into view rounding the curve in the road. She slowed her lathered horse to a trot, glanced behind her, and spurred Misty into the barn.

He stepped on the gas, pulled into the barnyard, and jumped out almost before the vehicle came to a complete stop.

"What's wrong?"

She rushed toward him, her head colliding with his chest hard enough she almost knocked the wind out of him. "A man. *Garb Eilean.* In the woods." She drew in great gulps of air, tears coursing down her flushed cheeks.

An icy hand wrapped around his heart. Fear pounded like an axe on a frozen loch. "Who? Are you hurt?"

"N-no. Gavin Gunn. I think. I was daydreaming. Oblivious. I don't know if he was watching or stumbled on me by surprise."

Angus came out of the barn office. "What's wrong, lass?"

"Bonny thinks Gavin Gunn approached her down by the islands. Did you know she went alone?"

The farm manager nodded.

He gripped her trembling shoulders. "Did he hurt you?"

"I jumped on Misty and took off. No one followed."

"You had no business out riding alone." He held her tight against him, but she balked.

"But it was all right for you to check on the *coos* alone. We agreed to be careful." The obstinate jut of her chin signaled trouble.

"I have a farm to run. You were out for what, rebellion?" He turned to Angus. "Take care of her horse. Bonny, we'll take our discussion inside."

"You weren't defiant?" Her voice was low and hard. "We settle it now. No one goes off alone. We listen to each other with respect and make decisions together. My needs are as legitimate as yours."

"Agreed. But first we call the police."

 COBO

Rivers of revulsion raced through Bonny's veins at the sight of the man from the loch seated at the plaintiff's table. She gripped Kieran's arm tighter. Gavin Gunn showed up for the hearing. The police had found nothing after he confronted her beside the loch.

Dark, stringy hair, waist-length, and tied with a leather thong. His kilt almost skimmed the floor in back, the wool stiff with soil, riddled with moth holes and small tears. At least he wore a shirt. Celtic tattoos covered the skin on his arms and legs. The boots, barely discernable below the kilt were crusted in mud, clumps of which littered the aisle but did nothing to detract from the decorum of the courtroom. The amber eyes burned with something she couldn't decipher. Hatred? Anger? Greed? Insanity? The man was an enigma.

What if the judge ruled he owned Greenfield? They would be cut off from the Laddie Wood and other prime grazing lands on the south side of Loch Garry. Fear of more personal harm haunted her.

Gunn uttered an expletive in Gaelic and glared in their direction, Bonny and Maggie seated behind Kieran, Hamish, and their solicitor, Lachlan Menzies. The other solicitor, she assumed to be Rory MacDuffie, turned and spoke quietly to him. Gavin shook a fist toward the judge. She wondered what he might attempt in the courtroom and reached for her mother-in-law's hand.

Scottish court procedures were somewhat different than American courts, at least from television shows and movies she'd seen. Pinpricks tingled up and down Bonny's spine when Gunn spoke, each time in Gaelic translated by MacDuffie. Maggie could translate, but she sat with eyes riveted on the backs of her husband and son.

Hamish testified in measured tones, eyes fixed on Menzies, never once turning toward Gunn. He described the terms of the deed and Diarmid's failure to return payment.

"Lies." Gavin leaped from the chair but the watchful bailiff grabbed him by both arms. A low growl issued from his throat reminding her of a wolf baring its teeth before an attack. "The land is mine by birthright. Stolen from my father."

He pointed toward Kieran. "No American belongs on MacDonell land. You'll never raise mongrels on Scottish land. I'll see you dead … I'll see you all dead."

"Enough." The judge pounded his gavel. "Bailiff, restrain this man for the verdict."

Two officers approached from the back of the courtroom, pulled Gunn's hands behind, and handcuffed him. Bonny was happy to not understand the string of Gaelic epithets.

"Mr. Gunn, you will remain silent or be removed from the courtroom." The judge looked over his glasses. "Due to the existence of the deed, duly signed, witnessed, and dated January 1, 1960, and the failure of Diarmid MacDonell to pay the amount due, we find the deed registered in Inverness-shire by Hamish MacDonell granting all lands comprising Stonehaven Farm to Kieran MacDonell to be legitimate. The court finds no evidence of the plaintiff's claim on the Greenfield lands. Said land therefore remains in the possession of Kieran MacDonell to be passed on to his heirs."

"Arrr!" Gunn wrenched free and rushed toward the judge's bench but the bailiff stopped him short.

"Mr. Gunn, in light of your outburst, and the alleged attack on Kieran MacDonell in the Bolinn Wood, you will be remanded to custody for thirty days while the police complete their examination of the evidence to determine if charges will be filed. You will leave my courtroom without further outburst."

Kieran turned and drew Bonny close while Gunn was escorted from the courtroom. Shouting Gaelic obscenities, he glared at them.

"Justice accomplished." Hamish held the door to the courtroom with one hand and grasped Maggie's hand with similar fervor to the grip Kieran kept on Bonny as they walked into the hallway.

"Aye, but not accepted, Da." An intense trembling accompanied Kieran's icy glare, and she edged closer. "I don't think Gavin Gunn will crawl back into whatever peat bog he crawled out of because a judge says so. We'll remain vigilant."

CHAPTER FIVE

The old stone farmhouse hummed with the voices of women in the kitchen and the laughter of men at work. Footsteps pounded across aged wooden floors, moving tables and furniture between house and barn. The delightful aroma of foods, both familiar and unfamiliar, issued from the hotplates and ovens of the old Aga cooker. Bonny's stomach growled with hunger.

Dressed in her MacDonell tartan, she sat between living room and kitchen, the designated supervisor of *ceilidh* preparations. No one appeared to need direction, so she indulged in people-watching, noted unfamiliar highland phrases, and marveled at the wide variety of clan tartans represented. Pride coursed through her veins at Kieran's easy camaraderie with farmworkers and neighbors, and their obvious respect for him. He offered a smile or wave whenever their eyes met, calling her Lady Bonny.

Maggie laid aside the load of tablecloths. "Should you rest, pet? If you're too tired, you won't enjoy the evening."

"How can I get tired when no one lets me do anything? I'm excited to meet our neighbors. I understood the farm's isolation, but nothing prepared me for the loneliness I'd feel after years of teaching."

Her mother-in-law's arm slipped around her shoulders. "Farm life can be lonely, but as you grow stronger, you'll get out more."

Bonny returned the embrace. "Right now, I'm excited about the music and dancing. Kieran owes me a few since we only danced once at our wedding."

"It's a wonder he could dance at all with a bullet wound in his side. If you don't keep up your strength, you'll be the one who can't dance."

"My blood count was normal. Dr. Moncrieffe says regaining strength takes time and patience."

"And we're here to see you do obey. I must say, you've made Kieran happier than I ever dreamed." With a pat on the arm, Maggie headed back toward the kitchen.

Kieran engaged in companionable conversation with a group of men gathered next to the wooden stage erected in one corner of the living room. Now larger by twice than the first time she saw it, her husband's vision of a gathering place for chapel and neighbors had become reality.

"Maggie said you needed tea. Everything looks lovely." Janet dragged a chair close.

"So many people brought boards and sawhorses for tables." Bonny sipped the too-sweet tea, Maggie's attempt to help her gain weight and energy. "We'll have a full house for sure."

"Are you ready for your debut as the Lady of Loch Garry?" Janet slipped an arm through hers.

"I didn't think I'd be this nervous. I'm happier than any time since the baby. It's a day for celebration since the judge decided in our favor. We should have no trouble tonight with Gavin Gunn in jail. And look at my husband, in his element in every way."

"What a relief. How are you feeling?"

"It helps to stay busy." Bonny accepted a scone when Maggie passed by again. "And I do know I'm loved."

"You are indeed." Janet stood and headed for the kitchen. "I need to stir the *cock a'leekie* soup and take a peek at the meat pies in the oven. Prop your feet up and *dinna fash*."

She laughed at the old Scottish adage not to worry and handed Janet her empty cup. Across the room, Kieran stooped and lifted the small daughter of a farmworker in his arms. The more giggles his tickling elicited, the broader he smiled.

The strong clan mentality of the MacDonells, as medieval as it seemed, caused him to question their ability to love a child not of their blood. How anyone could fail to want children who needed a family remained a puzzle, especially the way he enjoyed them.

The little girl skipped alongside as Kieran headed her direction. Bonny pushed her concerns away and smiled. He would make such a wonderful father. His playfulness and tender touch set the tiny mite at perfect ease.

"Who's your friend?"

He swung the apple-cheeked child with a riot of golden ringlets to his shoulders and laughed when she patted the top of his head. "I want you to meet Rowan. Her da and grandda both work at Stonehaven. She walked up, asked my name, and we became instant friends." He knelt with the child. "Rowan, say hello to Miss Bonny. Can you tell her how old you are?"

Face hidden, the little one held up three fingers.

"Three. What a big girl you are, Rowan."

Rosebud lips dimpled at the corners when blue-bonnet eyes met her own. "Misser Donell's my friend."

"Well, he's a friend of mine too." Bonny motioned Janet from the kitchen. "Could you find a biscuit for Rowan here?"

She nodded, curls bobbing. "Like biscuits." When Kieran set her down, she trotted after Janet.

"Where are her parents?" Bonny stood and smoothed Kieran's tousled hair into place.

"Her dad, Gordon McCrea, is setting up the microphones. I offered to watch her for a few minutes."

Bonny brushed his cheek with her fingers. "You're a natural with children, love."

Rowan ran back, a half-eaten cookie clutched in one hand before she deciphered the expression in his eyes. "Come, Misser Donell." Rowan grabbed one large finger, and led him toward her father.

"You see who's in charge." With a wink, he headed off, bent low to clasp the tiny hand.

She slipped upstairs and closed the bedroom door. It wouldn't do for the hostess to cry in front of everyone.

ೕ ೖ

Bonny's breath caught when her *braw* and *bonnie* Highlander mounted the stage, and she bounced on the balls of her feet in excitement. Fine and handsome, Kieran's deep baritone boomed over the din of gathering friends and neighbors dressed in everything from jeans to bright, varied tartans.

When he signaled, she joined him on stage, despite butterflies the size of eagles, grateful when he took her hand.

"I want to introduce my lovely wife, Bonny. She's learnin' a lot about sheep right now, and will love to hear your stories." A house full of highlanders brought out his thickest Scottish burr. "Please join us in singin' 'Flower of Scotland.' Then Bonny will perform 'Caledonia.' If you haven't heard her sing, you'll agree she's a special blessin.'"

The final notes of "Flower of Scotland" faded, and he left her alone at center stage.

"Welcome, and thank you for a lovely reception for a transplanted American. When I arrived at Fort William Christian College over a year and a half ago, I fell in love with Scotland and Kieran. I'll always be American, but I'm a Scot by choice. This song describes how I longed for your beautiful land when I returned home."

Cheers scattered the butterflies, smiles spread across the sea of faces, and her voice soared toward the vaulted ceiling.

"You tossed that caber straight and true," Kieran whispered when he rejoined her and faced their guests. "Her voice is one of many reasons my heart fell captive to the lovely Lady Bonny. Please bow your heads for a blessing. Dear Lord, we invite you to be present at our gathering today. Bless the food these many hands have prepared, and help us form new and stronger friendships. Amen."

Thank you, Lord, for home, friends, and family. A quiver of excitement skittered through every nerve when her handsome husband played "Scotland the Brave" on his bagpipes while the men cleared away tables to make room for the dancing. The woman who fled to Scotland, alone and crushed by loss of parents and a broken heart existed no more.

Kieran set aside the bagpipes and beckoned her up beside him while he explained their plans for Hope Chapel. The pressure of his hand on hers grounded her in the realities of this unexpected new life.

"Along with farming, I'll pastor the chapel when it opens." The powerful voice and presence commanded the attention of even the smallest child. "We invite you to attend a Bible study in our home each Sunday at ten a.m. It will continue after the chapel opens."

When they stepped down, Jamie and Seumas Matheson, the first farm employees to perform, took the stage with their fiddles. The crowd clapped and danced with enthusiasm from the first note. Even the old house seemed to join the celebration, so full of life after such a long time.

Kieran pulled her into the pantry and closed the door, gripping her fingers so tight they ached. She wiggled her fingers and gazed into a face growing redder by the second, lips pressed into a thin, white line.

"Did you see the woman in the long black cape with the mahogany hair? I tried to get close, but she disappeared."

"She's not a neighbor?"

"Not one I recognize, but something familiar about her makes my gut twist in knots. I never got a close look at her face." His eyes dulled to the blue-gray of the loch on a stormy day.

"You think she's related to the man who attacked you."

"Can I hide nothing from you?"

"Not much."

"She reminds me of Deirdre Adair, but heavier. Hair hung in her face and made it difficult to tell. Watch out for her."

Deirdre. The former student threatened her and made no secret of her desire for Kieran. His love for an American had apparently led to her aggressive behavior. Someone shouted a request for "The Rosebud of Allenvale," when they exited the pantry. In spite of the mind-reeling thought of Deirdre, her heart skipped at the memory of the waltz in flickering torchlight when he first confessed his love.

"Would you join me in a waltz, m'lady?" Kieran's smile stole the breath from her lungs and pushed unpleasant thoughts far away. He drew her into the circle of his arms and nuzzled her ear. "I love you more than the first night we danced to this tune, Mrs. MacDonell. *Tha gaol agam ort.*"

"I love you, Mr. MacDonell. Being your Lady of Loch Garry is the greatest privilege of my life."

When the song ended, they wove through the crowd to greet their guests, but her eyes searched for a glimpse of the woman who hated her. When people began to gather dishes and children, she shoved Kieran toward the stage. "Play 'Hector the Hero.'"

Her joy overflowed at the skirl of his bagpipes. How could she ever regret the decision to leave her old life behind for her wild, romantic sheep farmer? Whether their dream of children came true or not, she cherished the life God gave her.

In the middle of the tune, Deirdre's face came into view, hair dyed, the once-pretty face pie-shaped with added pounds, eyes glued to Kieran. Bonny inched her way through the crowd, confident her small stature kept her hidden. She wound her fingers around a flowing, black sleeve. "Deirdre. I'm surprised to see you here."

The woman yanked out of Bonny's grasp, eyes wide, mouth open. Deirdre could have escaped with ease but stopped. Her face twisted into a scowl of disgust. Her amber, cat-like eyes traveled over Bonny. "It still makes me sick to look at you. I … I wanted to speak to Kieran, but seein' him again so *braw*—I canna face him lookin' the way I do." Her eyes darted around, whether for an escape route or another person, Bonny couldn't tell. "I couldna care less for your sake, but he's in danger."

"Deirdre, please stay. If you're so concerned, help us." Kieran's back remained turned with no way to attract his attention.

The woman jerked away so fast her sleeve ripped in Bonny's hand. She knocked over two children in her run for the door and never looked back.

"Kieran, outside," Bonny yelled over the noise. "It's Deirdre. Run."

He sprinted through the crowd, but Deirdre disappeared into the night, leaving them alone in the middle of the lawn. Bonny quivered as he escorted her back inside, his hand pressed firmly against the middle of her back. "I'll send a few farmhands to look around. You did well, hen. Don't let her scare you."

When the ancient grandfather clock chimed three a.m., the last guests were gone, and Maggie and Hamish retired upstairs. Bonny collapsed into a kitchen chair, pulled off her shoes, and rubbed her feet. She survived and hoped her fatigue and the heaviness in her chest didn't show on her face. "Other than the unexpected visitor, it was fun. It will take a week to get the house back together, but I met a lot of wonderful people."

"You were the perfect hostess. Our first *ceilidh* was a grand success." Kieran dropped a soft kiss on her forehead. "I've never heard your voice so pitch-perfect. I'm proud of you, love."

"What about Deirdre?"

"I called the police. All we can do is remain watchful. Perhaps Alasdair will find a connection between her and Gunn since she mentioned danger."

"I saw the same hate-filled eyes the day she warned me to stay away from you at the college. Kieran, she'd only want to hide her looks because she still cares for you. Her appearance has changed, older, unkempt, and the body odor … she never used to be without cologne."

Narrowed eyes swept over her with concern. "We'll discuss it after some sleep. You look exhausted." He rose and gave her a hand up. "To bed, Lady Bonny. You'll take a day of leisure tomorrow, or I'll answer to Dr. Moncrieffe."

His phone rang. "Alasdair … keep me informed." The color drained from his face.

"Gavin Gunn escaped from jail."

☙❧

Kieran's pajamas were tossed over a chair, his side of the bed empty. Surprised she slept at all, after news of Gunn's escape, she must have fallen asleep before he finished praying. Despite orders to relax, Bonny pulled on old clothes, determined to help set the house in order, and headed downstairs to meet everyone for breakfast.

Angus swept into the kitchen with a cold blast of rain-laden wind and closed the door against the window-rattling gale. Muddy rivulets trickled onto the mat where he shifted from one foot to the other. Rain pelted the windows from a storm-blackened sky, while lightning flashed and thunder reverberated off the mountainsides. Face pale and mouth pressed into grim lines, he glanced around the room with haunted eyes.

Appalled, Bonny started toward him.

"It's Kieran and Hamish I must speak with. Alone."

Both set their spoons down and rose, their porridge half-eaten. Maggie and Eleanor startled when a crash of thunder shuddered the house.

"Outside."

Fear shivered through Bonny at his icy stare, a premonition that whatever he said would dwarf the storm outside. "You can say it in front of everyone, Angus."

"Nay, lassie, I *canna*." The work-toughened farm manager bit his lower lip and shook his head.

"You've had enough, *mo nighean*." Her father-in-law took her arm to guide her back to the table.

My daughter. She glanced at Kieran. "If it involves the farm or Gavin Gunn, I need to know."

"I prefer to tell you away from the women." Angus' eyes darted to Kieran's, and he backed toward the door.

Bonny wrenched free from Hamish and stepped in front of her husband. "Don't protect me. I married a sheep farmer. We're in this together."

The last time she saw such anguish in the old man's eyes, she led her horse into the farmyard with Kieran near death from a gunshot wound. "Oh lass, it will break your heart. Stay inside and call the vet and the police."

"Tell us." Kieran frowned and reached for his boots.

"Ach, I've never seen a case this bad. I'm fair certain it's copper poisonin'. Someone was busy durin' the *ceilidh*." Angus drew out his handkerchief and blew his nose.

Kieran's eyes darkened to midnight-blue. "Copper? How bad?"

"Fifteen dead and five times more dyin'. Whoever did it injected a lot." Angus clenched his fists.

"Bonny, call Alasdair Kavanaugh and Dr. MacKinnon." Kieran's strangled response sounded somewhere between a sob and a growl. He crossed the room to the gun safe, dialed the combination, and removed two shotguns. "I won't have you out there."

The hot lava of rebellion rose up inside. "I'm a farmer's wife. I'll be at your side."

"No. I won't have you around while we put down sheep even if you think you're strong enough." He glared, jaw set.

"But—"

"You're still weak. You worked too hard for the *ceilidh*—"

"We share the burdens. I hunted with my father."

Firm hands settled on her shoulders in a vise grip, eyes shooting flames of blue fire. "No."

"I—"

"Do as I say."

Maggie wrapped an arm around her waist. She'd lost.

"I must draw the line, *mo grádh*." He stroked her cheek with the back of his hand. "Mother, she stays inside until I come."

My love. Conscious of everyone's stares, she stepped back. "Will we lose all the lambs?"

Angus made a choking sound. "All the prize ewes and rams are either dead or dyin'. Whoever did it knew which to target."

"No one saw or heard anything suspicious?" Hamish's hands curled into fists.

"The sheep didn't spook, and the dogs didn't bark."

"Deirdre?" Bonny grabbed Kieran's sleeve.

"Gavin Gunn." He spat out the name like a bad piece of meat. "Mark my words. She may have provided the cover, but he'll be the cause." Garbed against the weather, guns in hand, the men headed into the deluge.

Her mother-in-law picked up the phone. "I'll make the calls. A wife needs to learn when to give in."

The first shot shattered the last shred of peace of the glen, and in Bonny's heart. She mopped her eyes with a napkin. Kieran was right, but she still reeled at his unexpected banishment in a crisis. Compassionate looks from Eleanor and Maggie did nothing to settle her inner turmoil.

The little porridge she ate turned to concrete in her stomach. Excusing herself to shower, she ran upstairs and collapsed to the floor in sobs. Gunshots echoed off the hillsides in a hideous clamor. Kieran changed during their passionate discussion. She knew it in her heart, heard it in his voice, and saw it in his eyes.

She picked up her Bible. The fifth chapter of Ephesians had a major influence on Kieran before they married, but now Bonny considered it from a wife's position. *Wives, submit to your own husbands as you do to the Lord ... Husbands ought to love their own wives as their own bodies. He who loves his wife loves himself. After all, no one ever hated their own body, but they feed and care for their body, just as Christ does the church—*

Men equate respect with love. How she missed her mother. The well-remembered voice whispered in her heart. *Submission isn't the surrender of your rights, but acceptance of your unique place in the God-given partnership of marriage. Make home a loving haven where your husband can escape the weight of the world.* Bonny slid to her knees, praying aloud to maintain her concentration. A battle raged outside the shuttered window with Kieran in the position of general. And there lay the truth her mother tried to communicate. He couldn't protect himself from the ugliness, but he could spare a part of himself—the wife he loved as his own body.

Maggie sat at the kitchen table, head in her hands when Bonny re-entered the kitchen. "I remembered a lesson from my mother and need to show Kieran I understand. I want to serve him a private dinner in our room tonight."

"What a lovely idea, dear. What do you have in mind? I'll help. You don't need to tire yourself." Maggie's solemn expression gave way to a smile, confirming her decision.

Bonny removed two Aberdeen-Angus steaks from the freezer. "To eat mutton will only further wound his spirit. I can fix salad. Would you make Sticky Toffee Pudding?" Perhaps a candlelight dinner in the privacy of their room might ease his raw, wounded heart.

"I'm proud of you. Kieran chose well."

At her mother-in-law's suggestion, they set a small, round table in front of the bedroom fireplace accompanied by deep-red upholstered chairs, and covered with a lace tablecloth. China, silver, and an antique candelabra completed the romantic atmosphere.

The choice to perform an act of love, a refuge for her husband, where strife could not enter, brought peace to Bonny's heart. In working to soothe her husband's hurt, she became more a partner with him than ever.

She looked around the beautiful room where the rich reds and golds of the down comforter blended with the draperies and gold, plush carpet. A red-and-gold-striped love seat stood in front of the marble fireplace, flanked by tufted gold armchairs. Her prayers had yielded the perfect means to communicate her acceptance of his role as loving head of their home. Dressed in jeans and Kieran's favorite soft-pink sweater, she waited in the library.

The sound of heavy feet stomping the mud off boots near the kitchen door alerted Bonny when Kieran returned. Muddy and windblown, mere slits of reddened eyes conveyed the depth of grief he suffered. He held out her coat. "Come outside, love." He smelled of sweat and gunpowder, his voice rough and hoarse. "You need to see why I didn't want you there."

CS ED

A cold breeze gusted off the storm-tossed loch. Bonny zipped her raincoat, pulled her scarf tighter, and gripped Kieran's arm, every sense on alert. She surveyed the chaos wrought against the barn and pastures of their serene, lochside farm.

Shafts of sunlight filtered through retreating clouds. Bits of blue sky created a stark contrast to the stench of the ravaged kidneys and bowels of the sheep caused by high doses of copper. She gagged and covered her nose with her scarf. What a truly *dreich* day.

Seumas, Jamie, and Gordon McCrea, the father of little Rowan, worked to move dead sheep into a pile at the far end of the pasture. A few sheep staggered around or slept in a pen outside the main barn where Dr. MacKinnon worked. The brilliant greens and blues which filled her heart with gratitude on any normal day looked muted and dull. How could anyone take out their spite on such defenseless animals? Her stomach knotted at the pitiful bleating. "Will they live?"

"Aye, if they're not down by now, most will." His voice sounded void of emotion, drained. "The most valuable are gone. If the feed or soil shows copper contamination, we'll lose more."

"But Angus said they were injected." How would he and Hamish handle the near-death of the successful tradition their family built over generations?

When he looked around, his glare hardened, and jaw muscles clenched. "Aye, but there's a slower way to poison them, and we can't afford to underestimate this maniac. If they've eaten poultry or cattle feed, or if animal feces contaminate the soil, we'll have to treat them all. Cattle and poultry can handle high amounts of copper, but even wee bits are harmful to sheep. Death is slower, but every bit as painful."

She listened while Dr. MacKinnon described the backbreaking process of drenching the living with ammonium molybdate, sodium sulfate, and penicillamine. It would take days. At his suggestion, they agreed to discard the feed, and Angus headed to Fort William for more.

"There won't be many lambs this spring." Kieran's voice wavered with weariness. Deep purple shadowed his bloodshot eyes. "Money will be tight. It could take years to rebuild the quality of our flocks."

"We'll pull through, love." She rubbed his back with her palm and sent up a silent prayer for God to guide the authorities. "Where were the dogs? How could anyone get past all six?"

"I don't know."

The English sheepdogs, Wally and Marion, remained around the barns and pastures nearest the house. Mary and Darnley, Kieran's beloved golden Labs, preferred to stay near the house, except for occasional romps through the pastures to chase rabbits, squirrels, and birds. Corrie and Bruce, the border collies, stayed out in the farthest pastures, except at mealtimes, when all six descended on the kitchen garden—a noisy, scuffling pack of fur and eager tongues.

He rubbed the backs and ears of Wally and Marion, milling around sad and confused. "Poor things, you're confused too. Why didn't you bark? There's the question. Alasdair and McLeod conducted their investigation. Da called Lachlan Menzies, the solicitor."

"It's late. We'll accomplish nothing else today." Hamish plodded toward them through the mud, followed by Mary and Darnley. He looked haggard and old. "Spend time with your wife. The ugly side of sheep farming can be a shock."

Bonny led him into the house and up the stairs. When he opened the bedroom door, smile lines crinkled around his eyes, and the corners of his mouth lifted in a weary smile. Firelight glittered off crystal and china, dancing across walls and windows in the darkened room. His arms slid around her, regardless of dirt. "You put your day to good use, *mo gràdh.*"

"I was wrong to argue. I prayed and received a lesson in submission from the Lord … and my mother."

"Your mother again?" His eyebrows rose.

"Before the cancer stole her ability to communicate, she used every opportunity to share her wisdom and teach me the lessons she wouldn't be around to give." Bonny smiled up at him. "I read the fifth chapter of Ephesians and remembered her talks about submission. It's not easy. Every time I heard a gunshot, I realized how it hurt to lose the fruit of your labor and passion. You couldn't shield yourself from the ugliness, but protecting me shielded a piece of your heart, because you love me."

Later, with Bonny asleep in his arms, Kieran battled to stay awake in a fervid desire to retain the greatest unity of spirit and love he had ever known. *Till death us do part* took on meanings he understood for the first time. And would never forget.

❧

Eleanor approached the kitchen table wiping her hands on her apron. The scent of bread dough clung to her, a delightful testimony to her gift. Bonny savored the smell.

"What's wrong?" Kieran laid down his fork and wiped his mouth.

She nodded. "It's best to plunge right in. The doctor diagnosed Angus with a heart problem. He said I could tell you. The stress makes him worse. It's time to slow down."

"Is it serious?" Bonny glanced at Kieran, who sat in stunned silence. He relied on his friend's opinions and had admired him since childhood.

Their housekeeper sat and folded deep-veined hands that testified to a life of hard work with little ease. "It could be if he doesn't stick to a strict diet and work less. He's not a young man anymore."

"Will he retire?" Kieran's golden brow furrowed above eyes the shade of a midnight sky.

"Without his blackies he'd have no reason to live, but this copper poisoning drained him."

Kieran covered Eleanor's hands with his own. "I'll find a way to keep him busy but not overworked. I don't know how Stonehaven Farm would run without either of you."

"None of us are indispensable. You two would do fine." Her eyes slid to the floor, a blush tinging her cheeks. "He asked me to marry him."

A smile tugged at the corners of Kieran's mouth.

"We'd like to marry soon and live in my cottage. I want to work part-time so I can care for our home and Angus. We lack your youth, but we've been good friends for years, and companionship means a lot. It will be a simple affair, just down to the *kirk* with two witnesses." Eleanor straightened her apron, her face still as water at dusk. "Would you marry us in the chapel? Our children are far away, so we don't plan to make a fuss."

A quiver of exultation tingled up Bonny's spine. At last, the good thing she prayed for had happened. Kieran considered the two like another set of parents, and they would remain on the farm. Here was a chance to offer kindness to a couple who meant so much to them both. "Nonsense. We can have a small cake and invite the farmhands for a little reception, can't we?"

"It's not necessary."

"Eleanor, please? You've been such a help to me—to us."

Soft brown eyes shone. "Aye, if you insist. Thank you. But keep it small."

"You'll take two weeks off." Kieran's voice was firm. "In order to move his possessions to your cottage and settle in, of course."

Bonny smiled at the last part, the only way this dear, loyal woman would agree.

She shuffled her feet and looked around the kitchen.

"I do know how to cook, and thanks to you, the Aga doesn't frighten me anymore. We ate on our honeymoon—and Kieran survived, in spite of my cooking."

"Thrived is more like it," Eleanor conceded. "I can see it won't do any good to argue." She stood, hugged them both, and walked out.

"What wonderful news. It's obvious how much they care for each other."

"Poor Angus." Kieran laughed. "As long as they've known each other, he should realize how she'll coddle him."

"It's perfect. Eleanor will put him on the right diet and make certain he gets plenty of rest. Her little cottage doesn't require much upkeep, and he'll still be around to advise you."

Kieran tugged at a curl dangling in front of her ear. "All right then, Mrs. MacDonell, decision time. Seumas makes the best choice for farm manager. He knows sheep, and the pay raise will help him own his own farm someday. Jamie will make a good assistant for his brother. The two complement each other. Angus can do payroll, order, and schedule."

⚘

"Dan says he's better on the prosthetic leg than on his own. He says he's a survivor, not a man who almost died in Afghanistan. It's a great way to relax and spend time together. You two need to have fun again too."

"Kieran and I are fine, but I have awful nightmares about the baby and a stalker chasing Kieran. They come every night, and I don't want to worry him."

"Honey, you've been through too much." In the background, water ran in the sink and dishes clattered. Kari sounded more like her mother than her best friend. "If you talk with him and pray about it, I think they'll stop."

"I've tried, but he believes I'm better. I hate to disappoint him."

"He won't worry if you're honest. Maybe you need some medication for a little while. Promise me you'll tell him. Other than my Dan, your Kieran's the easiest man to talk to. I'll check with you in a few days. If you don't explain the problem, I will." The fussy noises started with first one baby and then both. "Time to go, the wee ones are hungry."

"All right, Mama Kari. Kisses from Auntie Bonny."

"I love you. We're praying." Kari hung up.

Bonny curled into a ball. After a few minutes, she straightened. She should head for the dock and signal Kieran rather than mourn what would never be. She'd tell him about the dreams. But not today.

಍ ಏ

Heart hammering against her ribs, Bonny awakened drenched in sweat. She eased out of bed, grabbed her robe, and slid her feet into warm, woolly slippers. A glass of milk might help her forget the dream and fall back asleep. She'd do what Kari said and call Dr. Moncrieffe on Monday.

She switched on the light over the table, poured milk, slid a muffin from the bread drawer, slathered it with Eleanor's blackberry jam, and sat down. In the middle of the night, she found the Aga-warmed kitchen to be a comforting place.

The dream was too real. Kieran lay in a grave with their baby in his arms. She was alone.

Empty womb.

Empty arms.

Empty heart.

Groggy and confused, she looked around. The muffin still lay next to the half-full glass of milk. The warm, quiet kitchen had lulled her back to sleep with her head on the table.

Kieran's Bible lay nearby, and she turned to Psalm 113:9, the verse she read day after day, praying for his heart to open toward adoption. "He settles the childless woman in her home as the happy mother of children."

Lord, my arms ache, and my heart weeps. Forgive me for wanting more than you choose to give. I don't want pills. I want to be a mother, to see Kieran hold our child the way he held little Rowan. This old house needs laughter and life. Help me trust. Make me strong enough to accept if your answer is no, to sleep at night without fear. Enable me to desire no more than you choose to give.

Bonny rested her head on her arms, breathing in and out.

Listening.

Waiting.

Jesus, hold me.

Help me.

Strong hands rested on her shoulders. A voice whispered her name.

"Kieran?"

"I woke up and you weren't in bed." He knelt beside her, voice ragged with concern and smoothed curls from her face. "What's wrong?"

Shoulders stiff and hands numb from resting on the hard table, Bonny straightened. "A … a dream. It comes every night. I came for a snack to help me go back to sleep."

Reaching for the Bible, his eyes scanned the tear-stained page. "You were dreaming about a child?"

"In the nightmare, I stand alone beside the grave of you and our baby, like before God sent you. But if you die, I have no one. Kieran, Gavin Gunn wants you dead." Bonny wiped her eyes on her robe.

He pulled a chair close and drew her onto his lap. "How long has this gone on?"

"Since the hospital. Kari said to tell you or she would. I promised I would later today. She suggested I ask Dr. Moncrieffe for medication to help me sleep. But I don't want pills. I want a baby." Afraid to face him, she buried her face in his neck.

"I'm not ready to adopt, Bonny. I wish you could understand. I can't think with a farm to run, lawyers to deal with, dead sheep, and constant worry about you. You're still weak and emotional. My headaches are less but still there. A decision to raise an adopted child requires prayer and research. I'm not sure I can do it at all. And children are expensive."

She stood, pulled her robe tight, dug in the pocket, and wished for a tissue. "I'll shower and fix your breakfast. I need to be alone."

"Don't walk away, *mo chridhe*. We face our problems head-on."

"I'll do what Kari said. Medication can help me stop crying and sleep. You think you understand, but it's different for a woman."

Big fingers laced through hers and pulled her down on the bottom stair. "I, of all men, should understand, love. You feel to give birth and mother is a woman's role. Can you be patient with me a little longer?"

"Any child God gives us will be our own, Kieran. It will just grow in our hearts rather than my body."

The brush of his lips against hers began with tenderness but ended in a crush of longing and heartache. He pulled away. "Take your shower. I'll cook breakfast."

Her heart slowed. He hadn't said no. "Thank you."

"We'll try to see the doctor today. And don't hide things, remember?"

"Yes."

I don't want to be pacified. The desire won't go away. Dear Lord, change Kieran's heart.

⁂

The high cross of the chapel showed above the trees from the upstairs office window. Bonny and Kieran inspected it the day before, and only a few interior details remained to be finished. Their leisurely stroll in the warm sunshine, with her hand clutched tight in his, had assured her of their unity. In between redecorating and household chores, she accompanied Kieran to check the expectant ewes. If only life could always be this peaceful.

She'd met women who lived nearby at the *ceilidh,* and it had yielded a small but dedicated group to begin their Bible study. Grabbing a stack of lessons from her desk, she hurried downstairs to answer the kitchen doorbell. Three new families planned to attend the third meeting of their Bible study. The first arrivals were a dripping and *drookit* MacGregor family. "Welcome. Come in where it's warm."

"We brought potato soup." Mary nodded at the large pot Finlay carried over to the Aga. "Take off your muddy boots, girls, and get your clean shoes out of the bag."

Finlay shook Bonny's hand and headed toward the living room. "Is Kieran in there?"

She nodded. "He's setting up chairs. Thank you, Mary. I made venison stew, so we'll have more than enough. Wait a minute, you two, I want a hug." Six-year-old Charlotte and four-year-old Susan stopped in their tracks. Bonny held them close, admired the ruddy glow in their cheeks from the cool air, and inhaled the fresh scent of their clean hair. "You girls can get the books and toys out."

"Thank you, ma'am." Charlotte skipped toward the library.

"They are such a delight, Mary."

"I'm glad you think so. They love the lessons you teach. I had no idea how fast they would learn. We're grateful." Mary stirred the soup and set the lid back on the pot.

The rain streamed down in steady sheets. Its fresh scent filled the house the way fog blanketed the glen, cutting off the view of the loch. The New Mexican in Bonny still grew excited over each drop of rain, a great source of teasing for Kieran. "The potato soup will taste good in this *dreich* weather, Mary. I'm glad we decided to share lunch before you all head home. Here come Joseph and Allison."

Three-year-old James Miller threw his arms around her knees when she opened the door. "Mistis Donell!"

"Oh, my goodness, what a strong boy you are." She bent to help him out of his coat and savor the scent of a small boy.

"He talks about you all week."

Bonny glanced up to face Allison's baby bulge. *No.* She would not allow her loss to ruin time with their church members. Her new friend handed her a basket of hard rolls and sat to remove her boots.

"It's good to see you, Joseph." Kieran strode into the kitchen with Finlay at his heels.

"We wouldn't miss it."

She needed to free herself from thoughts aroused by her pregnant friend. "Would you watch James and the girls while I greet the others?"

With a wink and smile, Kieran headed to the living room with more chairs. For a split second, they were alone in the room.

"Aye, James can't wait to ride the horsey again." Allison took the hand of her boisterous son and headed down the hall.

The men carried another load of chairs through, and Bonny turned back to Mary. "Eleanor's old sitting room is the perfect Sunday school room."

"Don't you miss the space?" Kieran told her the MacGregors lived in a very small house.

"Not with only two of us. Eleanor, the housekeeper, moved into one of the farm cottages after we got married, and we decided it would work for a classroom. The adjoining bedroom makes a perfect nursery for when there are babies."

Mary stirred the venison stew and adjusted the heat. "You went to such a big expense for the Bible study?"

"We didn't buy anything. The rocking horse belonged to Kieran and his father before him. He and his first wife bought the baby furniture. I discovered it in the attic, and he agreed to use it for church functions at the house."

"You've had your share of trouble." Mary's affectionate arm around her waist caused a mountain spring of emotions to well up.

"God never promised freedom from trials, but to go through them with us." Bonny hurried to let the McAllens in, along with another cold blast of air. A shiver ran through her after standing near the stove.

"What did you bring us, Maev?" The shy sixteen-year-old, who shadowed Bonny the first two meetings, carried a large box folded shut.

"Mama said the little ones might enjoy the books from our attic. Padraic and I outgrew them all years ago. Mrs. MacDonell, could I help with the Sunday school? I want to be a teacher."

"I would love your help." The tall, lanky girl with thick black hair reminded her of Kari, though her eyes were a rich chocolate brown. "Go on in. I'll be there soon."

Maev beamed. "Thank you."

"With Maev to assist with the children, I can help Kieran with the music." Bonny headed for the door at the sight of Alex and Katie MacGyver.

Her heart swelled with joy to hear women's laughter fill the warm kitchen. Its new, red curtains and tablecloth added a cheery aspect to the dark day. God's gracious success in the Bible study offered hope for answers to deeper prayers.

Thank you, Lord, for so many hungry souls to begin our little church.

૦૩ ૪૦

Two and a half hours later, everyone bundled into their cars filled with food, excitement over new relationships, and promises to return the following week. Kieran stood next to Bonny near the kitchen window. The sound of thunder accompanied the last cars down the muddy drive.

A quick brush of his lips against her cheek tickled her ear. "Six families. I'm so glad we enlarged the living room. Are you certain caring for the little ones isn't too much?"

"You were the brilliant one who recognized the need for a larger room if I remember right."

Recent weeks had set a new pattern for their lives and filled her days with tasks to keep her mind off herself and focused on others. Days spent in study for Sunday school lessons, helping Kieran choose music, and prayer for church members lent new purpose to life. They were a team in both farm and chapel.

"This old house needs the sound of children's voices, though it does hurt a little to see Allison. She's due the same time I would have been. At only nineteen, Katie and Alex MacGyver will probably have bunches of babies. Jealousy is a devious monster, but I enjoy working with the children. It's good for me."

"It's good to have Maev help with all the little ones." Kieran's strong arms and encouragement provided a constant source of comfort and support. "In time, you can alternate with the other women and join in the study."

"We'll see." Bonny inhaled the pleasant, masculine scent of his aftershave. "I know a wonderful way to spend a rainy afternoon."

"What do you have in mind, Mrs. MacDonell?" The gleeful tone when he said her still-new name rippled chills from her head to her toes.

"How about a nice, warm *cuzzle* followed by a nap near the fireplace in our room." She glanced out at the relentless downpour and met his lips with eagerness. "Spring in Scotland is certainly different from home. Our constants are dust and wind."

"I'm all yours." He led her toward the stairs. "Do our Sunday afternoons help?"

She squeezed his hand in anticipation of the time they committed to spend alone before the new week began. "I forget the world exists, except for you."

Kieran lifted her hair to kiss the back of her neck. "No chapel, no farm, only us." He switched off the lights and guided her upstairs to their haven of peace.

A fire smoldered in the small fireplace, ready to be stirred into flames underneath the framed photograph of sunset over her New Mexico home, which now graced the mantle. The reds and golds of the fiery sky, a bond between her old life and the new, reminded Bonny of God's behind-the-scenes work. This afternoon she would focus on nothing but the new.

Bonny turned when Kieran walked into the storage room where she double-checked the list of supplies needed when they traveled to Fort William tomorrow. He hugged her close and rested his chin on her forehead in silence.

"What's wrong?"

"Katie MacGyver miscarried. Alex wants us to call the prayer chain."

For a friend to suffer the loss she herself lived with every day sent a painful stab through Bonny's heart. "I have to go, Kieran." She leaned into him and breathed deep. "They're so young. They need someone who understands."

"It's eight o'clock on a rainy night. First thing tomorrow, before we head to town."

"Nonsense. When does a Highlander allow rain to interfere with duty?" She took both of his hands and tugged him toward the back shelves. "Katie needs a woman who understands how she feels to pray with them. Alex won't know how to comfort her."

She pointed to a shelf stacked with baskets of various sizes and shapes. "Reach the rectangular one for me. I'll grab a few things, and we'll be off." After scurrying upstairs to the office, she located a devotional book, a copy of her poem, and a Bible bookmark embroidered with a verse about comfort, then tucked in a loaf of Eleanor's bread.

Kieran bit his lower lip, as always when faced with her hardheaded determination. "How am I to offer comfort to Katie or tell Alex how to help her? I don't know what to say to you. It's more of a woman's matter."

"A woman's matter? You know better, and you're a pastor who needs to give comfort in any situation. You can offer a lot." She grabbed a pair of fresh jeans and stopped. "You'll say the right things. Part of your flock needs their shepherd."

Garbed in wellies and raincoats, they climbed into the Land Rover and headed down the slippery, rutted, single-track road. Lightning crackled in every direction, illuminating dark, roiling clouds and whitecaps on the loch. Bonny's stomach churned much the same. *Lord, it's too soon.* Her own grief remained fresh, but if God called her to this, she wouldn't turn away.

It took close to an hour to reach the small stone cottage where Katie and Alex lived in a treeless valley north of Tomdoun. Once their rain gear hung on a hook by the door, Bonny stepped into the tiny corner kitchen to put the kettle on. "I'll make tea, and we'll sit with you for a while. We lost our baby before three months, and Kieran's first was stillborn. You're not alone."

"I don't know what to do for her." A red-eyed Alex sat next to Katie, one arm around her shoulders, while she dabbed her swollen eyes and pale cheeks with a handkerchief. Wind howled in the chimney, spraying ashes.

Kieran perched on a wooden chair near the hearth. "Tell her you love her. Share your pain. Give each other the freedom to grieve in your own way."

Bonny scooted close to Katie and reached for her hand. "Grief is personal. When you think you have it under control, the most unexpected event will trigger the emotions again. Alex, you hurt, but for Katie it's at the root of what it means to be a woman. She needs all the love, patience, and encouragement you can give. Reassure her she's not alone in her pain."

"God is big enough to handle your questions, your anger, and your hurt, but you must put the question of *why* out of your minds," Kieran said. "*Why* leads to depression and hopelessness." Bonny nodded her encouragement, and he smiled in return. "We live in a sinful world, and bad things happen. It's impossible to fathom the ways of God, only trust in his love."

Her heart rejoiced in spite of the sadness, which stirred her insides into jelly. The gratitude Katie and Alex expressed confirmed they were right to visit in the freshness of their grief.

Back in the car, Kieran leaned across the console and wrapped Bonny's hand in his. "I shouldn't have hesitated, love. Out of the comfort we've received, we did help Katie and Alex."

She breathed a silent prayer of thanks. "Let's go again next week. We'll take dinner and remind them it grows easier with time."

"Ah, lass, I wasted too many years focused on my own anger and pain. What a grand new experience to help others out of the loss I always tried to hide. You're a strong, brave woman. I'm proud of you."

Unable to see his face in the darkness, Bonny squeezed his hand. "By God's grace. Proud of what?"

"Your help and the gentle way you shared your grief for our little one." Emotion tightened her throat, and she choked back tears.

"I wanted to be strong for you and not make your pain worse. I long for our child and wonder if it was a girl with your russet hair or a boy with my lighter red every single day. Life would be very different if even one of my children had lived."

"Me too, but I believe God redeems our pain when we use it to comfort and encourage others."

Kieran withdrew his hand to navigate the swampy road, while rain pelted and wipers swished across the mud-spattered windshield. "I realize I make up excuses when you mention adoption, but I am praying."

"You avoid it, but it matters, and it's the only area where we're not together." Bonny leaned against the car door. If he were ready, he'd be eager to discuss it.

A deluge of muddy water blinded them to the point he halted in the middle of the road. One large hand reached across and drew her toward him. "I pray for help to deal with my doubts."

"We can't wait forever. You're already forty-three. It frustrates me when you refuse to discuss it."

He pressed her hand, grasped the steering wheel, and forged ahead.

Patience. She would try.

Prayer. She never ceased.

Kari's twins, Allison's baby bulge, James Miller's hugs, Kieran laughing with Rowan, and now Katie's loss, all made her long even more for a child.

It doesn't have to be a newborn, Lord. I want to be a mom, to hear our home filled with children's laughter.

◌

The first lamb was born. Seumas reported it to them during breakfast at four a.m.

Bonny jumped up from the table, her plate half-full. The car accident in New Mexico had caused her to miss the event when she and Kieran were dating. Weakness and fatigue aside, she planned to experience the whole gamut this year when there was such uncertainty over the future of their farm.

"We'll have precious little sleep for the next few weeks. We need every lamb if we're going to yield even a small profit." Kieran followed her to the sink with his dishes. "You'll love this. Do you feel ready for the hard, physical work of pulling lambs?" He underscored his caressing tone by the sweet way he tilted her head back and searched her eyes.

"You bet. I'm a lot stronger."

"I'll call my parents. Da thinks he's a more thorough teacher than I am. He plans to work with you a lot." He headed for the mud bench and grabbed his wellies.

"I want to work with you."

"Of course, and you will. He's so excited, though. We can't disappoint him. Since I learned about Brighde, I understand his love for you in a new way. Mother says you're very much like her."

"It will be great to learn from him, but you and I need time together. I'll finish the dishes, open their room to air, and change into old clothes."

Kieran tugged on a worn coat. "Call Eleanor to start the stew. She and my mother will keep everyone fed."

Dressed in long underwear, bib overalls, and a wool-flannel shirt, Bonny walked outside under a sky where stars faded into dawn. She lifted up a prayer for healthy lambs. Ducks still slept in the reeds by the loch, and hope wafted on the wind.

"Bonny." Seumas waved her over with his flashlight to where a ewe licked the membrane away from her lamb's face. "Sometimes one surprises us. Look."

"She's birthing another while she's walking around?" After the pain she suffered, Bonny found it difficult to imagine how little concern or discomfort the ewe showed.

"Oh, aye."

"Surely she won't let it fall to the ground."

"*Dinna fash yerself.* It'll be all right." He flashed a smile of reassurance. "Get to the barn. You'll do fine."

While she laughed at his admonishment not to fret, the second lamb plopped onto the grass. "Thanks for my first lesson. They're tougher than they look."

A long corridor of pens filled with pregnant ewes lined the sides of the old, cavernous stone barn. Though damp, it smelled fresher after they scrubbed the stone floors, then spread hydrated lime and clean straw. Kieran's second great grandfather built the original barn when he bought the land. How many births had these old walls witnessed?

They would take no chances with the remaining flocks, many of which were older. First-time mothers and those expecting twins or triplets would give birth in the barn. Experienced mothers with no problems in the past would have their lambs in the pasture closest to the house.

"Bonny, roll up your sleeves and get down here." Kieran peered out from a pen further along the corridor. "We have an old ewe, toxemic, and expecting twins. She's too weak to push out these lambs."

Her heart shifted into overdrive, and she hurried to his side.

"Kneel next to me. Do you remember her?"

She dropped to her knees beside the straining ewe. "I gave her Pepto-Bismol and yogurt in warm water through a feeding tube for toxemia. We made sure she had Vitamin B and steroids. You said she's a tough one."

"Aye, but she worsened overnight." He rubbed the head and neck of the ewe. "You're about done with mothering, aren't you, old girl?"

He knelt in the straw and rubbed the ewe's belly in a gentle, circular motion. The love and tenderness he showed his animals gripped Bonny's heart, one more facet to her husband's character, and each endeared him to her more. She understood better all the time why Scripture compared sheep to people. They were such simple, easily misled creatures.

"See where I place my hands? Can you feel the contraction?"

The abdomen turned rock-hard. In between contractions, he showed Bonny how to locate the heads of the twins. After about forty-five minutes, a nose and two tiny feet emerged. The first slid out with relative ease.

"Your first delivery, a strong ewe lamb." Kieran laid the limp, wet bundle under its mother's nose and watched her pull the sac away from her baby's face, licking it to stimulate circulation and breathing. Bonny wiped her cheeks on her sleeve. "Kieran, the sheep …"

"Are you all right, hen?" His eyes had taken on a steely-gray cast.

"Fine. It's just, well …"

One large, warm hand settled over hers, forcing her to meet eyes turned narrow and intense. "It hurts, aye?"

She nodded.

"Let yourself mourn. I'll finish with this one. Get a breath of fresh air." He nodded and turned back to the ewe.

"Thanks." A familiar car pulled in, and Bonny ran toward her father-in-law, who greeted her with a kiss on the cheek.

Maggie waved. "I'll be in the kitchen with Eleanor. Someone has to feed this crew."

"Come wi' me, lass." Hamish placed his arm around her shoulders. "See if an old man can teach you a thing or two."

To observe her father-in-law provided a glimpse of Kieran thirty years in the future. "I'm beginning to love the smell of sheep."

"*Guid.* You'll smell like one yourself soon enough." His belly-laugh echoed in the big, stone barn.

"Bonny!" The sharpness of Kieran's voice drew them to a nearby pen. "Da, you two should handle the breech in here."

"Are you up to this?" Hamish faced her with a question in his blue eyes and a firm set to his mouth.

She straightened her shoulders. "I wouldn't miss it."

Kieran patted her backside, and she smiled when their eyes locked. Of course, he understood. He faced lambing year after year with the memory of Liam, and now the newness of another loss. "Wash to your shoulder, and slather yourself good with the lubricant there."

"I'd rather watch." She took a step back.

"Nonsense, lass." Voice raised in excitement, her father-in-law threw his coat in the corner and rolled up his sleeves. "You learn better when you do it yourself. Hurry up. I'll be here."

Swallowing hard, she grabbed a rag to clean off the sheep's backside. History and literature were her areas of expertise for good reasons, but she had watched when her mother's mare foaled and her dog had puppies. No squeamishness allowed. Determined not to disappoint, she took a deep breath and pushed her hand into the warm, tight birth canal. "Okay, I feel the rump but no legs."

Hamish moved to the front of the ewe. "Cup the rear end of the lamb with your hand and reach around until you feel the little one's hind legs. Pop the legs back toward you. You can deliver the lamb back legs first."

"Got them." Just when she grasped the legs, the vet walked in. Relief, like warm cocoa on a cold day, flowed through her. "Great, you can take it from here." Dr. McKinnon shook his head. "Not on your life. I have other farmers to check on. Once you're in, stick with it. Neither the lamb nor the ewe needs more trauma to the birth canal. Keep pulling those back legs until the hips emerge."

The pressure of the contractions numbed her arm. Bonny's back and shoulders ached from the strange position. Dr. Moncrieffe had cleared her for "normal activity." Lambing probably didn't fall under the normal category. Meanwhile, her instructors urged her on, everyone concentrating on the life she struggled to save.

"Am I doing it right?" She gripped both tiny hind legs in her right hand and exerted slight pressure on the emerging lamb.

"Now, keep applying gentle pressure, backwards and downwards." Hamish placed his hand on her shoulder. "Good job, lass."

Sweat trickled down her back.

"A breech lamb stresses the umbilical cord." Kieran entered and knelt at the ewe's head. "It's vital to get the lamb out quickly."

"Kieran," Angus called from the other end of the barn.

"I've got to go. You're in good hands, love."

Just when her back and arm strength failed, the lamb plopped out onto the straw. She tore the amniotic membrane away, rubbing and cooing. "It hasn't moved. Come on, baby. Come on. The hard work's over. Breathe." She picked up a piece of straw and tickled its nose. Nothing. "Hamish?"

He reached for the lamb and grabbed the front feet in one hand, back feet in the other. Bonny sucked in a deep breath when he swung the lamb in an arc, one direction then the other.

"Oh, it's alive!"

Her father-in-law chuckled. "You did great, *mo nighean*. Anyone would think you're a veteran."

The ewe began to lick her lamb. Fifteen minutes later, the newborn stood, wobbled, tottered, and toppled over. Bonny hugged Hamish, and they both laughed to see the mother nudge her baby toward the food supply. Finally, it found the teats and began to nurse.

Bonny clapped her hands. "Amazing."

Muscles aching, she washed up, headed to the barn office, sat with her head leaned against the wall, and covered her face with her hands. The day neared an end, but not the births. Some came easy, others not.

Heavy footsteps pounded down the stone corridor, and Kieran entered. His strong hands kneaded the knots in her back and shoulders. "Are you all right?"

"Yes, I'm fine."

"You're exhausted, love."

"I'll be okay in a few minutes. I won't let you down."

He squatted beside her. "You never let anyone down. Did you remember the antibiotics?"

She nodded and looked into his beaming face. "Yes. And thank you."

"For what?" Kieran's eyes glowed the intense cobalt blue she adored, lips tilted up in a grin. "For this wonderful life. What's next?"

Kieran cupped her face gently, the wistful look in his eyes whispered he understood. "You helped with six deliveries and watched a dozen others. You've done enough for one day. Go eat dinner and rest tonight. Take a hot shower. Angus and I will handle the barn. Seumas and Jamie will take the outside."

"But it's my job too."

"Rest. It won't help anyone if you overdo." He helped her to her feet and walked her to the barn door. His lips claimed hers beneath the full moon, urgent and hungry before he pulled back.

"I wish you were coming."

His heart thudded under her cheek. "I want nothing more than to sleep beside you. We need every single lamb after all our losses. I'll stay in the barn tonight."

"I'll miss you."

Hamish cleared his throat and stepped out into the moonlight. "I'll escort the lady to the house. I need a little rest myself."

Kieran nodded, and Hamish placed a hand in the small of her back. "You're a special one, Bonny, a lot like my Maggie."

"Really?"

"Aye, and you'll get no greater compliment from me, ever."

Too exhausted to finish the giant bowl of mutton stew, she trudged upstairs for her shower. Joy and sadness danced a strange, uneven tempo through her cramped limbs. Joy in seeing their future come to life. Sorrow in the knowledge she would never bear a child to inherit this tradition from Kieran, cherish what he worked for, and carry on the proud MacDonell name.

His love for this place, this life, boomed in his voice, shone in his eyes, and pulsed in his caress of each laboring ewe. He was born to carry on the grand ancestral tradition of those stern people who stared down from the foyer walls and passed their way of life from generation to generation.

It ended with Kieran because he loved her.

Because she was barren.

Because he couldn't move past the genetics to see what miracle God might bring.

☙❧

Kieran tiptoed into the bedroom and paused, awed at the beauty of his sleeping wife. The warm reds of the room glowed in shadows cast by the bathroom nightlight and testified to the passion she brought to his life. He longed to crawl in beside Bonny and savor the sweet scent of her skin. Instead, he shook her shoulder and rubbed her cheek. "We need you, *mo gràdh*."

She stirred and opened her eyes. "What's wrong?"

"We have four ewes in active labor, one a young mother with her first pregnancy. The lamb looks dead. I put my finger in its mouth, and it's still alive. It won't be pleasant, but your hands are much smaller. Can you handle it?"

"I'm awake." She sat up and reached for her clothes.

He'd have to be blind not to see how the hunger in her eyes increased with each lamb born. Guilt tormented him over his inability to accept what she craved to the point of desperation. A fertility specialist offered the only way to satisfy them both, yet Bonny's fear haunted him as much as her desire to adopt.

When she dressed and donned her raincoat, he gripped her arm, slogging through deep, sticky mud into the well-lit maternity ward. She quivered beneath his hands when they stepped from the spring deluge into the warm barn. He pointed toward the second pen and grabbed her hand. "It's not pretty. They can live a long time this way. The sooner it's born, the better."

Eyes the color of mossy pools, she frowned at the dangling head of the lamb. The way she squared her slight shoulders and crouched next to the ewe, whose breath grew shallow between contractions, caused him to smile. His brave wife looked up at him. She started at the nose, let the sheep smell her, and then stroked its face. "Hello, little mama, let's go to work and get your baby out."

"Here I am." Hamish shed his raincoat, boots pounding across the stones. "Can you handle it, lass?"

"She's tiny. I'll create less trauma."

Kieran heaved a sigh of relief at her tenacity. "Lubricate to your shoulder." The smile she slanted his direction kindled tongues of flame deep inside him. She washed the mother's backside and baby's face, then maneuvered her hands inside on the periphery of the lamb's head.

"She has a small pelvis. Your hands would never fit." Her voice held new confidence since the breach birth.

Hamish signaled his approval with a wink. Kieran winked back with pride. The courage to leave her entire world behind and tackle a new life on her own made Bonny the wife he needed.

"What do you feel, lass?" Hamish knelt.

"The shoulders."

Kieran motioned his father away, the need to share the experience alone with her grew strong. He marveled at the silent determination with which she worked. Biting her lip, sweat glistened on her forehead, and her breath came fast and shallow. When she pushed her arm further into the cervix, the lamb's nose disappeared back inside. Angus walked in, but she never looked up.

"Quick, love," he murmured close to her ear. "Try to pull the front legs out so the lamb doesn't smother."

Clutching the front legs in her right hand, she pulled.

"Down and back."

She complied. And the lamb slid out.

"You did it."

The ewe shuddered. Angus dropped to his knees and rubbed her to stimulate breathing. "We're losing her. She must have ruptured internally."

Kieran's breath caught, captivated by the tender expression in Bonny's eyes, the pink bloom in her cheeks as she cradled the lamb. "You saved this wee one. It's yours to raise unless another ewe accepts it. The mama's gone."

Angus stood up from his futile work.

"What now?" Her shoulders sagged with an exhaustion they all shared.

"Rub it clean with this warm towel. I'll get fresh colostrum milked from an earlier birth. You can feed this baby its first bottle."

She accepted the bottle and steadied the lamb between her calves the way he demonstrated. Opening the newborn's mouth with her finger, she pushed the nipple inside and squeezed a little colostrum into its mouth.

The lamb took a few tentative sucks. Puddles formed in the corners of Kieran's eyes at her affectionate smile. He settled her on a stool from the corner and knelt beside her.

"Look. She's eating." The glow on her face reminded him of the day they discovered she was pregnant.

He brushed a stray curl from her eye. "Your first bottle baby. Every two hours for the next twenty-four, and then every three."

His heart overflowed with thankfulness for a wife who embraced his life with enthusiasm after the long, lonely years. Watching her cuddle the newborn lamb, he imagined her nursing their baby. Their dreams died together. She simply wanted to love a child, but he longed for a wee lassie with Bonny's russet curls and green eyes, and a son who loved the land. *Lord, help me desire your will.*

She hugged the orphan lamb closer. "No doll ever snuggled back."

He loved her with his life, and yet he denied the deepest longing of a woman who gained such pleasure from a lamb. Bonny brought joy to everything she touched. How could he refuse her the opportunity to use her gift? She loved them all—Kari's babies, little ones from Bible study, children without families, the lamb she brushed with her lips, and Liam's memory.

She was born to mother—to nurture.

CS 80

Shafts of sunlight streamed through the clouds above the loch when Seumas waved Kieran to the barn door. "Chief, there's a problem."

"What now?"

Seumas slid a glance toward Bonny and lowered his voice. "We had six healthy lambs born in the pasture last night. This morning there are four ewes without lambs."

Kieran shook as if the barn floor gave way underneath him. "Who was on duty?"

"Geordie, Jamie, and Duff staggered their rounds. No one saw anything unusual, and the dogs didn't bark." The farm manager looked at the ground and shuffled his feet.

Wally and Marion appeared to think the motherless lamb was theirs to protect. Bonny wrapped it in blankets and walked over, shooing the big English sheepdogs away. "What's wrong?"

"Your wee one will have a new mama. Four new lambs are missing, and the ewes are frantic." He'd give anything to shield her from another outrage. He turned back to Seumas. "Did you move them?"

"No."

Bonny's shoulders tensed. She cradled the lamb in one arm, rubbing her neck with the other.

"Let's take you to eat breakfast and rest." Kieran clutched her elbow and steered her toward the house. "I'll walk with you. Breathe. Slow and deep."

Jamie strode over, head hung low. "I spotted something under the trees when I headed to the kitchen for breakfast. There are four of them."

With gentle pressure on her arm, Kieran pointed toward the kitchen door. "Go. You don't need to see this." He turned back to Jamie and gestured toward the trees. "Show me."

"No." She jerked away. "You can't shield me from life."

The bodies of four newborn lambs lay in a row under the trees. Bonny let out a strangled cry and stumbled toward the loch, the lamb hugged to her chest.

Kieran reached for her, but she shook him off. "Go inside. I'll call Da and be there in a minute."

Her eyes grew wide with a mixture of fear and anger.

"Please, talk to me, *mo chridhe.*"

"Gunn is out to destroy us." Bonny's quivering voice reminded him of a frightened child.

"We'll make it through, love."

Green fire flashed from her eyes. "They'll ruin us, Kieran. Stonehaven Farm has lasted hundreds of years, but one day it might be you lying on the ground."

He reached out, but she backed away. A stab of pain knifed through his heart, and he steadied himself against the wall. "I'll protect you."

"And if you're *dead*?" Hysteria laced her words.

"They didn't kill me. And they won't get the farm. God is still in control."

"Then I don't like the way he controls things. We've had nothing but loss. Our baby, the attack on you, the sheep, our livelihood, now these helpless lambs."

Three long strides and he reached for her hand. The lamb squirmed between them. She wrenched away and ran toward the house. Helplessness and deep exhaustion overwhelmed him. What could he say? He entered the kitchen in time to hear Bonny's footsteps thud up the back stairs. Taking the steps by two's, he heard the lock to their room click before he reached the door.

Maybe time alone would calm her. Kieran headed back to the barn, convinced the earth had tilted on its axis. At ten p.m., with the barn quiet, he went to spend the night in the house. His wife needed him more than the sheep.

Maggie sat near the warmth of the Aga with Bonny's lamb. "She hasn't come down all day, son. I carried soup up at noon, but she didn't answer the door. I'm sorry."

"Take the lamb out to Seumas so he can find it a new mother." Worries rippled in ever-larger circles as he raced upstairs and pounded on the bedroom door. "Bonny?"

A faint sniffle drifted through the door. He ate dinner and knocked again. When she failed to answer, he took a blanket and pillow from a guest room and lay down outside the door.

At four a.m., his phone vibrated. He entered an empty room and closed the door. "Hello?"

"Kieran, it's Kari. Bonny called me from inside her closet." Babies cooed in sharp contrast to the quiver in her voice. "She's terrified, and I don't know what to say."

A shiver shot through him from head to toe. "What should I do?"

"It would help if the police found this Gunn character. Do they have any leads?"

"No." Rain slipped down the window in rivers as streams of fear iced him to the bone. He felt a hundred years old. "She doesn't think God does a good job of controlling things. How did she act when her parents died and Adam left?"

"She was too calm, too quiet, and couldn't escape fast enough. She'd never leave you and the farm. Try to talk to her again."

Relief rushed from his lungs in a sigh. "Thanks, Kari. I'll try."

The door inched open at his knock. She still wore soiled clothes from the day before, a blanket draped around her shoulders, bright curls escaping the knot on top of her head. She turned away when he met her eyes.

Kieran wrapped her in a gentle embrace as he would a wounded lamb. "*Wheesht, mo grádh*, I know life's out of control. Whatever will help you, we'll do it. I need you."

"I love you, but—"

When his lips brushed her forehead, her arms slipped around his waist. "As long as you love me, we can work out anything, *mo chridhe*—no cracks in those iron bars."

There was a knock on the door, and Maggie peeked in. "There's the lovebirds I know. I hope it's all right to bring your breakfast when I heard voices."

"Thanks, Mother." He accepted the tray of porridge and tea and set it on the table by the window. Bonny followed. "Are you hungry, love?"

"Yes."

"Eat first. Then we'll talk." He spoke as he would to a small child, half-afraid she would refuse.

"Bless our meal, please."

The small fingers he embraced were cold. "Father, I thank you for my precious wife. We come to you in confusion over the trouble we've endured since our marriage. Help us keep our eyes on you instead of our fear. Fill Bonny's heart with peace. Show her your special care. Thank you for providing food to nourish and strengthen our bodies. Amen."

They ate in silence until she pushed her bowl away and scooted closer. "I'm sorry. When I take my eyes off Jesus, the problems look too big. Kari and Dan helped me see what I've done. Those innocent little lambs tore my heart out. I'm afraid you'll end up dead too."

Kieran stroked her cheek. "My mother used to say when I let the bully control my thoughts, I might as well lie down and let him walk all over me. We can't allow the enemy to gain the upper hand."

A slight smile played across her lips, and his heart turned a backflip. "I've seen the pictures. You were bigger than all the others. Who would bully you?"

The laugh slipped out easily. "Bigger maybe, but not meaner. Bullies always go after your most vulnerable spot."

"You're my vulnerable spot. When I saw those poor dead lambs, I remembered leading the horse through the snow, afraid you would fall out of the saddle, and what it felt like to hemorrhage alone with a dead baby." She settled on his lap, where wispy curls tickled his neck and chin.

"It took me by surprise to see the most courageous woman I've ever known fall apart. Forgive me. I shouldn't expect you to always be brave."

"To not trust you is the same as a failure to respect you. Kieran, you're the most capable man in the world. Forgive me?"

"Of course, I forgive you. I fail too."

She sat up straight—her eyes and mouth open wide. "Who's with the sheep?"

"Da, Angus, and Seumas. Most that need help have delivered. The rest will straggle over the next few weeks."

"It was wrong to lock you out." Firelight flickered across her face, and she rubbed her eyes with the back of her hand.

"I slept on the floor by the door. Tonight, I'll hold you in my arms."

"Oh, Kieran, I'm sorry."

He raised her to her feet, tasting her honey-sweet lips. "I wanted to be close if you needed me."

"Your parents must think I'm a fool." Her cheeks bloomed a lovely shade of red.

He supported her elbow when they started for the door. "They understand, Bonny. We all love you."

"Kieran?" She stopped at the top of the stairs. "I can't promise not to do something stupid again."

"Neither can I. If it's Gavin Gunn, I can't imagine he believes killing more sheep will help his claims, but we need to be careful. I'll tell everyone you're all right. You might want to shower. The police will be here soon."

CHAPTER EIGHT

Detective Sergeant or not, Alasdair Kavanaugh and Kieran were long-time friends. However, Bonny still couldn't bring herself to call DCI Bruce McLeod anything other than Inspector. Polite and compassionate, the way he called her "my dear" set her at ease, but he was more of a kind boss than a friend.

A gentle breeze drifted through the open window, fluttering the curtains while Kieran led them out onto the patio. She had updated the white, cast iron furniture with new, apple-red cushions and an umbrella for the warm days of summer. For now, they enjoyed the spring sunshine. But even the spell cast by the sun glinting off the blue waters of Loch Garry wasn't potent enough to erase the vision of four white bodies beneath the greening tree in the nearby pasture.

Mary lounged at Bonny's feet, heavy Lab tail thumping. The playful dog accompanied her everywhere now, while Kieran kept Darnley close. The hunting dogs were their choice for protection over the border collies or English sheepdogs which roamed the pastures. The memory of her first day at the farm and the rowdy welcome of all six dogs made her smile. She'd always enjoyed big dogs. They gave her a sense of comfort, though recent visits of the sinister variety failed to arouse their ire.

Alasdair leaned over to rub Darnley's ears, which provided the chance to gain support for her newest idea. "We've contacted a breeder of German Shepherds outside Inverness. Kieran promised to take me up at the first opportunity. They rescued a pair once owned by a couple in the city who decided they were too large for their apartment. Can you imagine such big dogs in close quarters? Anyway, they're a better choice than these two, who would beat someone to death with their tails or play catch before they'd attack."

"Great idea. A well-trained watchdog can be a powerful deterrent." The Detective Sergeant, a well-known dog lover, offered the anticipated agreement.

Kieran tilted his chair back on two legs and laughed. "I knew she'd seize the opportunity to bring up her newest scheme. It seems we don't have enough of a menagerie already."

"German shepherds are perfect watchdogs. Too bad they'll already have names. Yours all have such character." Alasdair reached for the dog treats he never failed to keep in his pocket and tossed one to each dog.

"You won't believe it, but they're named Flora and Charlie. I guess others share Kieran's penchant for historic Scottish names."

Both detectives roared with laughter.

"This weekend, love, I promise. Before anyone else snatches them up." Kieran tugged on her ponytail.

"In all seriousness, you need security cameras and motion detectors around the house and barns, and a gate at the drive." Inspector McLeod refocused them on the immediate need. "Alasdair will provide names of the best companies for rural locations. Contact them right away."

DS Kavanaugh flipped the page in his notebook. "The most recent record for Deirdre is at Fort William Christian College the year you both taught. She's an elusive one, no job records, income tax information, driver's license, nothing. We found a birth record for a Deirdre Margaret Adair in Inverness. We're searching for the parents now, a Robert and Isobel Adair. There's a son named Gavin MacDonell living with them several years earlier."

Kieran's face paled, eyes round. "The name Adair isn't familiar. What age would this Gavin be?"

DCI McLeod looked at his notes. "About forty-seven."

"He could be related to Diarmid, the cousin who signed the land over to my father, but that would mean they're family." He leaned back, mouth pressed in a tense, white line, golden brow furrowed.

"If we can find the mother, perhaps we'll get some answers." The inspector stood and reached for Bonny's hand. "Thank you for the hospitality, my dear. Make the security system a priority. We'll be in touch."

After a vigorous tummy-rub and one more treat for the dogs, Alasdair followed the inspector toward their car. "Let me know if you get the Shepherds. I'll be out here again before long. Take care, you two."

Mary and Darnley followed, tails wagging. Bonny pointed. "Look how they beg for more. You don't suppose our intruders get past them with treats, do you?"

"It's possible. Something's not right. This unknown enemy keeps shoving us toward the edge of a cliff. It makes me uncomfortable, especially after what Da said about Diarmid's branch of MacDonells."

She released his hand and straightened the chairs. "I find their news, or lack of it, depressing. Let's take advantage of the lovely weather."

"I'll call these security companies and take you up on your offer." He headed for the office.

Humming "Scotland the Brave," Bonny danced toward the kitchen door. A relaxed afternoon in the spring sun might change both their attitudes.

ೞ ಬ

They saddled the horses, and Kieran led the way toward the far side of the loch.

"I love the view from the middle of the bridge where blue sky and still-as-glass-water meet. The loch mirrors the mountains in a seamless scene of serenity. Every time I ride into the cool shelter of the tall trees, my worries disappear. All I feel is gratitude for this lovely place." Bonny laughed as Mary and Darnley took off after rabbits. "Great watchdogs. An invitation to check on the *kyloe* is too good to pass up."

He slowed until she caught up. "You love those Highland cattle too."

"They're so cute." When she turned for one more glance, an eagle dipped down to the water, grabbed a fish in its talons, and soared skyward, majestic and proud. "Did you see the eagle? We saw the same thing the first time I visited the farm."

"Aye, I remember the electricity in the air with both of us wondering if love might grow to fill the empty spaces in our hearts. And it did."

"How I long to soar high above our trials the way the eagle flew over the trees and disappeared."

They left the horses, hiked up the hill, and sat on the grassy overlook. The loch shimmered below. She breathed deep, savoring the fresh, sweet perfume of clover and wildflowers, buzzing with bees, filled with bird song and the lowing of cattle.

"Remember the first time you brought me here?"

Kieran leaned back on the grass. The blue shirt brightened his eyes, and her breath caught. "I wanted you to love my home—to love me the way I already loved you. I grew more alive each moment, happy to breathe the same air with you. Bonny, those feelings grow stronger every day."

Her heart quickened along with the urge to wrap him in her arms and kiss him the way she wanted to then.

"We've been through a lot. Would you change anything if you had the chance?"

"Not a thing." She rolled sideways, pushing him down, then toed the grass with her boots to keep from sliding downhill. His chest rose strong and powerful beneath her. Kieran's lips yielded. His arms surrounded her and rolled her over, resting on his elbows, careful to not impede her breathing. Their lips never parted, matching hunger for hunger.

Love and joy overwhelmed her for this life, this man. And this place.

He pulled back. Cobalt eyes searched hers. "I miss that couple who only desired to love each other. I long for the freedom our hearts knew back then."

"So do I."

"Remember what I told you on our honeymoon, at the Old Town Christmas Stroll in Albuquerque? I understood for the first time why you refused my proposal and sent me home, why you craved familiarity while you healed after the car accident. I found myself surrounded by sights, sounds, and aromas, common to you, but curious to me. The rugged mountains where you grew up, chili, adobe, and the rustic wooden spires of the church meant to you what

Hogmanay, haggis, and glacier-carved lochs are to me. Home. Given time, you chose to leave everything you've ever known to marry me. Now I understand why you had to be so certain. To love and marry me, you had to turn your back on your entire life and accept everything about mine."

With a soft moan, her arms slid around his neck and drew him down to where their lips melded together. "I gained much more than I gave up. You're my home now."

"I'm not certain I'd have the courage to do what you did. And now we're faced with a situation neither of us knows how to handle. So, if you struggle now and then, we need to remember how much you've already accomplished."

She tangled her fingers in his hair and pulled him down again. The breeze sang in her heart because Kieran MacDonell loved her. "Just love me. Kiss me until all I know is you."

The caress of his eyes, his smile, melted her like sun on chocolate. He pulled back, panting. "Let's go home."

He offered a hand up, and they mounted the horses, urging them into a canter.

Hurry.

Don't stop.

When they crossed the bridge, the barn came into view. "I'll race you!" She urged Misty faster the nearer they came to the bridge. Bonny's sturdy little mare could never beat Storm. Kieran raced past, laughter floating behind him on the breeze. How wonderful he was. Strong, godly, romantic—hers.

He waited in front of the barn, laughing, the sun behind him turned his hair to gold. "I expected such a fine horsewoman to judge the capabilities of your mount with more accuracy."

"I only wanted to laugh and have fun. We need more laughter in our lives," Bonny answered in keeping with the conversation from their first wonderful day together on the farm.

Strong hands encircled her waist, lifted her from the saddle, and drew her to him. "I married the last woman who said that."

"And she would do it all over again." She threw her arms wide before wrapping them around his neck. "Would you care to accompany me to the house after we rub down the horses?"

"You don't have to ask me twice."

αβ

With the horses settled in their stalls, the newlyweds clasped hands and headed into the sunlight. Bonny leaned her forehead against the work-hardened muscles of Kieran's upper arm and gazed up at him.

He froze at the top of the hill. The kitchen door stood open, screen door blowing in the breeze. The magic of the pasture evaporated faster than fog on a summer day.

"What's on the step?" Bonny squinted to see.

"A dead lamb."

"No, Kieran, not more. I locked the door. You saw me."

"Stay here. Let me check things out."

"Call Alasdair. Please, don't go in alone."

Kieran led the way to the barn office, locked the door, closed the blinds, and dialed Alasdair. He paced while Bonny stared at the floor. Ominous notions about Deirdre and Gavin circled like birds of prey.

They stepped outside when the detective pulled into the drive, but he waved them back. Twenty minutes later, he entered the barn accompanied by Hugh MacFadyen, a local police officer. "There's not a big mess, but you'll have to examine each room to see if they took anything."

Kieran reached for her hand. "Bonny, don't look. Close your eyes and I'll guide you."

"Why?"

"Because, love, it's the lamb you were going to raise before one of the ewes adopted it."

"Why more dead sheep? I don't understand."

Hugh took her other arm. "They're trying to scare you, to convince you they'll take everything that matters unless you give in." He guided her past the lamb and into the kitchen.

"They're succeeding. And why my lamb out of the hundreds?" She opened her eyes. Muddy footprints covered part of the floor. The intruder's boots were removed near the table and replaced before he left. Tracks headed back toward the door, with no indication of where else they'd been.

"Maybe because we kept that lamb and ewe close to the house so you could watch them. They knew it was special." Kieran wiped her cheeks with his handkerchief and handed it to her.

"What else will we lose before they're done?"

Hand in hand, they scoured the house, hoping one might see what the other missed.

"One photo from the office is gone." Kieran dropped into a kitchen chair across from Alasdair while Bonny poured the tea. What a sad commentary on their life for a detective to be comfortable enough in their home to set a pot of tea while they searched. "The other rooms appear untouched."

"What photograph?" The detective nodded thanks to Bonny but glanced toward Kieran.

"Me with the Queen at the Braemar Gathering." He scrubbed his hand across his face.

"You're certain there's nothing else?"

"We haven't found anything."

"Why that picture?" The detective sounded puzzled.

"Deirdre Adair wants my husband for herself," Bonny said. "Now she has a picture to look at while she dreams of the day I'm gone. It was clear at the *ceilidh* she still hates me."

Kieran scooted closer and set his cup aside. "Don't go there. Remember the magic of the meadow, and let Alasdair handle the investigation."

"Our evil visitor overcame the magic of the meadow."

Alasdair stood. "I'll dust for fingerprints and make my report. Try to relax tonight."

She balled her fists. "I'll scream if one more person tells me to relax when people want to destroy us."

"*Wheesht*, love, sit with me while they finish."

"I can't sit still. Maybe I'll clean out the refrigerator."

By the time the police left, the refrigerator shone inside and out. Kieran even moved it for her to clean behind. He closed the door and caught her hands. "Come pray with me. Remember what we came home for."

How could she be angry when he cradled her hands while they knelt beside the bed? She opened her eyes and watched serenity transform him as he left his concerns with God, longing to recapture the meadow.

He finished, and she continued. "Lord, we don't know what faces us today or any other day. We entrust our lives to you. Thank you for this man I love with all my heart." Emotion choked her voice when he pulled her into his arms.

"Keep your eyes on the Lord, *mo chridhe*. Our strength lies in quietness and trust."

And there it was. The magic of the meadow. The reality of their love.

CB EO

The plain, white envelope with Kieran's name printed on the outside lay under Bonny's pillow when she fluffed it before climbing into bed. Her gasp brought him out of the bathroom, toothbrush in hand.

"What's wrong?"

Heart pounding, steps shaky, she walked toward him and held out the envelope.

He laid his toothbrush down and accepted it. The envelope contained a single piece of blue notepaper with handwriting in a delicate script. His hands shook. "I'm sorry for the actions of my brother. Please stay alert. If I had the power to stop him, I would. You're in terrible danger. He wants Kieran dead. Deirdre."

"She killed my lamb—came into our bedroom? I can't sleep on sheets she touched. Couldn't she leave it in the kitchen?" Bonny shivered. What evil possessed these people?

He turned the paper over, peered into the envelope, walked to the bed, and lifted the pillow to look for something else.

"Call Alasdair."

"Don't you see?" He laid the letter on the nightstand. "Deirdre confirmed Gavin's her brother, but it doesn't sound as if she's an agreeable participant."

"I wouldn't trust a word she says. Let the police sort it out. Please." She walked to the bedroom door. "Mary, Darnley, come."

"What are you doing?"

"They're not great watchdogs, but they're the best we've got. From now on, they sleep in here."

Clean sheets didn't erase the sense of violation, not only of their home but their private haven. By the time Alasdair arrived in the late morning, Bonny and Eleanor had aired and cleaned the entire bedroom.

"We questioned Brennan Grant again, told him we have reason to believe Deirdre might be in trouble. He admitted they have an older brother, Gavin MacDonell. He hesitated before, fearing he'd endanger his sister. Gunn's a family name." Alasdair began tapping on the table.

"Did you learn more about the family?" Kieran's jaw muscles worked overtime while Bonny gripped his hand in a vise.

"Aye, Brennan's a half-brother to both of them. We're looking in Caithness and Inverness-shire for more family records. He refused to tell us anything about their parents." Alasdair pushed back his chair and stood. "Taran MacDonell escaped prison and lived with them in Caithness until he died. They never hanged him. Brennan said Gavin takes after his father."

Bonny shivered, myriad implications running through her mind.

"We'll increase patrols in the area. It's all we can do for now." Alasdair laid a hand on her shoulder. "We'll get them. I promise."

When Kieran closed the door behind him, Bonny grabbed his arm. "A monster's chasing us. We'll never be safe until he's dead."

"If Gavin and Deirdre are Taran's children, Brighde may have survived and married Taran."

"Don't jump to conclusions. Taran was Diarmid's brother. He would have known about the deed."

⚜

Lambs frolicked in the pasture, and happy smiles shone on every face. Today, they would celebrate God's blessing on both Stonehaven Farm and Hope Chapel. The glassy loch mirrored a sky of *Saltire*-blue dotted with puffy, white clouds.

Kieran arrived at the chapel early and alone for prayer. The natural fir floor and pews, the stone walls, and timber frame construction made the chapel seem one with its surroundings. A round, rosette window of stained glass sparkled high above the double doors, hand-carved with Celtic crosses by his father. Two clear windows rose from floor to ceiling behind the pulpit giving worshipers a view of the loch and mountains, a simple wooden cross mounted between.

Readied for Janet and Graeme's wedding the day before, flowers graced the small stage, the top of the piano, and the pew ends. Two weddings seemed a perfect start for Hope Chapel.

How well Kieran remembered the lonely flight back to Scotland after Bonny sent him away, determined not to sink back into the deadly depression he had suffered since Bronwyn's death. "Dear Lord, I vowed to open this chapel, and minister to the isolated farmers of Glen Garry. I heard your call to my broken heart but never imagined Bonny would someday serve alongside me. Thank you."

The arrival of the women broke his silent contemplation, followed an hour later by the men and the guests. A sense of humility and grave responsibility filled his heart when Eleanor played the first chords of the wedding march on the new piano.

The door to the chapel office opened. Bonny, a fiery orchid in her lavender dress, started down the aisle. A radiant Janet, beautiful in her sister's wedding dress, dabbed her shining eyes with a lacy handkerchief and placed her hand in Graeme's.

Kieran took a deep breath. "Today, I'm filled with joy for our dearest friends. Before Hope Chapel opens, we've celebrated two weddings. It's an honor to perform the marriage of the couple who encouraged Bonny and me in our growth in Christ. What a blessing to see our dear friends united as one."

His wife's lovely smile reminded him of their wedding day and the oneness that blossomed anew now they were learning to let their trials draw them closer. What greater reminder of love and commitment than a wedding?

Graeme and Janet's faces glowed with peace and the confidence of answered prayer. They exchanged their Gaelic vows and gold rings with happy smiles and sweet tears of gratitude. Love baptized this little chapel before it ever opened for services.

Bonny's clear soprano kissed the crossbeams in the ceiling with "Be Thou My Vision" while the bridal couple took communion. The song carried him back to the first time he heard her sing "Heart of my own heart, whatever befall." Surely, those words spoke to her heart too.

"Your prayers are part of the reason we're here today." Graeme raised a toast at the reception. "When no one else believed we'd marry, you two never gave up. Thank you."

Janet's face glowed far beyond her usual beauty with the joy of dreams realized. Bonny hugged her hard. "*A beannachd*, Janet, my first and best friend in my new home. Many blessings on your marriage."

Surrounded by the remains of the simple reception, Kieran stood beside Bonny and watched the bridal couple head for a honeymoon in their New Mexico house. If God could bless them and draw Janet and Graeme together against all odds, he would resolve any problems they faced in his own time.

CHAPTER NINE

A calm, sunny day and the vibrant blue of the water stood in sharp contrast to the maelstrom in Bonny's heart as she stared out the window of the master suite. A report on the morning news showed video of the Corryvreckan Whirlpool off the west coast of Scotland, near the isles of Jura and Scarba and explained the mechanism of the third-largest whirlpool in the world. The apt description of the confusion swirling through her mind lingered.

The baby. Deirdre. Gavin ... They came together and formed a stone needle in her heart, similar to how the rocky outcropping on the sea floor caused the tides between the islands to spin in circles. Fear, depression, and her desire for a child made her emotions whirl out of control. Most often, Kieran ended up sucked under, never suspecting danger lurked in the slightest word he said or failed to say to his emotional wife.

Her Bible lay open to First Samuel, the story of Hannah, also a woman who suffered a fruitless womb. Yes, it said clearly, "the Lord had closed her womb." For unexplained reasons, God chose not to allow Hannah children. Or Bonny either.

Kari's days revolved around sweet baby smells, giggles, and warm little bodies to cuddle close. Her cup overflowed with the blessings of Annie and Willie. Without explanation, Scripture said Hannah's cup remained empty, while her husband's other wife bore children. God could have given her and Kari each a child. Instead, He chose to close Bonny's womb.

Hannah's husband gave her a double portion to sacrifice to the Lord because he loved her, the barren one. Kieran proved his love in more ways than Bonny could count.

She knelt and thanked God for his faithful, sacrificial love. Did she always show how much she loved him?

Dear Lord, help me prove my love for you and for Kieran daily.

Hannah eventually became pregnant, something impossible for Bonny. Yet the Scriptures also said the Lord remembered Hannah. He gave Bonny the poem about their child in heaven. He remembered her loneliness and doubt. In the midst of stalkers and her search for purpose, God did not forget.

Did Kieran realize God remembered his pain too?

She once believed infertility was something only women struggled with, but Kieran had lost two children. He struggled too. Genesis said Abraham and Sarah waited for a child until he was one-hundred years old and she was ninety.

Lord, I don't want to demand a child on my schedule if you have another agenda. If adoption is in your plan for us, help me be patient with you and Kieran. Help me wait for your best and not hold it over his head.

She retrieved her prayer journal from the top drawer of the nightstand to record her impressions and the encouragement of this morning.

A voice whispered deep inside, "in the fullness of time." Jesus came in the fullness of time. She would wait until God chose to make his will known to them.

The journal went back into the drawer, along with her Bible, while she pondered these matters. When God showed her the time was right, she would share her thoughts with Kieran. In the meantime, she needed to allow God to work in her husband's heart.

 C8 80

Bonny's Sunday school lesson was finished, the accounts balanced, and the house dusted. She was going stir-crazy. Eleanor only worked two and a half days a week to help clean the large house and bake. She had a lot of free time, but few friends. The women from the Bible study were busy with small children and lived too far away for visits when she couldn't go out alone.

Flora's leg twitched when Bonny rubbed her tummy. The German shepherd was now her constant companion. "It's you and me, girl. I'm not complaining about the company, but you're not much in the conversation department. At least the Labs are happier back with the rabbits and squirrels. Maybe Kieran and Charlie will take us for a long walk later, okay?"

Leaning back in her chair, she looked around the redecorated office. The selection of new furniture for the living room had filled several weeks. Kieran and his parents were both pleased with her changes to their family home. He smiled in undisguised pleasure when he saw Bronwyn's painting of Loch Garry, the trees dressed in their loveliest autumn colors, over the living room fireplace. The yellows of her sunflower painting in the kitchen blended well with the new red and gold. Three guest rooms upstairs included her paintings of the loch and farm in different seasons, while New Mexico art hung alongside. Rooms for their private use, the upstairs office and master suite, contained a mixture of items special to them alone. Now, she needed some new projects.

"Bonny!"

When the kitchen door slammed, she ran downstairs into her husband's arms. She lived for these moments but craved a purpose beyond this tiny world. Flora loped along behind and joined in a cheerful tussle with Charlie near the door while Bonny dished up two fiery bowls of green chili stew and carried them to the table.

Kieran splashed water all around the sink while they chatted about the details of his morning. Then he took a seat and offered a blessing. "How was your morning, love? Did you finish your Sunday school lesson?"

"I did. I still feel lost sometimes without papers to grade and lessons to plan. For the first time in my life, I'm lonesome and restless. Except for lambing time, the farm doesn't require much of me. I can't spend the rest of my life alone in this house."

His eyes searched hers and narrowed. "Do you feel down? Any nightmares?"

"The medication helps, but I don't have enough tasks to fill my days. I spent a lot of years being around people all the time."

"You haven't seen Janet since her honeymoon." He blew on a spoonful of stew. "Why don't you plan lunch in Fort William one day? Have you talked to Kari lately?"

"Kari's busy with babies and can't comprehend my lack of purpose. I would enjoy a visit with Janet. It's not depression, Kieran. I just wonder what meaning my life holds outside of the house and chapel."

A smile spread across his lips. "Come with me this afternoon. You need to get out, and I'd love your company."

She swallowed a bite of tortilla with butter and heather honey. "Who would think an afternoon in the mud could sound so delightful? I'd love too."

"Shall we take Misty and Storm? It's a nice day to ride out to check on the ewes and lambs." Those sapphire eyes twinkled whenever she showed interest in farm business. He spooned another bite of stew into his mouth and tore off a piece of a homemade tortilla. For a Scot, he loved New Mexican food.

"There's a pot roast in the Aga for dinner. My entire afternoon is free." She ran upstairs to change, grabbed a jacket, and stuffed her feet into Wellies while he placed the lunch dishes in the dishwasher.

Lagging spirits lifted when she stepped into the fresh air. Sun peeked through the clouds and warmed her face while Kieran checked the last of the ewes. The green-clad mountains dotted with white rocks and tumultuous waterfalls filled her with a love of her adopted homeland, though nothing close to her love for the man by her side.

Mist lifted from the water until the sky matched the brilliant blue of the loch below. The pasture hummed with bees while sheep munched the grass in placid silence. They sat on a log and sipped water, the sunshine warming her shoulders. "Kari has her twins, but I have your love, and this vast expanse of steep mountains, loch, and heather. I thank God for these moments of joy."

"The secretary at Faith Chapel quit last week. Would you help? You'd have a reason to ride to town with me every week. Then when I need help with counseling, I'd have you there, and we'd have the drive time to spend together."

"Are you serious or sorry for me because I feel useless?"

He settled his arm around her shoulders. "I wouldn't pacify you. When I have women with problems, like Emily, your presence would be beneficial. Will you come?"

"I … I'd love to. After dealing with my emotional ups and downs, any other woman should look easy. I've missed my work with young girls since leaving home." At last, a worthy purpose.

Kieran offered Bonny his hand. "It's settled then."

She smiled as she stood. It still wasn't the purpose she longed for in this life of limbo.

Chapter Ten

"Here's a letter addressed to you, hen. No return address. No postmark. Someone must have hand-delivered it."

"It's Deirdre's handwriting. Remember the note she left in our bed?" Bonny's shaking fingers tore a jagged hole in the envelope. Fear, sharp as a *sgian dubh*, stabbed her from the first words. "Oh no …"

"What's wrong?"

The paper fell from her hands, blowing toward the loch in the rising wind. "He's going to pull something else."

Kieran dropped the reins and chased the letter toward the loch, skimming over it and reading aloud while he walked back. "My brother Gavin is *aff his heid* with hate. Tell Kieran he's in danger. Gavin's desperate to get the land he believes belongs to him. Don't look for me. Deirdre."

"She wants you."

He was at her side in three long strides, reaching to lift her off Misty's back. "Do you believe this maniac?"

In spite of the sunny day, an inner chill penetrated her heart. She buried her face in his chest. "She wants to protect you, and I can die. Let's go back to the house."

"Shh. Quiet. In the grove of fir trees, do you see?"

She shaded her eyes with her hand. "There's someone near the shore."

"The horses could use a drink." They led their horses, the dogs trotting alongside. "They can't get away." He paused and held a finger to his lips.

She pointed to the mud. "Boot prints."

Charlie's lip curled with a snarl. Flora sniffed the prints, a low growl rumbling in her throat.

"Alasdair needs to come before dark."

"Don't call. She'll hear you."

He shook his head and mouthed, "Text."

The footprints led along the shoreline. "These look too big for a woman."

"She's a large one."

How far would Deirdre go to get him for herself?

Bang! Bang! Gunfire sounded from somewhere in the reeds.

More from instinct than fear, Bonny dropped prone into the cold mud. Misty headed home at a gallop. Both dogs took off in the direction of the shots.

"Where are you?" Kieran's voice sounded frantic.

If she called out, the next shots might find their mark.

He slogged through the mud toward her. "Bonny?"

"On the ground. Get down!" Better to frighten him than get both of them killed. *Please be careful.* She saw him.

He crawled the last few yards. "Are you hurt?"

"Shh! I landed on a rock with my elbow. I wanted you on the ground."

"She didn't shoot you?"

"No, but I might have broken my elbow. I didn't want to get us killed. Where is she?"

"The shots came from the trees to the right. They'll be long gone with the dogs after them."

"Misty ran home."

"Storm did too. Lie still. I'll text Seumas to come—armed."

Minutes seemed like hours. Bonny cradled her elbow until the truck rumbled up.

Kieran signaled silence. "I'll stand to show him where we are. Stay down."

"But—" *Show him respect,* she told herself. *Let him be your protector.* She held her breath when he stood to wave Seumas close. The truck stopped, and the door creaked open.

"Cover us. I'll bring her over." He bent, strong arms lifting. "Play out the charade. Don't speak and stay limp. I have the letter for the police."

Bonny nodded and let her head roll toward his chest, thankful for the truck.

"Get to the barn, fast." He spoke loud enough for anyone to hear, climbed in, and closed the door.

"I'm not shot, but my elbow is throbbing." Bonny winced with every movement of her arm.

"Let them believe they wounded you. I'll call Alasdair." He cringed every time she winced.

"What can I do, chief?" Seumus bounced the truck across the pasture toward the barn.

"Send Angus to drive us into Fort William. You stay and guide the police. There are footprints in the mud. Whatever you do, don't tell anyone Bonny's not hurt."

"The entire farm crew will be upset."

Kieran tugged a handkerchief from his pocket, wiping the mud from her face. "I don't care. I want her away from here for a few days."

Seumas stopped in front of the barn. "Bonny, I'm glad you're all right. I'll do my best to help the police."

Two muddy dogs ran up. Their culprit had escaped again.

ೞ ೡ

Her fear had grown into an uncontrollable monster. The fall dislocated Bonny's elbow, but at the detective's request, the hospital kept her for two days. Kieran watched her stare at the wall in silence for hours at a time, helpless.

"I recommend you hire a protection detail. We can't provide the protection you need." DCI McLeod was subdued.

"No, I'll handle it. She's mine to protect."

"Kieran, please? Who will protect you?" She cried herself to sleep.

He'd never forget the day Dan called to say Bonny refused Adam's marriage proposal because she loved him. The peaceful life he promised her had turned into a bizarre nightmare. He prayed for a way to remove her from this quagmire of tension and fear for a few days. The circles under her eyes grew darker, and she ate such wee amounts it wouldn't keep a mouse alive. He longed to make her feel protected and cherished.

She acted cool-headed and quick-thinking when the shots rang out, but the return home made it obvious Bonny had changed. She sought refuge in his arms whenever he was near. The rest of the time she remained upstairs, reading and sewing, windows covered day and night. They canceled the Bible study under the ruse of her recovery. In reality, fear consumed her.

Prayer time in the middle of a sleepless night led to a plan. "You've never been to the old *bothy* where I used to retreat to think." Kieran smothered a stack of Scottish pancakes with butter and raspberry sauce. "The cottage is isolated enough to be safe. If we take new furniture, linens, and clean it up, we could have a great hideaway to escape from the world."

Her lips trembled into a tentative smile. "When can we go?"

"This week? We won't tell anyone except Alasdair and McLeod. And of course, Angus and Eleanor."

She crossed the kitchen to her desk and returned with a pen and paper. "What do we need?" Her eyes glowed and her voice carried an excitement reminiscent of the wife he knew.

Two days later, Kieran loaded a new mattress, kitchen furniture, and bedding into one of the farm pickups while Bonny prepared food. Flora and Charlie jumped behind the seat, tails wagging, while Wally and Marion whined and followed them down the drive. She climbed in, and they headed up into the mountains.

Her eager smile and the warmth where her hand rested on his thigh indicated this trip might bring the healing he hoped. "I'm so excited to hide away in the mountains with you. It sounds heavenly."

Perhaps this weekend, they could leave trouble behind and concentrate on being two people in love. When he kneaded her shoulder, the knots relaxed under his fingers. "Your cheeks are pink, your eyes glow. I can't wait to see your expression when you discover how far into the mountains we're headed."

"You do know what makes me happy." She reminded him of a sponge soaking up beauty instead of fear, eager to remember each detail of this new adventure. "Mountains draw my eyes and my spirit upward. I couldn't live away from them."

In spite of the rocky road, overgrown with grass and heather, a deep sense of calm settled over Kieran's heart. Bonny talked and smiled more and more the further they traveled. "You wouldn't have married me if I lived in the lowlands?"

Biting her lower lip, she looked straight ahead. "I don't know …"

He frowned.

She laughed and patted his arm. "I would have married you no matter what. Tall peaks and rugged cliffs give life to my soul. No wonder you come here to think."

"I'm amazed at how well you express what I feel."

"We're God's gift to each other. It works both ways."

They bounced up the mountainside for an hour before an ancient stone cottage with a thatched roof and chimneys at each end came into view. She leaped out the second the pickup halted, inhaling the fresh, damp air, pungent with the aroma of decayed leaves, wet wood, and pine. The *bothy* stood in the open with one tall Scots pine next to it, but a few hundred yards away, dense forest covered the mountainside in varied hues of green dotted with rocks and *burns*.

"How old is it?"

"Three hundred years or more. Look around and then we'll unload the truck and get peat out of the shed for a fire."

Kieran unlocked the door and watched her nose wrinkle at the musty smell. She stepped inside and squinted into the darkness until he opened the shutters so light filtered through filthy windows. "It's shabbier than I remembered."

She examined the peat-burning stove and dry sink with a pump. A once-fine couch, armchair, and wooden table stood in front of an ancient stone fireplace, equipped with an iron spit and pothook. A small shelf held an assortment of favorite books, along with agricultural magazines and a few board games.

"It just needs a little care and cleaning." Grasping his hand, Bonny dragged him into the bedroom, furnished simply with a rusty iron bed and chest of drawers topped with an oval mirror. A washbasin and pitcher stood on a table in the corner and a small fireplace in the other. Across the tiny room, shelves were crammed with old clothes, blankets, and the necessary fishing rods, a first aid kit, and an old sheepskin.

"It's not fancy. Nothing's changed since my childhood. We can do more if you want." He was surprised how much he needed her to like it.

"There's nothing a good cleaning can't fix." Bonny wrapped her arms around his neck, bringing his forehead to rest on hers. "What an adventure to live in the wilderness alone. You'd be my entire world."

"You mean I'm not already?" He laughed. "Come see the best part before dark, but leave the dogs in here. They'll frighten the wildlife." A bubbling *burn* flowed through massive trees a short distance from the cottage. "Your source of water, in case the pump doesn't work or the well runs dry. And there, m'lady, is your luxury toilet."

Her eyes followed when Kieran pointed to a small stone structure. "An outhouse?"

"Do you have a problem with it?"

"Not in the slightest." She gave him a playful shove. "It adds to the adventure."

"There's an old chamber pot under the bed for when it pours rain."

"Which is most of the time." She giggled and tugged on his hand. "Show me the rest."

A quarter of a mile up, a graceful waterfall dropped thirty feet over a rocky ledge. "It's beautiful. I want to see everything."

"Not today, my insatiable explorer." He steered her toward the cottage. "I keep dry peat in the shed. Get the fire started while I prime the pump.

"Like the rest of Scotland, *dry* is a relative term." She filled the box next to the stove and one next to each fireplace. "Dad would have loved it here."

"Is your elbow up to helping with the mattress?"

"It should be with the brace. We'll find out."

Kieran heaved the mattress into place while she closed the door on the deepening dusk. "Did Bronwyn ever come here?"

"One glance inside and we headed back down the mountain—city girl, you know. Why?"

"Just wondered." She busied herself putting away the canned goods and poked into shelves and corners while he primed the pump and carried in the last box. The fire already filled the room with the sweet aroma of peat.

He winked. "Come tell me you love me."

"It's easier to show you." A smile he'd seen too infrequently of late, spread across her face.

"What do you have in mind?"

She twined her fingers in his hair and kissed him. "I plan to concentrate on only you the entire weekend."

"Sounds lovely." He deepened the kiss until the world disappeared, and only nameless sensations of mind-whirling delight remained.

"I feel the need to be held by the man of my dreams."

"Will I do?"

She took him by the hands and pulled him toward the bedroom. "Better than anyone in the world."

೮೦

Kieran busied himself hanging a rack for the fishing rods while Bonny dried the bowls from their breakfast. She stacked the last one on the shelf and hung up the towel. "It's time for a hike. Show me all your favorite places."

Dressed in layers, with waterproof boots, they headed up his favorite path behind the cottage. All the reasons he fell in love with her came back. A woman eager to tackle any trail, no matter the difficulty, didn't come along often. Eleanor long since admitted she'd misjudged Bonny's ability to handle farm life based on her petite size and delicate appearance. At her best, she could out-hike him any day. Right now, she reminded him of a wounded hummingbird, but perhaps their weekend trip would restore her indomitable spirit. "You'll tell me if you become too tired."

"The freedom of the woods gives such an adrenaline rush. Let's go."

They topped a ridge, and he pointed to one side of a large rock. A herd of red deer raised their heads and returned to grazing. Bonny's eyes shone. Her radiant smile confirmed her fascination with a place he'd loved all his life. They watched in silence and detoured through the trees to avoid disturbing the herd.

"At my grandparents' cabin we set out mangers. Soon, the deer weren't afraid of people. We had squirrel feeders and bird feeders. I loved it."

"I prefer the wilderness, where I'm the intruder." He stopped underneath a large pine and pointed to a red squirrel sitting high in the tree. "If the animals become pets, it will lose the magic. Other than letting out a few hunting permits to cull the herds and keep them healthy, I leave them alone."

"Thank you for sharing it. Show me more."

The wonder in her smile was part of what made his life worth living. The soft blush of her cheeks, her luminous eyes—never had God made a more beautiful woman.

Thank you, Lord, for more love than I ever dreamed possible.

og ꝏ

After a full day of hiking, they awakened much later than usual to rain lashing the windows. Kieran opened the shutters on a mountain shrouded in a thick lamb's wool blanket of fog. The trees nearest the cottage shimmered like ghosts in the heavy downpour, but peat fires kept the little cottage warm and snug.

Bonny's lips curved in a smile when he scooped up the last of the haggis. "I've never cooked for anyone who could eat so much, but then I never cooked for anyone your size."

"Did you just say I need to lose weight?" He tried to sound serious, but her laughter made it impossible.

"Never. You're solid muscle, but you have to admit you're larger than most."

"Have been since the day I was born. Come here, you." Arms around her waist, he drew her close. "What shall we do on such a *dreich* day?"

"Since it's too wet to explore, let's clean the inside from floor to ceiling. I have a kettle of warm water. I think I'll scrub the entire kitchen."

"I'll do the upper shelves. You take the lower ones."

When he reached the top shelf, she flicked soapy water at him, wetting the front of his shirt. He pulled her close, capturing her warm, willing lips until she drew back to catch her breath. Her sighs made his knees wobble and head spin.

Two hours later, dirt and cobwebs were banished from the front room, and Bonny admired their work with a satisfied nod.

"Set those dishes on the shelf and join me on the couch." Kieran plucked a cobweb from her hair and pulled her down beside him. "We've created a little nest where we can come whenever time allows. Now what?"

"I hesitate to bring it up, but since the rain's here to stay, maybe we should jump in and have the discussion about the matter dominating our lives like that big bull rules your herd of Highland cattle. We have to talk about our differences on adoption and fertility doctors."

He hated to admit it, but at times it seemed they tiptoed around an unexploded bomb. "I don't want to argue."

"Who said we had to argue? Your family's lived in Glen Garry since the mid-sixteenth century. You're the proud custodian of the familial lands. I'm a MacDonell now too, and I remember my grandmother's stories about the Frasers. Scots are serious about their national pride, their clans. You married an American against your mother's wishes, and my ancestry had nothing to do with it. You love me for me. How can it be wrong to accept a child into our family when they don't have one of their own?"

That hit a nerve. "I don't have all the answers, Bonny. My concern isn't with their heritage, but their differences from you and me, the risk of more disappointment, and the loss should something go wrong. We can teach them and provide opportunities, but who's to say they won't turn out like Gavin? We have no idea what they've inherited."

"Kieran, you're a sheep breeder. Pedigrees are what you do. Other than my Scottish grandmother, you didn't know anything about my genes. Maybe there's an ax murderer in my family tree. How do you know I haven't inherited a terrible illness? You suffered a rare form of depression. You don't pick and choose children, biological or otherwise, because of their gene pool."

She stood and placed another log on the fire, then paced back and forth in front of the couch. She sat with hands tucked under her thighs. "The procedures to enable us to have a biological child aren't without risk, and there's no guarantee we'd be successful. We could have a child with my infertility problems or my parents' cancer. Dr. Carson said it would be dangerous, and now we know it's true. Life is full of unknowns. You can't look at a child and foresee their adulthood based on their parentage."

This time, he started to pace. "To be honest, I don't want to think about it until I hear what the doctor says. We'll talk more tomorrow. I promise. Can I just enjoy my sweet, passionate wife for different reasons before we go to sleep?"

"I'm sorry for the lecture, love. It's no surprise I get carried away."

He cradled her small hands between his own. "I want to explore our options and make the best possible decision. Wouldn't you hate to miss the opportunity for a biological child?"

"In all honesty?" She freed her hands and folded them on her lap. "I'm afraid."

"If you're afraid, we won't do it. There's another matter we need to consider no matter which route we choose. Legal fees, medical bills, raising children, all are expensive, and we lost a lot of income this year. I'll find a way, but it won't be easy. Now, snuggle up, and let's enjoy the rain on the roof and the crackle of the fire."

She pulled back. "Come on, Kieran, adoption is less complicated here than in the States. In Scotland, an agency can't charge you a fee for the expenses. You pay for background checks and court fees. It's nothing compared to costs in the US, where couples pay thousands of dollars. Infertility treatments have a long waiting list, if you go the government-funded route, or are very expensive. You have a lot of excuses, none very good."

"I don't have all the answers. But I need to know our options."

They sat in silence, pondering the flames and the patter of rain on the roof. When she relaxed, curling under the arm he rested on the back of the couch, he drew her close. Time alone presented the rare chance for peace, and freedom from interruptions. He gave himself over to it.

ℭℬ

Morning dawned quiet and cold. The rain had stopped, but sadly it started again before they reached the meadow.

"The thunder sounds nasty. Let's go back and clean the bedroom." Bonny turned around and headed back up the trail.

"There's a deck of cards and a board game or two."

"Not until we're done cleaning," she called over her shoulder.

Two hours later, Kieran dumped the dirty water outside and flopped down on the couch. "Woo! Tell me we're finished. There's less dirt in the barn."

Bonny plopped down beside him. "It's enough. We didn't come to work the whole time. Want to play a game?"

"How about my favorite rainy-day occupation?"

"What is it?" She turned her face up.

"Did you make blanket forts in New Mexico? There's a grownup version. All we need are a couple of blankets and a nice, soft sheepskin in front of the fire, plus you and me."

"I love spending every day with you." She moved closer. Her warm breath tickled his cheek. "It's a relief to leave our problems behind. I needed this."

"Can I hold my wife and ignore the world?" He leaned closer, savoring the silk of her skin, the sweetness of her lips, and everything but Bonny vanished into the mist.

Charlie let out a low growl before both dogs leaped to their feet, barking and scratching at the door.

Bonny flinched. "Deirdre!" She sat up straight, faced the window, and pointed. "Kieran, she looked in the window."

Jumping up, he grabbed the shotgun next to the door and peered through the rain and fog. "I can't see anyone."

"I saw her. I'm positive." She crept close, peeking underneath his arm.

A clap of thunder rumbled through the hills, rattling the dishes on the shelf. He double-checked the ancient bolt, placed a board through the slats on either side of the door, and shuttered the windows. "We won't find anyone in this storm."

"It's creepy to have someone spy on our private moments. When will they stop?"

She quivered, their lovely day ruined by the same old troubles. "We'll push the sofa in front of the door if it makes you feel better. We've got the dogs, and they've proved their worth."

"I can't live this way." Tears puddled under lily pad eyes.

He smoothed the silken blaze tumbling down her back. "Dear God, we need the comfort of your presence. Strengthen those bars of iron and bronze around us, so no one can breach them."

All afternoon, Kieran tried to distract her with games and reading while her eyes roved from door to window, her quivering fingers twisting her hair in knots. She hovered near while he banked the kitchen fire for the night and placed the sofa against the door. When he secured the cottage in every way possible, the dogs curled in front of the fire. He lifted and carried her to the new bed, where she fell asleep, her head resting on his shoulder. What a feeling of gratitude at the realization he could calm her. If the time came when he couldn't protect her … what then?

ଓ ଓ

Kieran awakened to bright sun the next morning. Bonny still slept, her cheeks flushed from the cold, one arm cradled her head. Her pink lips reminded him of a partially open rose.

He crept out from under the new down comforter to build up the fire, then slipped back under the blankets. When she stirred, he kissed the sleep from her eyes.

"Were you watching me sleep?"

"Aye and thanking God for you."

"It's a bit off subject, but I'm hungry. Are you?"

"Bangers and mash for breakfast." He climbed out of the warm bed with reluctance, dressed, and moved furniture for a trip to the outhouse. "Get dressed. I'll help cook."

By the time he returned, she had one boot on and tugged at the other. He built up the fire in the stove and placed the large, enamel kettle on to boil.

"I'll be right back." She touched his shoulder, walked past, and opened the door.

"Where are you headed, love?"

"The outhouse. On the way back, I'll pick flowers for the table."

"You're not afraid?"

"I don't want to live in fear. The dogs will go along."

Pleased with her courage, he reached to the top shelf for a jar to put flowers in, and pumped it full of water.

"Kieran! Help!"

Both dogs growled and barked.

The jar crashed to the floor and he ran.

Thwack!

A man climbed into a rusty old truck at the edge of the clearing right before the dogs reached him. Bonny stood doubled over, panting, a fallen tree branch he intended for kindling in her hand. She cringed in pain when he wrapped his arm around her ribs, so he gripped her arm and led her inside.

"Gunn … he came out of nowhere." Her breaths were shallow and she splinted her side. "I bent to pick flowers and he … he came up behind me. I hit him with the branch."

"Are you hurt?"

"I think my ribs are broken. When I reached for the stick, he hit me with a rifle. A rabbit under the shed distracted the dogs or they would have had him." Her tight grip made his fingers tingle. "Please, don't let this monster separate us."

Her breath came in ragged gasps. He led her to the couch, crossed the room in three long strides, and grabbed his shotgun.

Bonny's eyes went wide. "What are you doing?"

Another shotgun stood in the bedroom. He laid it beside her. "I need to look around. Don't open the door until I get back. Charlie, come."

"Don't leave me, please."

He reached for the doorknob.

"No."

"You're safer inside."

"What if they ambush you? We stay together." Fear stared out from limpid green eyes, her face white as a newborn lamb.

"All right." Kieran laid the gun down, sat next to her, plucking leaves from her hair. "We'll gather our clothes and leave the food. I'll pull the truck from the corner of the cottage to the door. You'll only have to walk a couple of feet. Crouch low on the passenger side. We'll head downhill where a rough trail leads to the A82. We'll call Alasdair when we have mobile service. Sit here while I grab our clothes."

"Thank you." Bonny stood and followed close on his heels.

"I'll throw these in the truck and load the dogs. Close the door until I'm right outside. Don't worry about the padlock."

She nodded. "What if they shoot you?"

"Here. You have your gun, and the dogs will help. Fight for your life." He reached into his sock for the *sgian dubh* he kept there.

"You expect me to use a gun and a knife?" Her eyes grew wider. "I … I can't fight. I can barely breathe."

"You'll do whatever you have to. I taught you to plunge the *sgian dubh* up under the ribcage, and you're a crack shot. More than any woman I know, you can defend yourself." He reached out a hand to reassure her then drew it back. Comfort must wait.

"I … I can't." Her voice quaked.

"We *must* do this, Bonny. We'll be all right."

"You can't promise to keep us safe."

Her words penetrated deeper than any bullet. "Do what I say." He picked up the gun, opened the door, and ran the few steps to the truck. "Charlie. Flora. Come."

A white envelope lay in the driver's seat. He shoved it over, started the engine, and pulled forward. When he drew even with the cottage door, he leaned across to open the passenger door. Bonny climbed in, and he shoved her to the floor. "Here we go."

"Ouch! It hur … hurts."

"Sorry, it's rough going. Hold on." Rocks pinged against the fenders and jolted them from side to side all the way down the mountain.

"Are you sure we can get through on this road?"

"It's not used often, but it will do."

She winced with each bump, holding her side with one hand while the other clutched the door handle for balance. "What's in the envelope?"

"Our visitor must have left it. I'll read it at the hospital."

When the road leveled, Bonny lifted the flap and pulled out a blue paper with the familiar curling script. She read aloud, "*I tried to warn you. He watches every move.*"

Kieran reached for her hand but she jerked away, laid her forehead on the seat, and moaned. Her words seared into his mind. *You can't keep us safe.*

Lord, I would give my life for her, but she doesn't trust me.

Both detectives waited outside the emergency entrance at Belford Hospital. They opened the door and helped Bonny out.

Kieran waved them inside. "I'll be right there, love."

Her eyes were dull with pain. "Go. They have me." Alasdair placed an arm around her, and she smiled in gratitude.

They have me. The words stung.

By the time Kieran found her cubicle, a nurse wheeled her gurney down the hallway toward x-ray. Eyes shut, breath shallow, his hand brushed the top of her head as she passed.

"We'll stay at the farm if they send her home," McLeod spoke in grim determination. "Are you ready to hire those bodyguards now?"

Kieran didn't answer.

◁◈▷

The morphine had peaked when they returned Bonny to the room. She slept through Dr. Craig's review of the x-rays.

"Three ribs broken and severe bruises. She'll be miserable for several weeks."

"What can you do for her?" Kieran laid his hand on her forehead. *Dear God, I cannot take it if she loses faith in me.*

"Pain pills. Muscle relaxers. Time. The nurse will bring your prescriptions with the discharge papers." They shook hands and the doctor left.

McLeod stepped in. "We'll grab a few things and escort you home."

Kieran sank into a chair. The ache in his heart grew with each labored breath Bonny took.

Perhaps she spoke in the fear of the moment.

Or perhaps she simply didn't trust him anymore.

CHAPTER ELEVEN

An attractive couple accompanied Alasdair into the library. "Let me introduce former Detective Chief Inspectors Ross McIntyre and Eilidh Gordon-McIntyre, private investigators and bodyguards. Your special 'houseguests,' will protect you, intervene in any further difficulties, and aide our investigation."

"*Difficulties* seems a bit understated, Detective." Bonny narrowed her eyes in a deliberate glare.

Tall and dark-haired, Eilidh stood in complete contrast to the small, fair Bonny. She knelt next to the couch. "I can only imagine your fear. Ross and I do this all the time. We brought our own car. We find it best if you tell people we're your distant cousins, here to help out for a while."

"We will solve this." Ross stood only an inch or two shorter than Kieran. "We'll fit right in since I grew up on a sheep farm near Cromarty."

Bonny took her pain pills and eased into bed. Stormy waters on the loch churned less than the fears she lacked words to express. The pain of each breath discouraged any serious discussion, but the sad expression in her husband's eyes haunted her even when her own were closed. He responded with stony silence when she suggested Angus and Seumas run the farm while they sought safety in New Mexico.

Ross and Eilidh settled in the next bedroom. The dogs bedded down in the kitchen with free run downstairs, but sleep refused to come. She clung to Kieran and longed to absorb his strength while her heart pounded a rapid rhythm. Did people actually die from fear?

"Take us away from here. *Please.*"

"We have bodyguards, detectives, security patrols, and dogs." His tone caressed her. "God protected you and we have help now."

"You've been shot. I've been shot at and beaten. Who knows what he would have done if I hadn't hit him with a tree limb and the dogs chased him away? Those bars of iron and bronze don't look very strong right now." She gritted her teeth against the pain.

"They stopped the bullets, and God gave you the strength to fight. We can't just run away."

"Don't you see? Deirdre wants you. Her brother wants the farm. The answer is to leave and let the police handle it." Questions without answers. Nameless fears. Kieran's arms offered the only real security.

"*Wheesht*, love, I'll hold you all day long if you want." He began one of the Gaelic lullabies his mother sang to him as a child. His deep voice soothed, and she began to relax.

Father God, give us strength to endure this.

The next morning, Kieran served Bonny breakfast in bed before he headed out to acquaint Ross with the farm, workers, and security system. Eilidh promised to help Bonny any way she could, but sleep was her only escape.

"Life has degenerated into an endless nightmare," she told Janet on the phone. "Even if we agreed to discuss adoption, how could we bring a child into this horror?"

"Kieran isn't an unreasonable man, pet. Stubborn perhaps, but thoughtful. Give him time. You've lived in survival mode for months. If you need a few days away, come visit us. There's room for Eilidh too."

"There's another problem. Kieran said our tight finances impact any plans for a family. Hiring protection will drain our bank account even more. We're letting four farmhands go. He chose those without families but it's hard."

"You know God will provide everything you need but not one moment too soon. Trust, Bonny. He knows your needs."

"Thank you, Janet, you're right. I appreciate your offer but right now, I can barely get out of bed on my own. Ask a few trusted people from church to pray, and keep it confidential." She yawned. "These pills make me sleepy."

"Call whenever you need me. We'll come out to see you soon. Rest."

She hung up the phone and rang for help to the bathroom before her nap. Eilidh appeared to be a strong, capable woman with a kind heart. For now, her only comfort.

<·ɔ

Bonny rolled to her left side and yelped.

"What's wrong?" Kieran's sleepy voice sounded from the other side of their king-size bed.

"Is … is it time for a pain pill?" Sharp knives sliced through her chest and back when she spoke.

"I'll get them. I brought a cup and straw, so you don't have to sit." He turned the bedside lamp on low and stood with such care the bed hardly moved. Handing her a pill from each of the two bottles, he placed the straw in her mouth. The most tender nurse imaginable.

"Thanks."

"Do you need anything else, *mo chridhe*?"

My heart's desire. What comfort his words carried. "Maybe I should eat a little?"

"You're right. We can't let the pills make you sick. Toast?"

With a slight smile, she burrowed into her pillow. Each minute passed like an hour until footsteps sounded on the stairs. "I should sit up to eat."

Strong, gentle hands helped her sit, the way he learned in Albuquerque after her accident. At her nod, he helped her to a chair. Hugs were painful right now but she found his sleepy, masculine scent hard to resist.

Kieran raised the blinds to unveil the glimmer of moonlight on the loch. How could their dream have gone so wrong? He sat at her feet. The shadows under his eyes spoke of a pain greater than her ribs. "Don't you trust me anymore? When we left the cottage, you said—"

"Is that why you've been so quiet? Oh, honey, I have no idea what I said then. Of course, I trust you. I've never been attacked before, and I'm afraid. Don't be concerned if my fear speaks before my heart takes control. Thank you for hiring Ross and Eilidh. She was a real help today."

He sighed and stroked her cheek with his finger. "I thought you'd lost faith in me. I couldn't bear it, Bonny."

Tearing her gaze from the moonlit loch, she forced herself to meet his eyes. "I know you don't want to leave the farm. Janet suggested I stay with them for a while. Eilidh can come along."

"Everything I have means nothing without you, *mo chridhe*."

"I didn't say I'd go, but …"

"Let's get you back to bed. I'd rather not discuss it in the middle of the night." His voice sounded distant and reserved. If only she could remove the sting her words caused.

Once settled, she reached for his hand. "Kieran MacDonell, I love you with every fiber of my being, even the broken parts. We're made of the same stuff, you and me. I'd never go if you want me here. Come back to bed. I need your warmth beside me."

He eased in, sliding across the sheets to rest a hand on her hip. Her heart shattered, pieces flying every direction. Fear for him. Fear for herself. When trouble and pain drove sleep far away, her thoughts turned to children. Were they missing what God wanted them to hear?

଼ଓ଼ଈଠ

The dogs barked all the way down the drive, screams slicing through the peace of the clear morning air. Kieran grabbed his boots and chased Ross and Eilidh down the stairs, shirtless and tugging at his trousers. The kitchen door stood open wide. Bonny trembled on the doorstep.

"What happened?" He guided her inside while Ross and Eilidh dashed into the yard.

"Deirdre—right on the doorstep! I decided to start breakfast. When I opened the door for a breath of fresh air, we met face to face. She ran when I screamed. We'll never be safe. Never."

"The dogs didn't alert you?"

"They met me at the stairs. When I screamed, the dogs rushed past me down the drive after her."

"Bonny." She pulled away when he reached for her. The lump in his throat was like a fifteen-pound stone.

"You encouraged her. One dinner date and she still thinks you care." She turned away when their eyes met. "I just want it over."

The accusation, the blank eyes staring straight ahead, crushed his heart. Fear had paralyzed him through the deep depression after Bronwyn died. He understood Bonny's need to blame, her fear of the threats that plagued them like fleece worms on sheep. He would choose to lock away his own hurt and anger, to love and cherish. He would take the first step.

"Ross, Eilidh, I need time alone with my wife and away from here. Let's spend a day in Fort William. She can't tolerate a long day but a walk around town and dinner out while Alasdair and McLeod investigate might help. Can you shadow us?"

"What a perfect idea." Eilidh's arm circled Bonny's shoulders, guiding her toward the stairs. "Let's dress up for our husbands."

A sob erupted from Bonny's throat when Kieran entered the bedroom a few minutes later. He guided her to the couch and drew her onto his lap. He formed part of her bars of iron and bronze. He held the responsibility to lead them both closer to God. "I'm afraid too. We'd feel safer if I'd prayed with you more often about the threats. We'll pray together about a family too. I never mean to let you down, *mo chridhe*. Nothing should distract me from your needs."

Her breath tickled his cheek, soft as a spring breeze. "I fell in love with you because I trusted you. The danger outside frightens me. And the thought of never having a child."

"*Tha gaol agam ort.*" The anvil lifted from his shoulders, and he embraced her.

The need, which blazed in her eyes, ignited such passion his toes tingled. "I love you too, and I hate knowing I built the wall between us."

"You didn't build it alone. I make mistakes, but I always love you." He cradled her as he would a wounded lamb, then closed his eyes. "Lord, help us look to you to fulfill our needs rather than punish each other with our disappointments. Forgive my failure to show love and empathy. You hold the answers. Guide us."

She closed her eyes, relaxing in his arms. "Deirdre looked frightened."

"I can't say I blame her. You have quite a scream."

Laughter bubbled up, their shared hilarity a guarantee they were all right.

"Ouch. It hurts to laugh."

"I'll help you dress. We'll escape the gloom and enjoy a day away from here."

❧❦

Only a very special event would cause Janet to drive all the way to the farm. With ribs and bruises almost healed, Bonny prepared a salad of mixed greens, homegrown strawberries and blueberries, mandarin oranges, apple, feta cheese, walnuts, and chicken with red wine vinaigrette dressing. She prepared the table in the dining room where twin bay windows overlooked the loch and paired snickerdoodles with raspberry sorbet for the perfect dessert.

The new gold and burgundy accents added to the dark blues of the dining room and set off Bronwyn's blue Lochs of Scotland china, used only for special occasions. The sterling silver and Flower of Scotland crystal were handed down from Kieran's grandmother. It created a beautiful setting. Eilidh arranged a bouquet of mixed roses from the garden in the vase Kieran gave Bonny for her birthday.

"You don't need to include me. I'll eat in the kitchen while you enjoy time with your friend." Eilidh stepped back to admire the effect of their work. "Your dining room is incredible. We'll be so spoiled by your lovely home and views it will be hard to leave when we finish our job."

"It is pretty. But don't be silly. You're a friend now too. Janet wouldn't want me to send you to the kitchen. After all, you've seen me at my worst." Bonny sniffed the sweet fragrance of the tea roses and straightened a wrinkle in Maggie's crocheted ivory tablecloth with its thistle design. When the bell rang, she hurried to the door, greeting Janet with a hug. "It's such fun to have you come out for lunch. I told Eilidh you wouldn't mind if she joined us."

"Of course, she should." Janet laid her purse on the bench near the front door, took off her blue sweater, and extended her hand. "Eilidh, I'm glad to meet you. I hear you two are good friends already." She stopped at the door of the dining room, hand over her mouth. "You went to a lot of work, and you used Bronnie's dishes. She would be pleased."

Bonny relaxed. Janet and Bronwyn had been good friends. "There's no need for new ones. I have my own but I love the Scottish china and the Buchan Thistle pottery in the kitchen. It's silly not to use it. Come, sit down. Lunch is ready."

The three chatted about weather—a common topic among Scots—Janet's classes, and the fast-growing lambs that romped in the pasture near the house.

When they settled in the library with dessert, Janet took a sip of water and folded her hands in her lap. "I came out here today to give you our news in person rather than over the phone."

Bonny set her spoon down and held her breath.

"We're expecting a baby. The doctor confirmed it several weeks ago. I waited until we reached three months to tell anyone. At forty-three, it's risky. We're a little nervous, but the doctors seem pleased." Janet implored Bonny with her eyes. "I know it's not easy for you, but I had to say something before it becomes obvious."

"Congratulations. Kieran will be excited too. Kari felt guilty about her twins, but our disappointment doesn't change the joy we feel for friends. You've waited a long time for marriage and children. I'm thrilled. I know how much you both want a family." Her voice caught, and she reached for her water to hide it.

Eilidh stood and began gathering dishes. "Congratulations."

Janet placed a hand on Bonny's arm. "Are you all right, love? Graeme and I prayed for you to be prepared."

"I'm fine. And so happy for you." Bonny balled her fists in her lap. "I'll even give a shower." It had happened. God chose to bless the one friend who feared she would never have children. How could you prepare for the time when all your friends have children and you don't?

"We want you and Kieran for godparents. Will you do it? Graeme plans to tell him, by the way." Bonny wondered if Janet practiced sharing her news in gentle tones to soften the impact, but pregnant was pregnant.

"Of course, we'll do it." A voice whispered *God remembers,* and Bonny smiled. Sometimes she could make excuses to skip baby showers, but she would give one for Janet and celebrate. God would remember her, whatever His final answer.

Chapter Twelve

Sirens from the direction of Tomdoun provided the reassurance Bonny needed. Help was on the way. She glanced at the clock. Half an hour since Kieran awakened to orange light flickering through the bedroom blinds. If he imagined she could wait in peace while their chapel burned, he was mistaken. She shared his dream of their farm and ministry in this rugged, rainy place with equal passion. In spite of recent scares, she wasn't a sit-on-the-sidelines girl.

Tongues of fire still streaked the night sky, and anger flared at the memory of his attitude. The narrowed eyes and insistent tone when he told her to remain inside were uncharacteristic. He tugged on jeans, retrieved his boots from under the bed, and lunged down the stairs with Ross in stony rejection of her promise to stay out of harm's way. Unlike when the sheep were poisoned, the chapel symbolized the dream God gave him on his return to Scotland after she refused his proposal of marriage. She had shared the dream since the day he told her about his calling. Their ministry and a fire were different from dying animals. The first chapel service, scheduled for next week, would be delayed.

Bonny grabbed her jeans from the chair in the corner, yanked a wool turtleneck over her head, and reached for her boots, wool socks still tucked into the heels. If he didn't return within an hour, she'd go out there.

She descended the back stairs by nightlight, but the kitchen light burned bright. The analogy struck hard. The darkness of fear, rebellion, and arguments had to give way to the light of unity and peace with God in order to defeat their enemies. Disagreement led to defeat.

At least she could make tea and set out the leftover gingerbread. Tea made any situation better for a Scot, no matter how dire.

Before their marriage, nothing sounded more peaceful than marriage to a sheep farmer and pastor. Even when Brennan shot Kieran prior to their wedding, they couldn't imagine the turmoil they now faced. How did anyone learn to respond with calm to shootings and fires? Perhaps Bronwyn had been happy in the background. Sitting quiet and obedient while someone destroyed their livelihood and ministry wasn't Bonny's nature, but perhaps God could help her learn.

Eilidh stepped into the kitchen, dressed for warmth, long dark hair caught up in a ponytail. "You weren't going out there alone?"

"I considered it. Kieran refused when I suggested going with him. I belong at his side. Maybe we can tell if the fire is under control from the window in the upstairs hall."

The sky toward the chapel still glowed red, but only occasional flames escaped skyward. She wiped her eyes, breathed a jagged sigh of relief, and started back to the kitchen with Eilidh on her heels. "Perhaps it won't be a total loss. We've prayed and worked so hard." How would they afford to rebuild if insurance failed to pay the complete cost?

Flora growled and bounded downstairs, barking and pawing at the front door.

Thwack!

The loud thud brought to mind the TV Westerns her father loved. Both women flattened against the stairway wall. Bonny's heart thudded. They stood silent. Waiting.

After five minutes, they removed their boots and padded downstairs toward the living room. Flora whined near the door, but no shadows filtered through the drapes.

Headlights shone through the trees, moving toward the house. Eilidh remained near the door while Bonny rushed to grab the kettle before it whistled. Her heart slowed when the garage door rumbled and Kieran's Land Rover pulled in. She flung open the door and halted at the top of the stairs.

Her husband leaned back in the passenger seat, eyes closed. Ross stepped out from the driver's side.

Bonny rushed to the passenger door and yanked it open. "Are you hurt? Surely the fire's not out yet."

"Someone shot at me."

She closed her eyes and sucked in a deep breath. "Who? Why?"

Indigo eyes met hers, mouth pressed into taut lines of disbelief and fear. He stepped out and stooped to wrap her in quivering arms, his face buried in her hair. The tang of smoke permeated his clothes and tingled in her nostrils.

"Perhaps whoever shot at you? Ross forced me into the truck. Alasdair and McLeod are there."

"And the fire, how bad is it?"

"We suspect the shooter started it. The stained-glass window shattered. The walls will be charred, the floors, beams, and stage, are a complete loss." He scrubbed his face with his hands. "Someone's out to destroy us."

"I was frustrated when you refused to let me go along. Now, I'm afraid."

One finger tilted her face upward in a gesture she loved. "Correction. You were *angry*. Thank you for not arguing. We won't live in a box, afraid of our shadows, but I couldn't put you in danger. They can investigate better by daylight."

"Come inside. You're shaking. Someone came here too. Something hit the front door, Ross. Eilidh's on lookout in the foyer. We didn't see anyone."

Kieran stiffened. "What do you mean?"

"We heard a thud against the door. Harder than a knock. We couldn't see any shadows through the drapes."

The two men headed toward the foyer, Bonny taking three steps to their one. "You saw nothing?"

"It happened right before we saw your headlights."

"Stay back." He shoved her behind him.

Ross eased the door open, gun barrel first. "Look."

A poisonous snake of fear slithered through her veins at the sight of a note pinned in place with a *sgian dubh*. The small knife glinted silver in the porch light.

"The detectives need to see this." Ross closed the door and slid his cell phone from his pocket. "Come to the house. Now."

Within a few minutes, the kitchen doorbell sounded.

Ross opened the door to Alasdair and Hugh. The detective nodded in their direction but focused on Ross. "What's wrong?"

"You tell us." Ross stalked to the entry hall and opened the door.

Alasdair snapped a few photos, drew on latex gloves, and pulled out the knife. Note in hand, he shut the door. "It angered our Mr. Gunn when the court ruled in your favor." He held the paper up for Kieran.

He read the bold, childlike printing out loud. "Other MacDonells want their due. Honor the deed, or the price is on you."

⊗⊗

DCI McLeod's steely glare matched Kieran's tight-lipped grimace.

"It took a little over an hour to put the fire out. Arson investigators are there now." Alasdair accepted a glass of water rather than tea and drummed his fingers on the table. The knots in Bonny's stomach grew with every beat. A mere threat to the police symbolized their dream, the tangible sign of Kieran's recommitment to the Lord. Christened with love by two weddings, prayed over and cherished through the Bible study, its destruction seemed a classic denial of God.

"The chapel isn't a complete loss, but it's close," Alasdair said. "Your doors, the floor, and the stained-glass window suffered. Some of the timber frame may have to be replaced. We found casings from a .30-06 rifle near the bridge and footprints to the chapel and back. We'll examine the boots of all your employees. Someone had parked an ATV near the bridge on the far side of the loch."

Bonny reached for the hand Kieran rested on the table. "30.06. The same caliber Brennan Grant used. Are they common over here?"

"They're more popular in America. I wouldn't expect the average poacher to have one." Alasdair's eyebrows rose. "You're familiar with firearms?"

"She used to hunt with her dad. She's knowledgeable and an excellent shot." Despite the tension, his eyes twinkled whenever he could brag on her.

"An unusual caliber should make it easier to trace, right?" She reached for the teapot, but the men shook their heads.

"You know we never found Brennan Grant's rifle. However, if the bullets match. we'll know there's an accomplice." DCI McLeod's gentle tone engendered confidence.

"Nothing you've said indicates you're on the trail of Gavin Gunn or anyone else, Inspector." Bonny's voice choked. "A man's intent on killing my husband, on destroying our livelihood and dreams."

"He's elusive. They're conducting a thorough search of the premises." Bonny felt like a microscopic specimen under the steely glint of Alasdair's eyes. "The chaps at the *nick* were discussing your daring rescue of Kieran last fall."

Her cheeks warmed with the praise. "Instead of sitting around the station discussing me, they'd better get busy and find our stalker."

"Bonny doesn't think it matters if she's feminine and petite when it comes to what or who she takes on. She's one of a kind, and I recommend you stay on her good side." Kieran placed a hand on the back of her neck in warning but beamed with pride.

"A resilient woman is the right woman under these circumstances." DCI McLeod shot her a smile. "No one can predict Gunn's actions. We're doing everything in our power, Mrs. MacDonell."

Kieran settled his arm around her shoulders, a hint to calm down. She had nothing to prove, and rehashing the past did nothing to prevent future danger. "I'm no heroine, gentlemen. I did what was necessary when your department failed to come to our aide. Just do your job now, before anything else is destroyed. The culprit must be caught. Soon."

The inspector met her eyes. "Of course. We won't rest until we apprehend both Gavin and Deirdre. Now, about this note and its unorthodox method of delivery. If it's Gunn, his attacks are growing more aggressive and personal. You must stay with your bodyguards at all times."

"Don't worry. I wouldn't even go into the garden without Eilidh and Flora."

When Ross closed the door behind the police, Bonny leaned her head on Kieran's chest. "I want the attacks to stop. Why destroy a chapel meant to honor God? I don't understand."

She glimpsed Eilidh from the corner of her eye. Perhaps it was wrong to voice doubts in front of their kind but unbelieving sentries. She couldn't help it.

θ

Bonny knew she'd rubbed more tears than polish off the small area of the chapel floor left untouched by the fire while Eilidh scrubbed soot from a section of wall. One fire set near the pulpit, destroyed stage, pews, and the stained-glass window. A second fire burned Hamish's beautiful hand-carved doors. Gasoline and matches seemed to be the method of ignition. More gas, sprinkled around the lochside wall, away from the house, destroyed the timber frame.

The extensive repairs would take time, despite the decision to clean the least damaged timbers. Scars provided a visible reminder to forge ahead in the Lord's work, in spite of obstacles. What if opening the chapel led to a worse attack?

To replace the stained-glass window required at least three months. Hamish's beautiful, hand-made doors were burned beyond repair. "I know it's pointless to demand answers from God in my own timing, but my heart's full of questions. No baby. A sheep herd reduced to a fraction of its original size. Our beautiful chapel scorched and scarred. I believe in God's control but everything seems too much at times."

"Yet you still worship and pray every day. I don't understand." Eilidh's quiet comment, eyebrows raised in question, startled her.

Before she could form an answer, motion caught Bonny's eye through a window at the back of the church. "I see a patch of red moving through the trees near the loch." She dropped her cloth and hurried to the window. "Over there, near the bridge."

"A woman." Eilidh pulled out her phone. "Ross." Both women sighed in relief. The men, moving sheep from one pasture to another, had phone service. "Come to the chapel. Now. Someone's in the trees near the bridge." She hung up and placed her hand on Bonny's arm. "They'll try to sneak up. We're to wait inside."

What frustration to watch the men creep through the trees, uncertain if they would be met by gunfire, and unable to help. When they neared the chapel, Eilidh opened the door and stepped onto the porch.

"Ross, let's get them safe in the house. I'll lead you to the spot. Stay inside. No matter what." Her tone left no room for argument.

Minutes later, they climbed into Kieran's Land Rover and headed to the house.

"What exactly did you see?" Ross asked.

Bonny moved into the curve of Kieran's arm, grateful for the throb of warmth and security that coursed through her. "A woman approached the chapel on the loch side, then moved away when I looked up. By the time Eilidh reached the window, she'd moved too far into the trees."

Parking near the kitchen door, their protectors headed back on foot to search for the mystery woman.

"Why don't you lie down, love? You've worked hard all morning." The bags under Kieran's eyes testified to restless nights since the fire.

Her worst enemy, the monster of defiance, stiffened her back, but she swallowed the ugly comments before they caused hurt. "Sleep while they search for a maniac bent on more destruction?"

He put on the kettle while she paced between the table and door. Within half an hour, Ross and Eilidh returned. "We called Alasdair to make casts from the footprints in the mud before dark.

Bonny covered her face with her hands. "I can't handle any more. Kieran, please can't we go to your parents' house or to New Mexico for a while? The strain is wearing us both down."

"We've discussed this before, it's our farm. I want it to end, but I can't leave. You can visit my parents, Janet, or even Kari. I need to stay."

"Leave without you? Not after another attempt on your life. It's for *our* protection—not just mine."

"Was it Deirdre?" Kieran grimaced and ruffled his hair.

"It had to be. She's bigger than some men."

Ross looked up from the notes he kept for DCI McLeod. "She seems to be the spy. With her tendency to peek through windows, perhaps we should offer opportunities." He leaned back and tapped his pen on the table. "Suppose Eilidh and I hide out a few days, rent a car in Fort William, and check into the Invergarry Hotel disguised as hikers. You leave blinds and drapes open in the evenings. Carry on conversations outside about the romantic evenings you plan with the house to yourselves. Try to draw her out."

"Absolutely not. Invite her to spy on us during romantic moments?" Bonny's ire rose like a pot boiling over. "Invite danger? I can't."

"He's right," Eilidh said. "We bait the trap and wait for results. Nothing private, just a little *cuzzle* on the couch. We'll be nearby to intervene if anything happens."

"Think about it, Bonny." A smile played over Kieran's lips. "We get time alone, and it ends in the capture of Deirdre and Gavin. It's worth it."

"Few things excite me less, but if you believe it will work, it appears I'm outvoted."

؃؄

Resting next to Kieran in her lacy, wedding negligee with pink satin robe and a fire crackling in the library fireplace, Bonny struggled to remember they were on alert.

Soft strains of classical music and an evening alone were a part of marriage she had almost forgotten existed. When she opened her eyes in the middle of a kiss, she glimpsed movement through the darkened window. Flora and Charlie, shut in the bedroom, made no sound.

"What's wrong?" Kieran didn't move a muscle.

With her mouth next to his ear and arms around him, she hoped their spy failed to notice the movement of her eyes. "There's someone outside."

Kieran stiffened and moved one hand to the back of her head. "Who?"

"Deirdre?" He nuzzled her ear and Bonny whispered, "Does she have radar tuned in for romantic evenings?"

"I have no idea. I'll suggest we go upstairs. Don't look toward the window. Turn off the kitchen lights and call Ross. Meet you by the front stairs."

Phone call made, Bonny headed for the foyer.

"Oww!"

The front door stood wide open. "Kieran?"

"I'm fine, love. Come on out."

She flicked on the outside lights and ran.

Ross lay prone on the ground. He righted himself and massaged his head.

"Ach, are you all right, man?"

"Man, that woman can hit hard." A large goose egg began to rise on his forehead.

"It was a shovel." Kieran rubbed his own forehead. "You have a nasty bump there. My head connected with your knee."

"Honey, are you all right?" Bonny dropped to the ground, clutching the neck of her robe.

Ross shook his head. "Just a wee headache for a day or two."

Eilidh ran up, panting. "What a fiasco. There are footprints under the window. The others went after her, but they won't find much in the dark."

"What a foolish thing to do, Kieran MacDonell." A grenade couldn't have exploded with more force. "You don't belong outside with a madwoman around. You could have left me a widow."

"I'm sorry." He stretched out his arms, but she stepped back.

"You take a stupid risk with lookouts everywhere and all you say is you're sorry?"

"Bonny ..."

She shoved him away and headed for the house.

"You're not rational."

"Neither are you. I'm always afraid. And you take unnecessary chances."

"Please, stop. We work things out together, not separate." He grabbed for her arm, but she jerked away.

"I'm too angry." She stomped toward the house, vaguely aware of their audience. "And we don't work anything out—ever. To hear you, we're experiencing some grand adventure."

"You're being unreasonable."

"It's not me. And you can stay on your side of the bed. I might take you up on a trip to visit Kari."

She stomped inside and slammed the door, leaving him on the step. How many times must she explain her fear of their stalkers and voice her frustration over his continued procrastination about adoption?

CHAPTER THIRTEEN

Kieran sat on the bed in his pajamas, eyes blazing with an anger Bonny had seldom seen.

"I can't believe you argued in front of the police and anyone else out there. If we're divided, the battle is ten times harder to win, love."

A geyser of rage seethed inside her, worse than any time since her former fiancé Adam left her for another woman. "I thought we were united. You're the one who ran outside with professionals here for that purpose. And my tongue is sore from biting it and acting the part of Little Miss Quiet and Obedient when it comes to stalkers, adoption, and fertility doctors. You don't listen. Ever."

His face grew redder. "I know things are tough, but you're never happy anymore. You're upset over my discomfort with adoption. I see hunger in your eyes every time you look at Emily, Janet, or the women at Bible study. Do you think I don't notice the reproach in your voice? You chafe at security and circumstances, our every move dictated by others. Well, I don't enjoy it either. I don't know why God allows us to be attacked from every side but I'm not the enemy."

Her throat stung as if she'd swallowed a prickly pear. "Think about something while you lie alone on your side of the bed. My life is unrecognizable and out of control. I came from constant sunshine but I'm trying to adjust to an isolated farm in the rainiest part of Scotland. I have almost no friends, and I don't know where I fit in. Add in bodyguards 24/7 and insane people who want to kill us. All I want is to love you and learn to be your wife." Her knees gave way, and she crumpled on the carpet, wiping her eyes on the hem of her gown.

"I feel inadequate because my body doesn't function the way other women's do. Yet you refuse to discuss what I desire most in the world. You try to act like a hero without thinking what might happen. I have a right to be scared. And angry."

"Yes, you do." He moved to the floor. "I'm ready to listen. Explain it to me. How does not being able to carry a child make you feel?"

"I'm not sure now's the right time to talk about it."

"The best time for me to listen is when you're upset. I promise I'll take to heart every word you say."

She drooped against him, unable to hold herself upright. "I come from a dry, parched land where a heavy rain never satisfies the thirsty ground. My heart longs for a child the way the New Mexico desert pleads for water. Now, home is a *dreich* and *drookit* place where the rain seldom stops, and neither does my crying. I have no hope the sun will ever shine on my dreams of motherhood. Not even the Lord penetrates the hopelessness in my barren life any longer. I'm lost in a fog. And nothing changes because we can't agree over what constitutes family."

Calloused but gentle hands wiped her cheeks with the edge of the sheet. "We won't go to bed angry, even if we stay up all night." He tugged a blanket from the bed and draped it around her shoulders. "I'm so sorry, *mo chridhe*. I thought I took into account the challenges you face, but I didn't. I was an *eijit* tonight." His voice soothed like a lullaby. "Forgive me. Bonny, love, having a baby doesn't make you a woman. To love me, complete me, and remind me when I do idiotic man-things makes you a woman. I never intended to hurt you. I'll listen to whatever you want to say when we're not exhausted."

Her voice had gone missing. She touched a finger to his lips, unable to deny the emotions stirred by his warm, comforting scent, the heat where their bodies touched, and the whisper of his voice. This kind, gentle man asked for nothing except love. "*Tha gaol agam ort.*"

His lips touched her forehead, warmed, caressed, reached to the deepest part of her pain. "Don't stay on your side of the bed. Meet me in the middle. Let me hold you." Kieran stood and offered her a hand up.

The whisper in her heart reminded her of all the promises God had fulfilled. *Cease striving, dear child. Remember Hannah, and leave it with me. The question of children isn't Kieran's to decide or yours. The decision is mine alone.*

⋅ CʒꝹ ⋅

Bonny's open Bible lay in front of Kieran next to a half-empty glass of milk when she came downstairs. Her cheeks warmed with the memory of the way his arms encircled her in the night, the sweet whispers whenever she stirred. In the two days since their argument, he kept his promise to listen and asked questions without disagreement. This morning he was all smiles.

"Why are you grinning like you won grand prize at The Royal Highland Show?" She walked over, ruffled his seldom-tamed hair, kissed his freshly shaven cheek, and breathed deep of his woodsy cologne.

"Let's take the day off and drive to Glasgow. I emailed a pastor who works with Forever Family. He's free this afternoon. I want to find out how we might collaborate to find homes for children in the Highlands. It's a good way to explore adoption. Talking to someone involved might help sort out my own feelings. Ross and Eilidh are ready whenever you are." He put a finger under her chin and closed her open mouth. "Mind you, I haven't changed overnight. I still want to visit the fertility clinic, but I'll look into adoption. We need to make decisions based on facts."

"Thank you."

"You might stir the porridge. We should get on the road whenever you're ready. Wear something feminine to make you feel lovely, *mo gràdh*. We'll eat at a nice restaurant and shop or sightsee, whatever you want." He pointed to a highlighted passage in her Bible. "Forgive me. I thought if I looked at the pages where you've put sticky notes and highlighted verses, it might help me pray for you."

Something melted deep inside. She never expected him to make such a big concession.

"'He settles the childless woman in her home as a happy mother of children,'" he read aloud. "And Hannah's prayer. 'Lord Almighty, if you will only look on your servant's misery and remember me, and not forget your servant but give her a son …' It tore my heart out to hear you say you felt inadequate. Bonny, the moment I laid eyes on you, I knew you were a woman who would challenge me every day of my life. Forgive my failure to understand the strength of your desire for motherhood. Having lost two, I thought I knew."

"Oh, Kieran, you're such a dear man. I don't expect you to fathom what I can't explain. My emotions aren't under control these days."

He pointed to a verse above those she'd highlighted. "Remember this one too. 'But to Hannah he gave a double portion because he loved her ….' My love for you is greater because you've suffered such pain. I promised to cherish you, *mo chridhe*. You've never allowed childlessness to prevent you ministering to other women. I learn from and am blessed by you every day."

She reached for a napkin and wiped her eyes. "It's good I didn't have mascara on yet. I love the heart and soul of you, Kieran MacDonell. You make me feel loved." She caressed his cheek then headed for the stove. "Right now, if I don't see to the porridge, it will burn in the pan."

ೞ ೲ

The drive to Glasgow took forever, and she wished for a full day with the pastor. Each story of birthmothers, children in need of families, and women who longed for children pierced Bonny's heart. The way Kieran paled and his eyes widened made her realize how he lacked even basic knowledge about adoption. Both had underestimated the immense demand for adoptive families.

Ross and Eilidh sat across a quiet restaurant to allow them privacy. Kieran pushed his half-full plate away while she nibbled. "I never made the connection between the adoption of believers into God's family and adopting a child, giving them a new name, raising them with benefits they would never have known. The idea of a family as a ministry to children who might never hear about the Lord is new to me. I'm overwhelmed."

Bonny sipped her water and compared the light in his eyes to exhilaration he showed when he grasped a Scripture for the first time. "It helps to hear other women's stories and know I'm not alone in my roller-coaster emotions."

"It helps me understand you better." Kieran stared out at the Clyde Arc Bridge, the breeze from the open window ruffling his hair. "Perhaps God needs to do a little bridge-building in my heart, help me rethink my view of family. My whole life's been about ancestry, inheritance, and clan. I'm learning about a different kind of love altogether."

"I'm sorry I failed to appreciate your struggle. Most Americans come from a variety of backgrounds. They have little idea of their heritage and don't care. Family history is a hobby. Not a way of life." She reached across the table, the heat from his hand warming all the way to her heart. "In the church where I grew up, adopted children were common. It wasn't a stretch for me to consider it because I never thought their families different from my own."

"Before, Emily was just another troubled kid. I can't imagine having no choice but to give your baby to strangers, to never see your own child grow up, to not know what happened to them. It shocked me to discover how many children in Scotland need homes. No one does enough to raise awareness and find permanent families. Two hundred and forty thousand in foster care is criminal."

She speared a tomato and stuffed it in her mouth. *Wait on the Lord.* Allow him to think aloud without comment. God worked better without her help. He could handle her fear of fertility doctors. She still struggled with fatigue and weakness from the hemorrhage. The thought of more medical procedures terrified her.

∞

The four enjoyed a decadent dinner at the Lodge on Loch Lomond and arrived home late to discover all the lights on. Angus, Eleanor, and Seumas waited in the kitchen with downcast eyes and frowns. Bonny watched Kieran's brows lower until his frown matched theirs. The hopes raised by their peaceful day in Glasgow evaporated in an instant.

Angus stood when they walked in. "It's not good, lad. The entire *Garrygulach* flock of ewes and lambs is gone. Tire tracks lead toward the slopes of *Meall Tarsuinn.*"

"Ach, if I could get a hold of Gavin Gunn, there wouldn't be enough left for fishing bait." Kieran dropped into the nearest chair.

Ross pulled the phone from his pocket. "Did you call the police, man?"

"Aye, they've been and gone." The old farm manager nodded. "I asked them not to call until tomorrow. We have to set a watch, lad. Whoever it was, passed the house or chapel in order to reach the bridge. A truck shouldn't go unnoticed, even at night."

"Did they get anything off the camera at the driveway or chapel?" Eilidh questioned.

Angus swiped his handkerchief across his forehead. "The police downloaded the video."

Seumas stood and headed for the door. "I'll spend tonight in the barn office, chief."

Kieran crossed the room to examine the map over the desk. His face turned a dark reddish-purple before his fist hit the wall, knocking pictures to the floor. The fearful glare in his eyes suggested the outcome if he found the thief. "Thanks, Seumas, we can't watch over all the flocks, but we can watch the road and do random checks on different pastures. We'll have to go by horseback. An ATV or truck would alert them, and we need to catch them in the act."

"I agree," Ross said. "It's certain Gavin's armed. We can't afford to leave ourselves without protection. How can one man accomplish such a job alone?"

"There goes our peaceful day." Kieran pressed her hand to his face. "Dear God, we trust you, but we can't understand what you're doing."

They sat, while Eleanor placed hot cups of tea in front of them.

Tea. Bonny shook her head. She had remained silent during the exchange between the men. One more sign they were losing the battle. One more loss of valuable property. How much more could they survive? There wasn't enough tea in Scotland to solve this problem.

03 80

The night brought little sleep, and the next day held nightmare discussions with contractor after contractor of security measures for hard-to-reach pastures.

Alone at last, Kieran's pacing reminded Bonny of a caged bear, his anxiety palpable in the atmosphere of the room and tension of his muscles. His hair stood out in a fiery glow like a maple in autumn, eyes more gray than blue. Perhaps from the dark notions crowding his mind.

"Brooding won't bring answers." She closed her book without reading a word.

The bear paused in front of her. "With the flocks in the lowest pastures, there are still too many for one man to watch."

"Who will make up your patrol?" She tossed off the blue-and-green MacDonell tartan blanket, which warmed her feet from the cool evening air, and went to close the windows against the dusk. Would she ever grow used to how late it stayed light in the summer?

"Angus, Seumas, Jamie, and Duff can take turns. Ross and I will share the load."

Ross nodded and Bonny waited.

Kieran sat with hands clasped and stared at the floor. "We'll go out at random times."

"I hate for you to face armed men." She pressed her hand against his knee to still its nervous bouncing. "There's no other way? You'll stay close to him?"

Eilidh had nodded off, but Ross paid close attention. "Aye, you know I will. It's a sound plan."

Her husband's slight smile failed to reassure. "Seumas offered to accompany Jamie to the pubs he frequents in Tomdoun and Fort William. He'll keep an ear out and call the police if necessary."

"It's late, my love. Let's pray before we go to bed. You can puzzle it out in the morning with Angus." She stood and folded the blanket and knelt by his side while their Ross and Eilidh sat in silence across the room.

Kieran slept little. She rubbed his back while he tossed and turned, falling asleep just before dawn. He reminded her of the stories Hamish told about ancient shepherds who protected their flocks against the *reivers* and wolves that once roamed the Highlands.

Up at four a.m., Kieran devoured his breakfast in a few bites and wrapped her in a firm hug before he headed out with Ross. "Thank you for not giving me a hard time about the patrols. God knew the wife I needed for such a time. Try not to worry, love."

"I'll pray instead, my *braw* Highlander. Be safe." No matter what they thought of her bravery, she quivered inside.

∽∾

"Kari, do you have time for a confused man with a lot of nosy questions?" Kieran settled into his chair in the barn office. With Bonny and Eilidh off to Fort William to eat lunch with Janet, he had time. He'd promised to address all the problems that turned his wife into a quiet shadow of her normal, high-spirited self.

"Sure. I'm out for a run while Dan watches the twins. What's on your mind?" She breathed hard into the phone, and then he heard her sipping water.

"It's about adoption. I know so little, but if I don't settle my confused emotions soon, Bonny may arrive on your doorstep. I don't blame her for being impatient. I assume she told you about our visit to the pastor with Forever Family." He traced lazy circles in the margin of his list of questions.

"Woo! It's hot here. She did tell me. Ask whatever you want. Adoption is the greatest blessing next to salvation. My parents gave me a chance to be a normal kid and live a life I only dreamed existed. I don't know where I would have ended up." Her enthusiasm set him at ease.

"I'm not certain about raising kids who don't look or think like us. How will we know what's right for them?" Seumas walked through the door, but Kieran motioned him to leave and close it behind him.

"Most adoptive parents have the same concern. You've met mine. Mom's a natural blonde and Dad's hair was medium brown when he was younger. Most of their biological kids inherited Dad's medium brown hair, and a couple look like her. They adopted three, me being the youngest. Two were Hispanic twins who at least had each other. Then I came along with dark hair, blue eyes, and a fifteen-year-old, rejected-too-many-times attitude. I created the biggest challenge. By then, most of the biological kids had left home. The friendship of Bonny, Dan, and super-committed parents prevented me from failing the way I did in all the foster homes."

He stared out the window, uncertain how to take what she said. "They would have given you back?"

"A little secret, Kieran. An adopted child is *placed* for adoption, not given away or given up. It sounds like semantics, but the sense of rejection runs deep no matter how you phrase it. The placement could have failed. They might have had to search for someone more equipped to deal with my rebellion. Even the word *failed* sounds better than rejection. Every day my parents said God gave me to them because I belonged in their family. I believed they liked me, though I was an athlete, and their biological kids were all musical or artistic. I only draw stick figures."

"What made them choose a fifteen-year-old so different from the rest of the family?" He traced a heart in the dust, added Bonny's initials, and then his own.

Kari laughed. "My dad said the sparkle in my eyes, the freckles on my nose, and a spunky attitude made him believe I could defy the odds. Even then I wanted to be a teacher. School was the only place I ever fit in or felt happy. The foster families weren't bad, but for a kid who parented her drug-addict parents until the age of twelve, obeying the rules of others created a major struggle. Foster parents have to make rules stick in homes where there are at least two or three other kids. My rebellion presented a bad influence, but I didn't see a need for adult supervision."

"How did your adoptive parents treat you different from the foster families?"

"They asked what rules I believed were fair. We made a list and signed a contract to stick to them. I became an adult too early because of my birthparents. My adoptive parents respected my maturity and believed I could learn to obey because I excelled in school. I began to see love as a choice because they chose to love and accept me. No matter what."

"Wow." Kieran moved to the floor and leaned his back against the wall. "What commitment."

"They were there for me." Her voice grew soft. "My mom, the artist, became the best soccer mom around. She learned the game and became my biggest cheerleader. My dad, the singer, claimed to love every sport I tried. They encouraged the older kids to support me, because God picked me for their family, and accepted me without reservations. My parents made a great example."

"You have an amazing story, Kari." If only he could parent children with the same success.

"Bonny's probably told you there were a lot of adopted kids in our church. We weren't much different from the others."

He waited in silence.

"I don't know what conversations they had behind my back. I didn't always respect the others, but beyond the normal teenage arguments, we got along. They were my real parents because they were kind, loving adults who saw me as an individual with unique needs and capabilities. Never once did they suggest they didn't have to take me in. They taught their biological kids to respect my athletics, and I was to respect their music and art. Then along came Bonny, the singer and poet, different in every way, and she became my best friend."

He checked the list of questions and sat on the desk to see if he missed anything important. Most appeared irrelevant in light of Kari's explanations. "Your parents made a concentrated effort to ensure a supportive family unit. Did other people point out the differences between the adopted and biological children?"

"Mainly with the twins because they were Hispanic. They asked if we were adopted or said how lucky we must feel. When the twins and I realized other people thought we had something special, we developed even more respect for our parents. They had five children already. It wasn't a matter of building a family. They adopted out of love and a commitment to help children. The twins had developmental difficulties, and I was a fifteen-year-old foster home reject, so we weren't considered adoptable. They wanted us because no one else did."

She sniffled. He did too.

"I don't know what to say. No one would ever believe you didn't grow up in a normal, biological family. I'm not certain I have what it takes, for a baby or an older child. Your parents are very special and unique people."

"No, Kieran, they're simple, obedient, loving Christian people. I do have my insecurities. Dan could fill you in. I'll never make light of your apprehension. My parents used to take us to adoptive parent classes where most people shared concerns similar to yours. The majority also went on to adopt. A few took kids like my brothers and me, others chose babies or young children. Most important, they formed happy, healthy families. I know God will guide you to the right decision."

"I'm not so sure. I don't think I have the skill to handle every unexpected situation."

"Do we ever, in any relationship? When you hire a new farmhand, are you certain he'll work out? When you met Graeme, did you think you'd become best friends and end up a pastor yourself? If your first son had lived, would you know how to deal with every situation because he shared your genes? Kids are kids, each unique in their own way.

"You and Bonny have faced many challenges in your short marriage. Adoption requires you to take a step of faith. It's what all parents do. Dan and I have no guarantee our twins will grow up happy, healthy, and well-adjusted. How do we know they won't inherit my parents' tendency toward drug addiction? All we can take for granted is the Lord's guidance."

He rested his head in his hand. "I guess you put me in my place. Thanks for your willingness to talk to me, Kari. I see Bonny and Eilidh turning into the drive. I need to pray about our talk for a while before I'm ready to discuss it with her. Thank you."

"Bye, Kieran. We love you guys. I'd better run back to the house and rescue Dan."

He rested his head on the desk and took slow, deep breaths to prepare to greet Bonny. He knew one thing for certain. Her plea forced him to become educated about adoption and pray. God had a plan, and they needed to discover it.

෴

Night descended cold and clear. Kieran turned his collar up against the wind and urged Storm toward the pasture where the sturdy little cattle lay bedded down in knee-high grass under the full moon. The hoot of an owl provided an appropriate accompaniment for their mission.

"Why check on the cattle tonight?" Ross rode up beside him and pulled the zipper on his coat higher. "It's the sheep they've targeted up until now."

"Call it a second sense." Storm skirted a large boulder and nickered when Ross's horse passed too close.

The bodyguard fingered the stock of the shotgun in his scabbard. "Bonny wouldn't approve of us going so far at night, and neither will the detectives."

"No one will know unless we discover a problem. The stolen sheep came from the same area. You do your job. I have to do mine."

When they rounded a grove of trees along the fence line, Storm tensed and snorted, ears alert. Kieran halted first, and they both dismounted. With shotguns ready, they picked their way along the fence to gain a clear view of the pasture. The cattle moved about, lowing. Kieran knelt behind a rocky outcrop, and Ross hunkered beside him.

"There." He pointed toward two figures near the gate to the stock pens.

"Let's get closer, see if we recognize them." Kieran started to stand, but Ross held him in place. Hunched down, they skirted the tree line until Ross pointed to where he spotted movement. A shiny object glinted in the moonlight. "They have knives. Look, over there. It's hard to tell in the darkness, but I see three dead animals."

"I'll take the lead." Ross stepped into the open, gun ready. "Stop, thieves!"

He fired a shot and gave chase. Kieran passed him and fired another shot. The cattle killers topped a hill and entered the dense forest of the Laddie Wood.

"Stop!" Ross ran up, breathing hard. "It's suicide in the dark. We'll come back in daylight with help."

"Ach, I almost hit the shorter one." He lowered his gun.

"Did you recognize them?"

"I couldn't see enough." Disappointment stoked the fiery blaze of frustration.

They picked their way back to the horses and rode home in silence, where their sleepless wives met them in the kitchen.

At daylight, a dozen uniformed officers, along with Alasdair and McLeod, accompanied Ross to the pasture. Bonny slipped her arm around Kieran's waist, her touch cooling his anger a bit. "He's right, you know. It is too dangerous, though I understand why you hate to stay behind."

"Yes, you do. No wonder you try to convince me otherwise." Hand in hand, they headed for the house with Eilidh. A game of ball with Flora and Charlie killed time until Bonny spotted the police Land Rover heading up the single-track from the bridge. She walked with him to meet Ross, Angus, and the detectives.

"Three bulls with slit throats." McLeod's intense gaze settled on Kieran. "A few footprints are all we have to go on."

Angus shaded his eyes from the sun. "Your three prize bulls, lad. I'm sorry."

"They knew what they were after. I wish one of us had succeeded when we shot at them. First, the sheep and now the cattle. We may have to let more employees go." Kieran turned his back and headed for the barn.

Ross waved Bonny back. "Give him time. You can't take the sting away."

Chapter Fourteen

Graeme and Janet were expecting a boy. At forty-three years old, the doctor said she had a healthy, normal pregnancy. Bonny survived the baby shower without public emotion, but her private anguish carried undeniable pain. She dreaded today's events.

The flower gardens, which dotted the broad, green lawn needed attention before they headed to Glasgow. She cared for Bronwyn's rosebushes with reverence for the woman who still held a place on this farm and in her husband's heart. A woman who, like herself, struggled with the desire for a child and died because of it.

In her private thoughts, she considered the first appointment with the fertility specialist a highway to heartbreak. No doctor hid a miracle up the sleeve of his lab coat to help her bear a child. Was it fear from the past or premonition?

No matter how many times Bonny swore she couldn't go through with it, Kieran insisted they owed themselves a chance. His assurances were insufficient to balance her doubt. "Let's pray first."

Ross parked the car in the shade in front of a modern stone and glass office building.

"Father, we ask you to give the doctor the wisdom and insight to see whether or not his methods are right for Bonny. Give us the information to make a wise decision. You know our desire for a child. We lay our hopes in your hands." Kieran stepped out and rounded the car to open her door.

Eilidh offered a handful of tissues, which Bonny stuffed in her purse. She realized with surprise how natural it had become to have Ross and Eilidh privy to the most intimate details of their lives. They were now good friends.

"We'll stay in the waiting room," Eilidh said. "Good luck."

"I'm not ready, love." Bonny leaned her head against Kieran's broad chest. The steady beat of his heart helped slow her breathing. She prayed to maintain a semblance of calm.

He stroked her hair. "I won't force you into a procedure you're not comfortable with, the same way you've been patient with me about adoption."

Decorated in soft shades of blue with classical music in the background, the office would be cheerful under different circumstances. They signed in and sat down, hand in hand. Dr. Dougal Forbes had already received their completed paperwork and her previous medical records. When the nurse called them, Bonny forced herself to put one foot in front of the other, hoping medical advances might make the news better than expected.

The nurse called their name and escorted them into a private office. When Dr. Forbes entered a few minutes later, he shook their hands and seated himself behind an art-deco desk where files covered every available inch. Bonny sensed a genuine warmth from the tall, forty-something, dark-haired man with hazel-green eyes and a ready smile. "Loch Garry. Lovely spot. I used to fish there. It's been far too long."

"We love it." Kieran patted Bonny's shoulder, where his hand had rested from the moment they sat.

The doctor opened the top file and folded his hands. "I've reviewed your records, Mrs. MacDonell, and spoken with both Dr. Moncrieffe and Dr. Carson, fine men with excellent reputations. We agree it's too soon to consider a pregnancy and recommend a wait of no less than a year, preferably eighteen months. Dr. Carson expressed sympathy for your loss."

A reprieve from the ordeal she feared. Kieran kept his arm around her, solid and comforting. If only he'd decide it was too dangerous.

"I compared the images of the ultrasounds after your original surgery with those Dr. Moncrieffe did following the ectopic pregnancy. I would order many more tests to determine the degree of success we might expect from any procedures I could offer. However, with the severity of your endometriosis, any pregnancy would be extremely high-risk. You'd be on bedrest most of the time, and I'd perform a Cesarean section. The baby would be in intensive care due to an early delivery."

"What are the dangers, Doctor?" Kieran's voice took on a deeper, tentative tone.

"More than twice the normal rate of miscarriage, a high-risk of placenta previa, a condition where …"

Kieran's face paled to a grayish hue. "My first wife and child died from placenta previa. I'm a sheep farmer. We face it occasionally."

"Then you understand the danger of hemorrhage both before and after birth, including bleeding into the abdomen, which she already experienced." He cleared his throat, stood, and leaned against the corner of his desk. "Mrs. MacDonell, I perform these procedures daily. Your disease is stage four, meaning several courses of in vitro fertilization might be required, with uncertain success. We would harvest every egg possible, then fertilize and freeze them for future use to minimize the number of surgeries."

His words resurrected the dead babies that haunted her dreams. "Doctor, are we talking about the possibility of unused embryos or selective abortion if too many implanted?"

"Both situations are very much a reality."

She wrenched loose from Kieran's embrace. "I can't do this. I'm sorry for wasting your time."

"Bonny." When she pressed the elevator button, Kieran caught her arm. "We need to hear him out."

"No. We have to discuss the medical ethics involved. I won't be responsible for the deaths of unborn babies. It's too frightening." The doors opened, and she stepped into the elevator.

"I should go back and tell them we'll call when we've had time to talk." His voice quivered.

She swallowed hard and fisted her hands. "Do what you have to. I'll meet you at the car. We're heading home tonight."

ʕʖ

He spoke with the receptionist, then sat on a bench next to the elevator, granting Bonny time to pull herself together. Who was he kidding? He needed time before he faced her too. His dream, his prayer, his hope, even with knowledge of her prognosis, brought them to this point. He wanted a child to carry on the MacDonell name and the proud tradition of Stonehaven Farm's award-winning Black-faced sheep and Highland cattle. Kieran craved a son with the soul of a farmer and heart of a pastor. A MacDonell.

His lungs emptied like bellows, but instead of fanning flames of hope, the breath extinguished it altogether. How could he ask her to face more surgeries, disappointment, and danger? He couldn't lose her or bear to see more small stones in the kirkyard.

Lord, I need to hear your voice. Can I be a loving father to an adopted child?

When he stepped outside, the angle of the sun on the Land Rover revealed Bonny's shape in the back seat, hunched over, head bent. He opened the door, braced for whatever storm awaited him.

The floor of the Land Rover looked as if she tried to staunch a flood with tissues. Eilidh patted Bonny's knee, a fragile, wee lass, instead of the strong, passionate woman he married.

"Ross, drive us to where we can walk, the university or the river." Bonny's eyes were swollen and red, but her voice sounded calm. "Shadow us while we talk this out."

"Take all the time you need. We'll be nearby." Eilidh's voice cracked.

They stopped near Kelvingrove Park, and Kieran reached for their jackets. Bonny stepped out, shivering while he held her raincoat.

She set a brisk pace, and he trudged alongside her past Kelvin Way Bridge, dodging bicyclists and walkers out for a pleasant stroll. Near a pedestrian bridge within view of the Prince of Wales Bridge, she slowed and waited while a group of boys wheeled past on bikes, then crossed over to a bench under a spreading horse chestnut. Seating herself near the end, Kieran settled a few inches away and waited.

"Your calm reaction when I first explained I couldn't have children surprised me. You said, '*Wheesht*, it's all right.' But you weren't. And you disappeared to the *bothy* for days." Bonny stared toward the bridge. "I struggled to get up the nerve to tell you, and then you accused me of lying because I knew your desire for a family. You say you love me the way I am, but you still want a blood heir. I've never doubted your love but neither have you come to a complete acceptance of who I am."

He closed his eyes. "Aye, it's true. There was no living without you. I love you more today than I did then."

"I never told you Adam went with me to discuss our options with the fertility specialist after my first surgery."

"No. I assumed your mother went." The thought of such intimate conversations with Adam made him cringe. "Did Dr. Carson express the same opinion?"

"Yes. It's not worth it to me, Kieran." Emerald eyes bored into his soul. "Understanding the strength of your desire for children, I chose not to use birth control after we married."

His sharp breath reminded him of the pain when he was shot. "You … you decided on your own, without consulting me?"

"I never imagined I would get pregnant." She tucked her head and dabbed her nose with a tissue pulled from her pocket. "I wanted to give you a child if God allowed me to become pregnant in the natural way. The danger is real. I can't do what Dr. Forbes suggests."

"Bonny, love, did adoption come between you and Adam the second time?" He waited, listening to the flutter of leaves in the breeze.

"Along with his controlling attitude. He wouldn't adopt and had no problem with the fertility methods. A lot of people don't have trouble with it, but I do." She appeared mesmerized by the flow of the river, the tone of her voice flat and lifeless. "I thought you consented to adoption when you asked me to marry you. Now, I realize you breed your sheep to produce the desired genetics and want the same for your children. You sound like that horrible Gavin Gunn. There are two babies buried in Fort William. I can't add to their number in my desire for motherhood."

Unable to remain still, he paced circles around the tree and bench. Words like *placenta previa* and *hemorrhage* resounded in his mind. He knelt in the damp grass, reached for her hands, and waited for her tormented eyes to meet his. "Bronwyn and I never considered adoption because she believed she'd become pregnant. I've lost a wife and two children. While we were in Dr. Forbes' office, you concentrated on the risk to the babies. I only heard the danger to you." He sat and drew her into his arms. "I agree, *mo chridhe.* It doesn't fit my beliefs either. I only need you."

"Thank you." Bonny wiped her eyes. "It's late. Let's stay overnight the way we planned, have a nice dinner, and go home in the morning. If adoption is to be, God will guide us."

A church bell rang in the distance, the death knell of his dreams.

෮෨

Strolling hand in hand with Kieran along the shore of Loch Garry had become their favorite way to unwind. After a morning of counseling at Faith Chapel in Fort William, they visited the MacGyvers to fill their freezer with meals from the women of Hope Chapel. Pregnant again, Katie's morning sickness made it difficult to cook, and Alex failed more than he succeeded in the kitchen. The glassy waters mirrored a sky of amethyst, rose, and gold clouds above dark, violet mountains.

"You're quiet." He stooped to skip stones.

"Tired, but happy. Emily's thrilled to have chosen a family. She's uncomfortable in this heatwave with such a few weeks left." She met his raised eyebrows with a smile. "You don't need to worry. After hours spent traveling to the agency in Inverness, I could never adopt her baby. I know her too well. Strangers will make better parents for her child."

The warmth when he grasped her hand sent a thrill through her like the ripples spreading from the stones he tossed. His lips brushed hers, then teased, deepening the kiss until tidal waves rushed through her veins. She twined her fingers in the springy curls at his neck and allowed him to sweep her away to where only he remained in her consciousness.

The clouds darkened, but Kieran's lips softened and moved to her cheeks, her eyelids, and her forehead. She settled her head into the hollow of his chest, and he kissed the top of her head. "It's time to head upstairs."

She roused from the dreamlike state of his caress. "Tea in our room?"

"Let's skip the tea." His soft laugh throbbed beneath her cheek. "A shower and the lovely perfume I bought you in Glasgow?"

"The one I can't pronounce?" She raised her head and kissed the hollow of his throat. The ever-present Ross and Eilidh stayed in the trees, also enjoying the evening ritual.

"Aye." He turned and waved to Ross. "It's time to go inside."

Ross waved back. "Right behind you." Hand in hand, they stepped out of the trees and followed up the hill.

"What's on the schedule for tomorrow?" Kieran asked.

"Eilidh and I plan to meet Janet for lunch in Fort William." Bonny held him back until their friends caught up. "Kieran mentioned fly fishing on the Garry for you guys, Ross, unless you're in for a lot of girl-talk."

He laughed. "I'll head to the barn and check out my fishing gear now, given the alternative."

Kieran held up his hand. "You can wait until morning. It's Friday. We could sleep in and still not miss the best fishing. I'll finish my sermon in the afternoon."

"We might decide to shop a little before we head home. Do you mind?" Bonny stopped to inhale the fragrance of the evening primroses bordering the driveway.

"How many clothes does a farmer's wife need?" Kieran pulled her behind him toward the door. "We don't have money for unnecessary shopping."

"None. It's a way to extend the girl-time. I know money's tight."

Eilidh's laughter chimed in like bells. "I've shopped more since we've lived with you than in my entire marriage. I don't need any more clothes."

A little later, Bonny lay snug in Kieran's arms, enjoying the comfort of his heartbeat, the rise and fall of his chest beneath her head. "I can't imagine a more perfect life."

"I haven't given you everything, *mo gràdh*." He pressed a kiss on her forehead, tightening his arms around her. "I remember the look on your face when you nursed the motherless lamb. You have endless love in your heart, a quality I don't possess. I'm still uncomfortable with your greatest desire, and it makes me feel guilty."

"God's in control. The more love you give, the more you have. I see you grow every day. I want to fall sleep right here. I'm content. We'll take the future as it comes."

But sleep didn't come. His words of regret stirred the plea of her heart. To see Janet blooming with new life made her feel dead inside. A soft snore escaped Kieran's lips, and she rolled over. The future might hold hope, but her heart ached with an emptiness impossible to suppress in the here and now.

☙❧

"Look at the tartans. I haven't been in here for ages." Eilidh stopped walking and whisked Bonny into a tourist shop along the High Street in Fort William, picked a tartan skirt off the rack, and hurried her into a dressing room at the back.

Her shoulder muscles tightened at the abrupt change in Eilidh's light-hearted mood. "What's wrong?"

"We've been followed since we left the restaurant. Stay here while I look around and pretend to get another size."

The way the first crack of thunder from an approaching storm startles, a few weeks without dread lulled Bonny into a false sense of comfort. She sank into the corner chair and hugged her purse to her chest. "Who?"

"Gavin Gunn." Eilidh checked the revolver in her purse and opened the door a crack. "I won't go far. The skirts are right outside the dressing room. Call 999 for a police escort. With so many tourists in town, he could force us to go with him, and no one would notice. If I tried to take him down here, someone might be injured."

She withdrew her phone from her purse with trembling fingers. The police said five minutes. *Breathe. Just breathe.*

When the door handle turned, she jumped, relieved when Eilidh entered with another skirt. "He's in front of the store with his back to the window. Did you call?"

"Five minutes."

"Stay here. I'll keep watch." She stepped out again. Bonny prayed.

After a few seconds, Eilidh knocked. "We have two gentlemen here ready to return to the farm. Are you finished?"

"I don't like the fit. Let's go." She opened the door to find two men in plain clothes alongside Eilidh.

"We're parked just down the street." The officer looked too young for the job, but his partner, Donal had stood watch at the hospital after the shooting by the loch. She fell in beside him. Gavin had disappeared.

The officers drove them to their car and followed at a distance. Near Invergarry on the A82, an older model black Toyota pickup passed the police, decreasing the space between them too fast. It pulled alongside and encroached on their lane.

"Hold on!" Eilidh shouted. The Land Rover bounced into the ditch at a crazy angle, stopping with the front wheel against a large stone. She shifted into four-wheel drive and backed up the incline, sliding in the wet grass and mud, until they rested on level ground.

With a screech of tires on pavement, the police vehicle halted alongside, and both officers bounded out. Donal signaled Bonny to unlock her door. "Are you all right, Mrs. MacDonell? Eilidh? We never should have allowed so much space in between."

No way would she and Kieran survive. "His … his eyes. Those evil eyes. Didn't he realize who you were?"

"We may have been mistaken for farm employees." Donal's voice sounded too calm. "Take a drink of water and breathe slow and easy."

Half the water spilled in Bonny's lap. She ran for the ditch retching.

"I'll drive you ladies the rest of the way home. Tom can follow."

Eilidh let Donal take the driver's seat. Bonny crept into the back, huddling under a blanket.

Alerted by a call from Eilidh, Kieran and Ross met them at the end of the drive. Kieran half-lifted her from the car, leading her up the back stairs to their room, where he drew her onto his lap on the bed. "No more trips to town alone. I can't even trust the police to take proper care of you. Ross and I will protect you from now on."

She managed a nod. Fear eclipsed the safety and peacefulness of last night. Bonny crawled under the covers. "Just let me sleep. Please."

He scooted over and placed an arm around her.

"Go. I don't need anyone here. If Eilidh and XXX shouldn't leave alone anymore, perhaps you and Ross shouldn't go to the pastures by yourselves either. Gavin's determined to succeed. I saw it in his eyes."

Chapter Fifteen

Some days prayers refused to come. At other times, they rushed forth like the waterfall behind the cottage. Bonny ached to return to a place she had sworn never to visit again. Kieran's *bothy* in the mountains seemed the perfect place to discuss their problems and pray for answers, in spite of the attack she suffered there. Her desire for motherhood throbbed with every heartbeat.

She cowered in bed, spent hours alone, and refused to eat. Kieran worried when her moods turned black, but she lacked strength to change. And God remained silent.

Today, however, the roiling emotions gelled in her mind. By mid-afternoon, she showered, dressed, warmed the cold scones from breakfast in the microwave, and settled on a plan of action.

Why she longed for the cottage was a mystery, but the immense beauty and solitude, which brought peace to Kieran in the past, offered seclusion to seek answers now. Demands of the farm and the constant presence of Ross and Eilidh made time alone almost impossible. How they'd manage in a one-bedroom cottage was a mystery, but she determined to find a way.

A private conversation with Eilidh confirmed the police possessed an unmarked vehicle with a bed and bathroom used for stakeouts in remote highland locations. DCI McLeod granted unexpected permission.

Kieran sat alone in the upstairs office, chair tipped back, feet on his desk, staring out at the loch. This room provided a place of unity, a haven where they worked on chapel plans, Bible study lessons, and held deep theological dialogues. A room where they saw their prayer for ministry answered.

Bonny watched in silence from the doorway, heart kathumping like a drum in a pipe band. She glanced at the ruby and diamond ring on her left hand, awed at the bond between them. She knew his thoughts.

Her best friend, lover, and the man she trusted above anyone on earth, Kieran MacDonell held her heart in his hands. She caused the pensive mood. Guilt surged through her, watching him contemplate another day of her moodiness.

She drew a deep breath and knocked. "Am I interrupting?"

Her heart's rhythm changed to a staccato when he turned and his lips lifted into a smile. "You never interrupt, love. Are you ready to talk, or should I ask?"

"Would it upset you to know I schemed behind your back?" She grabbed the chair from her desk, pushed it toward him, and sat, needing physical distance to keep her emotions under control. "The time is right for a little trip."

His sigh of relief showed welcome acceptance of how she dealt with emotional issues. "What kind of scheming?"

"I want to visit the *bothy*."

Elbows on knees, chin on hands, he waited.

"Are you surprised?"

"Aye, but your dark days seldom come without a monumental decision."

"We need time away, so Eilidh and I figured it out."

His eyebrows arched. "Why does it amaze me when you face your fears and conquer them? What do you have in mind?"

"If you're ready, I want to talk about adoption. I need to know. For certain."

He scooted his chair closer and stroked her cheek with one finger. "We can talk. I make no promises."

"Praying wouldn't push you too much, would it?" She took the hand he rested on her cheek and kissed his palm. "If you're not ready …"

"I'm delighted you want to go again. When shall we leave?" His lips curved into another smile as she explained her plan. "You never cease to astound me."

"Whenever you can get away."

Kieran's eyes glittered like the loch through the window behind him. "Remember the night after the Fort William Christian College faculty banquet when I said the beauty of Loch Linnhe couldn't compare to the woman next to me? You grow lovelier every time life circumstances reveal the true depth of your heart in a deeper way. Shall we leave on Monday?"

"Perfect. I'll tell Eilidh. I'm sorry about today. Sometimes we're both better off if I stay in bed."

"I know." His lips brushed her forehead. "Some days the men must think they work for an ogre instead of a pastor. I'll discuss whatever you want, love. You're not afraid of Deirdre and Gavin?"

Bonny straightened her shoulders. "I refuse to allow them to dictate our lives. We have capable people to protect us. We need to face our fear and defeat it."

He scooted closer until his lips touched hers, feather-soft. Nothing indicated his thoughts, but whatever he concluded, she had to accept it.

ോ

Bonny tucked her hands under her thighs and attempted a smile. Whenever worry caused her to twist her hair in knots, Kieran's forehead wrinkled in concern. "Sorry. It's more difficult than I imagined."

"We don't have to go to the cottage. We can go to a hotel instead." His voice held the same tenderness she noticed on the first night they talked when he offered to listen to her heartbreak over Adam.

Three broken ribs, a spy at the window, and attempted kidnapping weren't something easily forgotten, but Bonny ignored the flutter in her chest. "I'll be fine. Buying a sleeper sofa for the front room, in case we need Ross and Eilidh inside, is brilliant. I will *not* be hostage to fear, though I do feel like a rabbit stalked by a mountain lion."

Determination flooded through her at Kieran's pleased look. "Gavin Gunn would be more dangerous even if Scotland had mountain lions. I'm proud of you."

"Distract me. Tell me what you're thinking." She turned to glance toward the van, which kept the pace with no trouble. Eilidh waved, and Bonny waved back.

He shifted to a lower gear and steered around a deep rut in the road. "I want to raise a family with you, Bonny. I want to be a father." His fists tightened on the steering wheel, knuckles whitening.

She waited. Silent.

"I still have reservations about adoption, though I agree we have more than enough love to share with any child. Your comparison of the brief length of pregnancy to a lifetime of parenting made me think. I do feel love for Rowan, James Miller, and other children from the chapel. If they needed a home, I wouldn't hesitate. I have no problem with being guardians for Kari and Dan's twins, or for Janet and Graeme. At least, we're acquainted with their parents and their background. I still can't imagine raising children of strangers." The ruts and rocks in the road matched the rugged emotion in his voice. "I'm still frightened of getting our hopes up and someone taking it all away, like my friends."

"Kari shares a lot of traits with her non-adopted siblings. Either God worked it out, or she took on characteristics of the family she loves. Half the people at church don't remember she's adopted."

Kieran pointed ahead. "There's the cottage. The door's closed even though we didn't lock it. Chances are good no one's been here at all. Ross suggested they park in front of the door at night, then we can climb into their vehicle if necessary."

"I'll be fine unless there's another threat." Bonny's stomach rolled over, and she swallowed hard. "I make no promises otherwise."

They put the food away, replaced the threadbare couch with the new sleeper sofa, and headed for the waterfall near a rocky overlook where the farm and Loch Garry appeared in miniature far below. She scrutinized each tree and rock, expecting a bullet or arrow to fly out of the woods at any moment.

When they had walked out the knots from bouncing up the rough road, they headed back for dinner. Bonny and Eilidh worked side by side in the tiny kitchen area while Kieran entertained them with tales of boyhood adventures in the nearby woods.

ରଜ ଓଓ

A misty rain enveloped the mountain in fog the next morning. Ross and Eilidh settled on the couch with books while Bonny and Kieran relaxed in the bedroom. Leaning on pillows propped against the tarnished brass headboard, she listened to Kieran pray for open hearts and clear direction. The ache in her own heart tugged like stitches in a healing wound.

She traced a circle on the back of his hand, making the reddish hairs stand on end. "If you agreed to adopt, would you consider any age other than a newborn?"

Golden brows furrowed, and Kieran stood to add a log to the fire, hung the poker on its hook, and stared at the wall. "I assumed you wanted a newborn. Do you want an older child?"

"Don't get me wrong, I long to hold a baby in my arms and experience the different stages of growth. But it breaks my heart to read about older children without hope because people want babies. What would you think about a young sibling group? We'd have our family all at once." The chimney didn't draw well in wet weather, and she rubbed her eyes, stinging from a slight haze of peat smoke.

His fists clenched and relaxed. "I haven't considered either. What age?"

"A toddler group. I'm not ready for teenagers. It would half the paperwork and waiting, plus keep siblings together."

Big fingers traced the pattern on the quilt. "I guess they teach you how to discuss adoption with kids. It seems they might feel afraid of strangers." Kieran bit his lower lip.

She ruffled through brochures and information, coming up with a yellow envelope. "Most articles say to tell babies they're adopted from day one. With older children, you become well acquainted before taking them home, day trips and all. They encourage total honesty at a level the child can understand."

Fisted hands and pursed lips revealed his concern. "How do you know what they're ready to understand?"

"I remember one of my friends at home said each child asks when they're ready. Her daughter didn't question much. At about three-and-a-half, her son wanted to know why the lady who grew him in her tummy didn't want him.

She reassured him it wasn't because she didn't want him, but the birthmother's inability to care for any child. It's sad. All parties in adoption have their own hurts—children, birthparents, and adoptive parents. It will keep us on our knees, but think what a wonderful home we could provide on the farm. You look so right with a child in your arms."

"I'm not smart enough to know all the answers. But I'm willing to talk with an agency." Kieran twisted to the side and rubbed his back. "I called Kari a couple of times."

"When? She never said a word."

"Not too long after we lost the baby, and again before we went to the fertility doctor. They were a couple of eye-opening conversations. She said my doubts are normal. I didn't tell you because I had to digest it all. I'd do anything to make you happy, Bonny. I promise to explore the details, but ..."

She clenched her lips and closed her eyes. "I'm glad you talked with her."

"A walk would feel good, but it's raining too hard even for a Scot." He stood and looked out the small window above the bed. Rain pounded like a jackhammer on the metal roof.

"How about playing a game with Ross and Eilidh? I'm certain they're ready for a diversion."

He scooped embers from the hearth back into the fireplace. "Sounds good. Later, we'll list the pros and cons about the different agencies and write down our questions."

"There are plenty of those." She wrapped her arms around his waist before he opened the door. "Thank you."

"Thank you for making me a better person than I'd be without you." He bent to place a kiss on the end of her nose.

CB ബ

The peat smoke and lack of space wore on all four of them. The rain let up while they played a game of gin rummy and ate roast beef sandwiches. With full stomachs, they donned rain suits and hiking boots and headed into the woods. About a hundred yards from the cabin, a knot the size of the boulders jutting through the thick carpet of grass and leaves formed in Bonny's stomach. Kieran's firm grip on her hand, and the fact they were armed, kept a tenuous hold on fear that alerted her to every sound, including the beat of her own heart.

Birds called in the trees where a herd of red deer leaped through the bushes. Woodsy sounds, the chatter of squirrels, a woodpecker tapping overhead, soothed her. Wet leaves muted their steps and trees dripped under the disappearing clouds.

"Did you two ever think about having a family?" It didn't seem so intrusive to ask Eilidh when children were the reason for their trip.

"Aye, but we love detective work. Providing personal protection allows us to develop relationships with people." She moved up alongside Bonny. "I never desired motherhood. If I hadn't met Ross, I wouldn't have married. It's not for everyone, but it works for us. We refuse jobs when we want time off to travel or visit family."

"You won't miss having kids as you grow older?" Bonny lifted a branch out of the way, and Eilidh ducked under before Kieran raised it higher for him and Ross.

"We enjoy our nieces and nephews. I'm forty-five. It's too late now." Eilidh offered a hand at a stone higher than Bonny's short legs could manage.

"It's all I've ever wanted."

"I hope it works out."

They returned to the cottage in time to light lanterns and cook dinner. Bonny added peat to the stove, exchanged her boots for warm slippers, and put the green chili enchilada casserole into the oven. Half of the dish contained the hot chilies she and Kieran preferred, half the mild chilies Ross and Eilidh tolerated.

Crickets and frogs chirped outside when she and Kieran headed for the bedroom to begin their list.

"Forever Family." Kieran pushed the pile of brochures and printouts to the foot of the bed. "They're faith-based, and it makes sense to work with the agency we'd like the Faith and Hope Chapels to become involved with."

Hope flickered in Bonny's heart. "They offer the counseling and a wide range of services to help us become the best parents possible to a child."

"Or children."

"Are you certain?"

He nodded. "If we're doing this, let's be open to the family the Lord wants to create."

She rolled onto her knees. "Tomorrow's Saturday, and I want to get started. We're going to be parents, Kieran!"

"Hold on, love. Things move slow and go wrong. And I haven't agreed to do more than look into it."

"I refuse to dwell on the negative. If God leads us to adoption, He will guide us through it. Any delays are only because our child—children—aren't ready yet."

"Bonny, please don't let the process or my hesitancy break your heart. I can't bear it."

Sleep refused to claim either of them. Throughout the night, they whispered hopes, concerns, and the excitement—the joy of seeking God's plan together. When the sun rose, Bonny propped herself on one elbow. "I'm exhausted. You're right about the need to stay busy with other things."

"If we pack early, we can take another hike before heading down the mountain."

When they carried their bags and sheets into the main room, Ross and Eilidh came through the door.

"Brace yourselves," Ross said. "We had a visitor during the night."

Kieran rubbed a hand over his face, an action she saw him make more and more often. "What now?"

"There's an arrow stuck on the outhouse door with a note, in spite of our truck parked right outside. It says, 'Vacate Greenfield and the Laddie Wood or lose your lives.' We called the detectives on the SAT phone." Ross rested his hand on the gun at his side. "Ride in the van with us. Alasdair will bring your truck later. Leave the keys."

Shivers raced through Bonny's body, and she pulled her sweater tight. "My appetite's gone. Get us out of here."

Kieran guided her toward the door. "Stay calm and focused, *mo gràdh*. He won't beat us."

"Let's go." Eilidh grasped her elbow.

"Ooh." Bonny stomped her foot so hard it hurt her knee. "I'm so angry. When I see Gavin or Deirdre, they better hope I'm not armed."

"All Deirdre has done is warn us." Kieran climbed into the van, and Eilidh slid the door shut while Ross started the engine.

"I don't trust her for one second."

Eilidh insisted they crouch on the floor of the van. "Heads down."

"Are the keys in your truck?" Ross rounded the corner of the cottage.

"Aye." Bonny pushed his head back down.

Ross drove right to the kitchen door of the farmhouse. Kieran led her to their room and clasped her hands to pray.

"Once again, a peaceful getaway ruined." Her mood darkened and she grumbled. She couldn't escape for a moment.

In defiance of threats—and despite her pleading—Kieran refused to move his flocks from Greenfield or the Laddie Wood. Bonny wondered what bizarre act he might provoke, but knew he stood on principle, in spite of her sleepless nights.

C3 80

"At times I thought today would never come." Kieran and Bonny walked into Hope Chapel one hour before the opening service. The new doors his father carved after the fire were perhaps more beautiful than the originals, polished wood and carved crosses sanded smooth and varnished with love. Colored light danced across the floor from the new stained-glass window.

While Ross and Eilidh took seats near the back, Kieran led Bonny to kneel at the front, cherishing her sweet warmth against his arm. "Bless us, Lord, in our new endeavor. We fail to trust you far too often and become discouraged. Thank you for your patience, your sufficiency in our need, and your grace in our weakness. Enable us to accomplish your purposes here and protect us from those who would prevent it. Gird us with strength, and make Hope Chapel a mighty work able to change each life it touches."

When they finished praying, Ross and Eilidh came forward. "What a victory considering everything you've gone through."

Kieran floated in weightless joy and thankfulness, in spite of the threats surrounding him and his family. When the dream began to take shape, he never dared hope Bonny would share in his life or ministry. He acted out of pure obedience to God, and a promise never to allow loss to defeat him again. To have her for his partner in life and ministry made him want to dance in front of the altar.

She reached for his Bible and read the highlighted verse from the Contemporary English Version aloud. "'Weapons made to attack you won't be successful; words spoken against you won't hurt at all.' Perfect for each moment of our lives."

A brisk wind off the loch ushered in Finlay and Mary McGregor. Their girls ran to Bonny with hugs and giggles while Finlay shook Kieran's hand. "We'll put song sheets on the chairs, Pastor. You have plenty to do."

His parents walked through the door, Da stopping to polish the brass handles with his handkerchief. Kieran stooped to kiss his mother. "*Madainn mhath, Mathair, Da.* It's here at last!" A glimpse of Bonny, over his father's shoulder, revealed her smile at their Gaelic.

"*Madainn mhath.*" She returned their hugs, kissing each on the cheek.

"Lovely Gaelic, Bonny," Hamish said, following Maggie to the front row.

The chapel was half-full when Bonny took her place at the keyboard. Kieran moved to center stage with his guitar and nodded. Her clear soprano, complimented his deep baritone, precious memories of how music drew them together before they married. Light from the stained-glass window shone on her hair like the first time he heard her sing. The emotions stirred by love for her and the God who brought them together were difficult to blink back.

When the last worship song finished, she took a seat right in front of him. Filled with a sense of the unreal, he moved behind the pulpit, another gift from his father. "I'll read the statement of faith for the chapel and then let Graeme MacDholl explain the cooperative relationship between our Hope Chapel and Faith Chapel in Fort William. My sermons will begin with the book of Genesis, the foundation for all of Scripture. Our Bible study will continue after the worship service, and we hope you'll stay for the covered dish meal each week before your drive home."

Maggie and Hamish visited with old friends and met new neighbors during lunch at the farmhouse. When the last car drove away, his mother tiptoed to kiss his cheek. "You're so like your Grandda MacKenzie. And the people love you already. It's a delight to watch you both grow into your new roles."

"Mother, Da, there's something we'd like you to pray about. Could you stay and talk a wee bit?" He led the way to the library. "We visited a fertility specialist in Glasgow to see if their methods might allow us to have a child."

Bonny's mouth dropped open, an earthquake of surprise and hesitance registered on her face. They planned to wait for a discussion about adoption with his parents because of his uncertainties. But he continued out of his own need.

"We can't undertake the risks or agree to the moral implications of Dr. Forbes' methods. They may not bother some people, but they're wrong for us. I won't endanger Bonny's life or those of unborn children. She's convinced God is leading us toward adoption, and I've agreed to explore it. We helped a young girl from Faith Chapel find a family for her child and Bonny's done thorough research. We'd appreciate your prayers."

His mother's wide, startled eyes didn't bode well for her reaction, and he held his breath, the memory of her protests when he told her he planned to marry an American still fresh. She looked at Bonny and cleared her throat. "My heart broke when I saw how the children at the chapel love you. Since Kieran says he agreed to explore it, I assume you're more enthusiastic than he is. I have my reservations, but we'll see where God leads."

"Maggie," Da placed his hand on her arm, "a serious decision like this belongs to them alone." His eyes rested on Bonny. "You're a blessing to our family, lass. We want to see you two happy and fulfilled. We'll pray God's will is done."

"Hamish, they need to make certain a child who will carry on the MacDonell name comes from a good Scottish background."

Kieran stood and crossed the room to stand in front of them. "Mother, Da, we have to obey God no matter what direction he leads. There are thousands of children in need of homes—infants, older children, and sibling groups. We're open to the family God wants for us. Though we hoped for your complete support, you'll have to work through your reservations the same way I'm progressing on my own."

Bonny rushed toward the library door, stopped, and leaned against the wall. "You should have waited, Kieran. Why hurry into this discussion before we have all the information?"

"Lass," Da crossed the room and placed his arm around her. "We'll accept whatever child the good Lord sends us. We've more than enough love for a dozen children."

Relief flooded through him. Da could be counted on. "Mother, you were wrong about Bonny, and you're wrong about adoption." Suddenly, she broke free from his father's embrace and stumbled up the stairs. "Thank you, Da, she'll be all right."

"I'm sorry we upset the lass. Prayer can work marvels, the chapel is proof, and you have ours." Da embraced him and reached for his mother's hand. "Maggie, we'll be leaving now."

◊

A crumpled heap of clothes lay on the bed when Kieran walked into their room. When it moved, he realized it was Bonny.

"I had no idea you planned to speak with them before we met with an agency." The pillow pulled over her face muffled her voice. "With your doubts, it's no surprise your mother reacted the way she did."

"It changes nothing. You heard Da. Set up the appointments. Leave the rest to God." Ready or not, the decision to speak with his parents moved them further along.

The moon rose over the distant mountains outside their bedroom window. Despite some niggling uncertainty about their course, his heart swelled with love for the wee woman whose courage and faith never ceased to challenge him. The first day he saw her at the faculty meeting, how little he imagined the changes Bonny would bring to his world. The outburst by his mother cemented his own commitment to seek God's will about adoption.

CHAPTER SIXTEEN

Bonny sat on the top stair and drew slow, deep breaths. *Calm yourself. It will all go fine.*

"I put fresh bouquets of roses in the living room and dining room, the last of the season. Yellow chrysanthemums for the library and a small arrangement for the table in your room." Eilidh climbed the stairs with a crystal vase of yellow and dark-red mums. "Are you all right?"

She laughed and smoothed her load of towels with shaky hands. "I dropped these twice on the way upstairs. I'm a nervous wreck. We have one hour until the social worker arrives, and I think we're ready. I sent Kieran to sweep the front porch."

"Aye, Ross decided to rake leaves." Eilidh offered her a hand up. "I'll put on the tea. It might relax you both. I'll have a fresh pot when the social worker arrives. What's her name again?"

"Rhona Pentland, from the Forever Family Adoption and Foster Care Agency where we went for our initial interview and prep group in Aberdeen." Bonny laid the towels in the linen closet, straightened the stack, and took the bouquet. "Thank you for helping. My hands are so sweaty and shaky. I hope I don't drop it before I reach the table. I wish we didn't have to explain security details and cameras."

"Your acceptance process will all be over soon. If you straighten one more thing, I'm going to lock you in a closet until she arrives. No one will check to make certain your towels are straight. Now change your clothes, and I'll send the men to do the same. You explained your situation. Gavin's been quiet for a while. I honestly don't believe he's smart enough to accomplish what he wants." Eilidh pulled the door closed.

"He's so unpredictable," Bonny called through the door. "Today, the serious questions start."

"*Wheesht*, don't borrow trouble. You two are the most stable couple I know with educators, friends, and pastors on both sides of the Atlantic for references. Remember all those prayers you've prayed."

Footsteps receded down the hall and she closed her eyes. Did her faith make a positive or negative impact on Ross and Eilidh?

The brown skirt, hip-length top of crochet lace, and wide, leather belt hung on a hook inside the closet. The final touch, her mother's gold cross necklace, surrounded her neck like a hug.

When she reached for the hairbrush, Kieran came through the door and enfolded her in his arms, smelling of the outdoors and damp leather. "The rain started again, but not enough to create problems on the single-track. Should I do anything else before I change?"

Cheeks red from the chilly air made his eyes such a deep cerulean blue, it started a different kind of flutter in her chest. "No. We'll pray after you change. Can Ross direct her up the circular drive to the front door?"

"She's a Scot. A little rain won't melt her." He placed a kiss at the nape of her neck and walked into the closet. "You're the most perfect potential mother in all of Scotland. We'll answer her questions, introduce Ross and Eilidh, and leave the rest to the Lord. If it's necessary to wait until the Gavin Gunn mess is sorted out, then we will."

"Eilidh reminded me of all the prayers we've prayed. Do you think my fear and questions look like a lack of faith? They aren't believers, after all."

He tucked his shirt in and tightened his belt. "I suppose it might. We need to be more careful about how we say things. They weren't sent to protect us by accident." He glanced toward the window. "She's here."

A car pulled up to the front steps at the same time they reached the door. She breathed deep and followed him onto the porch. "Welcome." He greeted Rhona, took her umbrella, and ushered her into the house.

"Mr. and Mrs. MacDonell, thank you for having someone let me know I was in the right place. My, but the road becomes muddy where the pavement ends. Your directions were perfect. I'm Rhona." She offered a firm handshake to each.

"I'm glad you had no trouble." He pointed her toward the living room. "Please, take a seat. May we offer you a cup of tea?"

The social worker chose a chair near the bay window, surveyed the room, and opened her briefcase. "Tea would be lovely. Thanks."

"Just coming." Eilidh entered with a tray of tea and biscuits. She set the tray next to the crystal vase and handed around Edinburgh Blend in the old Scottish Lochs china.

"My grandmother had dishes like these." Rhona held up her cup, turned it around, and smiled.

Bonny breathed a little easier at the discovery of common ground, no matter how small. "I like them too."

"I anticipated a small cottage when I saw you lived on a sheep farm on Loch Garry. What an impressive home, and such bright, cheery colors. I was pleasantly surprised to see the big sign announcing Stonehaven Farm. Your home is lovely and inviting from first sight."

Kieran's chest expanded with pride when anyone complimented Stonehaven. "My second great grandfather built the house. We consider ourselves privileged caretakers."

"Let's save the farm tour for my next visit. Did you grow up here?" Rhona looked out the window, her mouth curving in a smile. "I'm a city girl, but it seems like a wonderful place for children."

"Aye, I spent my childhood roaming the countryside with sheep, horses, dogs, and boats. My parents set strict boundaries, though I wandered as boys will. The portraits in the entry hall are an ancient history of the MacDonells."

"I'll pay attention when we tour the house. Perhaps we should get better acquainted first. Mrs. MacDonell, do you care for this big house on your own?"

"We have a wonderful housekeeper who's been with the family since before Kieran was born. It's still new to me, but it's a wonderful place to live."

Rhona held up her hand at the offer to refill her cup. "It must be quite a change, coming from New Mexico. Did you have trouble acclimating to our weather?"

"I don't have webbed feet yet, but I love it most of the time. Before Kieran and I married, I taught for a semester and a half at Fort William Christian College, though I'm still not used to weeks of rain."

The grandfather clock chimed three times while they discussed family, childhood, marriage, and infertility. The house tour became a lesson in MacDonell family history and the New Mexico climate. When they returned to the living room, relief washed over Bonny. A family seemed achievable for the first time. Kieran leaned back and crossed his legs.

The social worker selected several forms from her briefcase and slipped out a legal pad. "I want to cover a lot of details today. You'll come back to Aberdeen for your individual interviews, to meet with one of our support groups, and get acquainted with some other staff members."

The rest of the interview passed quickly. By the time Rhona headed back through the puddles, a sense of elation set in. The next visit would explore the farm and chapel, the environment their children would experience.

"I think it went well." Once Rhona turned the corner onto the single-track, Kieran closed the door.

"The discussion of our safety issues isn't finished. Ross and Eilidh's explanation of the situation concerned her, I could tell."

His arms slid around her waist, warm and secure. Her head, resting in the curve of his strong biceps gave her a sense of security, a homey peace, and she breathed deep. His physical strength always reminded her of the emotional and spiritual strength he brought to her life. "The marathon's begun. We need to be at the top of our game for these meetings."

"No, love, we need to be on our knees."

Cℬ⅋

Who would place children with people whose armed protectors stuck closer than shadows? They must be crazy to believe anyone would give them children under these circumstances.

Bonny squeezed a chamomile teabag into her mug. Her Scottish husband would cringe at the American method of tea-making. She crossed the dark hall to the library and curled into her favorite armchair like a cat. Charlie and Flora took up sentry duty next to her in the dim glow of the hallway nightlights. The mug warmed her cold hands while she leaned her head back and prayed for sleep.

The elation, which followed their interview, vanished by midnight. Snuggled close to Kieran's warm back, sleep failed to come, so here she sat. Nighttime had lost some of its charm with security lights outside, but nothing marred the silence, broken only by night birds and small wildlife scurrying through the bushes beneath the windows. The nearby hoot of a barn owl hunting a lamb to snatch reminded her of the way Gavin awaited his chance to steal their dreams.

She flicked on the lamp and reached for the Bible. A loud *snap* followed by what sounded like a yelp of pain outside the window caused her to almost drop the heavy book.

Thankful they closed the blinds at night, Bonny slid to the floor, crawling toward the hallway. Whoever sneaked around the yard, the dogs didn't respond. She rounded the corner and paused. Someone pulled their foot from the mud in the flower garden next to the kitchen door and stepped onto the stone step, rattling the doorknob.

"Charlie, Flora, door." Both loped into the kitchen, bared their teeth, and growled.

Who in the world? Standing, she tiptoed to the stairs, hugged close to the wall, and slowed to avoid the squeaky treads. At the top, she pounded on Ross and Eilidh's door before opening the master bedroom door. "Hurry, someone's outside."

Robes cinched tight, all three joined her in seconds, guns in hand. How she hated the control a madman held over their life.

"Why are you out of bed?" Kieran shoved her behind him and followed their protectors to the stairs.

"I didn't want my restlessness to bother you."

"Stay in the hall, away from windows. No lights." Ross started down the back stairs while Eilidh headed toward the front.

Kieran stuffed the gun in his robe pocket and drew her tight against him. "Couldn't sleep?"

"It's a good thing. I heard a branch break and a cry outside the library windows. The dogs growled a little but settled down and didn't bark. We keep them with us. How would they know the stalker?"

They heard Ross phone for backup. Eilidh crept back upstairs. "They tried to pry open a library window. Hopefully, someone responds fast enough to catch them before they get away. With the road conditions, it will take a while. No lights."

Thunder cracked, and the rain returned in torrents. A short time later, Ross opened the back door where Hugh MacFadyen dripped on the doormat. "No sign of anyone, but there are footprints all over. Rain will obscure them by morning and make the cameras too grainy. Go back to bed. We'll look more in the morning."

A gloomy report, once again. Back upstairs, Bonny slid her feet out of her slippers, laid her robe on the bench, and climbed into bed on Kieran's side. "The more incidents, the less chance anyone will let us have a child. I want a normal life, free of constant stress."

"We're in God's hands, *mo chridhe*. We need to rest there." He kicked his slippers under the bench, tossed his robe next to hers, and crawled in beside her. "Worry makes you unable to eat and rest to regain the weight you lost."

"Are you complaining?"

"Never. I'm forever thankful I didn't lose you."

☙ ❧

Bonny awakened to the sound of Kieran in the shower and Ross and Eilidh downstairs in the kitchen. Outside the window, pea-soup fog covered the loch like a blanket. Deep puddles in the yard assured the road would be a muddy mess.

Ross and Eilidh shrugged into jackets and wellies when they entered the kitchen. "We're going to check out the road and cameras. Stay inside until Hugh and Alasdair finish their search."

"Another morning lost to fruitless investigation." Kieran waited at the table while Bonny started breakfast.

"Work on your Bible study lesson. Seumas can handle things outside. I'm glad to be in here alone."

Feet stomped on the porch, and Ross entered, crowbar in hand. "We have a lead. Our intruder cut himself when he attempted to pry the window. He dropped this on the front porch. We have blood for a DNA sample. Now, if they find a match in the database."

Two days later, Alasdair called while Bonny worked with Kieran and Ross to vaccinate the sheep. They failed to find a DNA match.

◦◦◦

"The Granite City. I didn't notice much on our first trip here. My nerves got the better of me." The streets of Aberdeen and traffic of a busy petroleum center on the North Sea made Bonny cringe after the quiet of their loch-side hideaway. Her stomach knotted tighter than a traffic jam at the thought of their interviews at the adoption agency.

"We can relax after the interviews." Kieran gave her knee a squeeze. "I'm eager to visit a support group and meet other couples with our same concerns."

"I doubt anyone else brings bodyguards."

"They'll think you're famous," Eilidh teased. "I'm certain government officials and wealthy people with protective details adopt."

"You're right. I'd feel better if they had a match on the blood, though."

Kieran grinned. "Bonny, you'll charm them into forgetting Ross and Eilidh altogether."

Ross took a sharp right and pulled into the car park at a white, three-story dormered house. "Here we are."

"We're staying in such an elegant hotel? How can we afford it?" The gorgeous, white house sat among ornate gardens and flowering trees.

"My mother knows the owners, so we got a deal. They have a lovely suite where the four of us won't feel crowded. Enjoy the next chapter in our big adventure." He opened the car door and helped her out. "I want you to feel relaxed and special."

"Don't argue with him." Eilidh pointed at a spectacular flowering tree and then back toward the building, which reminded Bonny of a graceful southern plantation. "I plan to enjoy every minute."

She pushed down her anxiety. "Let's check in. We could all use a break from the tension at home."

Èî

A stray sunbeam filtered through a gap in the draperies when she awakened next to Kieran in the king-sized bed. A shared living room connected the two bedrooms. What a blessing to have private space at such an emotional time.

After a sumptuous breakfast, Ross stopped the Land Rover in front of the long, Greystone building with multiple offices. The large, white sign near the steps boasted an artful adaptation of the *Saltire* proclaiming Forever Family Adoption and Foster Care Agency. An equal desire to jump up and down in excitement or make Ross drive away warred inside Bonny. Kieran's grim stare and pressed lips brought her back to reality. "We're not headed to our execution, you know. Let's smile and get on with it."

He opened her car door, clasped her hand, and led her up the stairs. "One more step in our adventure of faith, Mrs. MacDonell. And by the way, your new green dress fits perfectly. You look lovely."

Their bodyguards followed. "We'll wait here."

"Bonny, Kieran, welcome." Rhona met them in the lobby. "You took the office tour the last time?"

"We did." The cold, gray exterior hid warm, comfortable meeting rooms, a conference room, kitchen area, lounge, and attractive offices. Bonny drew in a deep breath and settled into a chair in Rhona's office, while Kieran awaited his turn. Rhona's friendly, relaxed demeanor allowed time to think about her answers. An hour later, they exchanged places.

"Before you leave, Isobel McGuinness, our director, wants to meet you both. She'll accompany me on your final home visit."

"The director? Does she always do home visits?"

"It's not unusual."

"How did it go?" Ross looked up from the magazine he was reading.

She stretched out the kinks in her back before sinking into the chair. "Not bad, but they asked a lot about you two."

"Don't worry." Eilidh smiled. "We'll explain whatever they want to know."

"If people had to go through such a strenuous process to get pregnant, there would be fewer children who require adoption and foster care."

"Too bad it's not required." Ross headed for the coffeepot. "Bonny, you want any?"

"Water, please. When Kieran's done, we're free until seven p.m. when we have the support group."

"What kind of questions did they ask?" He handed her a bottle of water and sat next to Eilidh. "I've always wondered. It might prove helpful in handling domestic situations."

The cool water trickled down Bonny's parched throat. "We talked a lot about my family, growing up, and my career. We discussed my acceptance of infertility, our marriage, my adjustment to Scotland, and farm life. She asked about the ages and backgrounds of children we'd consider and our attitudes about discipline. We talked about the effect our faith would have on discipline and teaching, any background of abuse or criminal charges, and my emotional state. They're nothing if not comprehensive."

Eilidh's eyebrows couldn't arch much higher. "Had you and Kieran talked about all those topics?"

"I doubt any couple thinks about them all, but there won't be much difference in our answers. You know how things come up when you're around friends or see a report on the news. We'll differ in some areas, but nothing essential."

She pulled a book from her purse, hoping to withdraw into solitude, when a petite woman with short-cropped gray hair opened the door. "Mrs. MacDonell,

I'm Isobel McGuinness. Would you join us, please?" Her piercing blue eyes held a mixture of intensity and *joie de vivre*.

Back in the office, Bonny took a seat next to Kieran and reached for his hand to ground herself.

"Mr. and Mrs. MacDonell, I want to discuss your security problems." The cadence of Mrs. McGuinness' speech held a peculiar familiarity.

Kieran's eyes widened, head tilted to the side with his mouth open. Did he sense the odd familiarity too?

"I spoke with DCI McLeod at great length. We've worked with couples who have security details before. Most of the time, they're high-profile people, but I find your situation disturbing."

Kieran squeezed Bonny's hand while she steeled herself for the rejection sure to come.

"You may be far safer than the average citizen in many respects," Mrs. McGuinness continued. "I'll accompany Rhona on her next visit. You have the ability to provide an excellent home for children. Go ahead and prepare your family notebooks for birthmothers. I have no doubt the board will approve you. We need more couples with your priorities of family and faith. However, placement will wait until any danger passes and your life is more stable. I'm excited to see your farm. Please don't let the delay discourage you or keep you from the support group tonight."

The walk out of the office was reminiscent of the walk away from the cemetery when her father died. The mist in her eyes blinded her. A cloudburst threatened in her heart, though the sun shone bright outside.

Kieran placed an arm around her shoulders and patted her for reassurance. "It's not forever, love. Perhaps our child isn't ready yet."

"How do we sit in a support group and act normal around people who are waiting for children, or have already received them? I can't do it. I can't."

"We're not the only ones who've experienced a delay for one reason or another." He urged her toward the car. "Delays don't take God by surprise and he's still in control. We weren't blind to the probability. We'll be fine."

"Tell me one thing that's gone right since we got married."

"We're more in love than ever. We had a lovely honeymoon. The chapel's open and growing." Gentle fingers massaged the knot between her shoulder blades. "It's sunny today. Mrs. McGuinness said we'd make perfect parents. We prayed for God's will and he didn't say 'no,' he said 'wait.' We'll come through the process stronger than ever, as individuals and as a couple."

Why were the tissues always in the bottom of her purse?

"What did they say." Eilidh's voice from behind sent a quiver through Bonny. How could she forget they followed?

"In the car." Kieran's hand moved to the door handle. "We'll head back to the hotel for a little while. Gavin's done it again without even showing up."

಼಼

An early autumn breeze scented with heather ushered Mrs. McGuinness and Rhona into the house. Bonny gave them her best smile, encouraged by their commitment to finish the approval process. "Welcome to Stonehaven. We have a lovely day to show you around the farm. I see you wore your wellies." Where in the world were Kieran and Ross? Of all times to be late.

"I'm a country girl, born and raised." Mrs. McGuinness tilted her head back when she stepped into the foyer, staring at the two-story portrait gallery of Kieran's ancestors. "There must be something in the air." She wiped watery eyes with a tissue. "These old homes are full of history. Is there a place reserved for your family, Mrs. MacDonell?"

"Call me Bonny, and yes, my pictures are in the hallway. My American family were poor farmers and pioneers. They lacked the land and wealth of the MacDonells, and had no grand family portraits, though I'm no less proud of my heritage."

"You should be. Pioneer stories fascinate me. Courageous people."

Kieran and Ross entered through the kitchen door, muddy and disheveled with Charlie at their heels. "Mrs. McGuinness, Rhona, sorry. We were delayed by a ram with its horns stuck in a bush." Kieran turned and pointed. "Charlie, bed."

Charlie settled next to Flora, and Mrs. McGuinness knelt beside the dogs, petting until both were eager to follow. "Call me Isobel, please. I assume you want to clean the mud off, though you don't have to worry on my account. Bonny can show me the downstairs. We're ready for our farm tour when you are. I love the smell of fresh, country air."

Kieran met them on the back stairs. "We'll take the Land Rover out to the pasture when you finish here or stop at the barns first. You ladies decide."

"Let's talk while we walk to the barn. I love your home, Kieran. Farms are the best place to grow up. Rhona tells me you might be interested in up to three children. We're excited to work with you."

"Only two children if they're older than toddlers. We want to be able to give them the individual attention they need." Kieran's nod reassured her. The delay wasn't difficult for him.

"Bonny, I assumed at your age and with your recent loss of a child, you might be more interested in newborns." Rhona's tone sounded much more serious than their previous conversations.

"I … I would love a newborn. But we know they're more difficult to adopt."

"Surprising things happen, the more flexible you are." Isobel headed for the coat rack. "Please allow the dogs to come. They add such enjoyment to life."

"Six more might show up at any time."

"The more the merrier." Isobel set a quick pace at Kieran's side leaving Rhona and Bonny to follow. "I'll hate to return to the city after a day out here. Tell me, Kieran, how many sheep and cattle do you have?"

What a perfect day to showcase the glory of Stonehaven. The loch shimmered in the sunshine, the grass beneath their feet sprinkled with the first fallen leaves. Spots of citrine, carnelian, and ruby winked amidst the evergreens, while patches of heather clothed the hillsides in purple splendor. Water lapped at the shore, the surface a glassy mirror for the clouds overhead.

"I love the smell of sheep and damp grass." Isobel pulled a sack of breadcrumbs from her pocket. "As a wee lassie, I passed many happy hours feeding ducks. To spend the day on a farm is a vacation day for me."

Eilidh smiled and winked as if to say, *I told you.*

"Rhona, have you ever spent time on a farm?" Bonny hoped to discover some subject to interest the quiet social worker.

"No. I grew up with Aberdeen's paved streets and granite-walled buildings. I enjoy the country, but I've never spent enough time to become comfortable here. How far are your nearest neighbors?" Rhona watched each step on their way across the pasture. Her boots still showed the sheen of newness, while Isobel's showed signs of hard use and wear.

Bonny motioned her to the gravel path. "About five miles, but a few farm workers and our housekeeper live in cottages on the other side of the barn."

Isobel stopped just inside the barn door, inhaled deeply, stared overhead at the ancient stonework, and commented on the spotless conditions. Her questions about the size and types of flocks hinted at more than a passing familiarity with sheep farming.

The tight lines of Rhona's face relaxed when they climbed into the Land Rover and headed toward the chapel. Perhaps she'd enjoy it more if she didn't worry about where she stepped.

"You can't cross the bridge with the ladies today." Ross, who had gone on ahead, stomped toward them, his voice terse with warning. Bonny's heart thumped out a couple of extra beats. "There's a problem on the far side. I've phoned the detectives."

The Land Rover sat near the chapel door and they all jumped out. "Go ahead and tell us. We can't keep secrets from these ladies."

Ross motioned toward the bridge. "Wally and Marion are lying dead just inside the gate to the Greenfield pasture. We'll download the video from the chapel cameras before Alasdair and McLeod arrive. Perhaps we caught something."

Bonny's lungs deflated like a punctured balloon. She brushed her sleeve across her eyes.

Eilidh held the dogs by their collars. "I'll drive you back to the house while Ross sorts it out. Gavin Gunn chose a fine day to break months of silence."

"Wally and Marion?" Rhona's eyes matched the size of the giant mums nodding outside the chapel door. "Employees?"

"Ten-year-old English sheepdogs." Kieran's voice choked. "Faithful friends."

"How could anyone kill those sweet, loveable dogs?" Bonny's voice quivered. "They were so gentle and dependable."

"The same way they could kill lambs or threaten you. They're sick." Eilidh looked back when she climbed into the driver's seat.

They rode to the house in silence. "Leave Flora and Charlie outside for now." When they were all in the kitchen, Eilidh began locking doors. "Eleanor, please serve our guests. Thanks for coming to help on your day off."

"I'm sorry we can't give you the tour." Bonny motioned them back into the living room. "By the way, I want you to meet Eleanor, our housekeeper. She's more family than an employee, a second mother to us both."

Mrs. McGuinness nodded and turned her attention back to Bonny. "Please, don't feel your chances are ruined. We still have to go over all the reports before the board approves you, but I don't anticipate a lengthy delay. It's obvious you have excellent safety precautions though the constraints of such security must be trying." The director's words were reassuring.

Eleanor set the tea tray down and stopped, staring at Isobel, eyes widened, though the social worker's attention remained on Bonny. She scurried from the room. Her startled eyes gave the impression she'd seen a ghost.

"How do you deal with the constant uncertainty? The loss of long-time pets feels like you've lost friends."

"It's become old in a hurry. Everyone on the farm loved those dogs." Bonny struggled to keep the bitter taste in her mouth from tainting her words. Eleanor's tea and biscuits held no appeal now.

"And the police have no leads?" Rhona's voice quivered.

"They have a person of interest, but he's proved very elusive. Don't worry. The police will escort you to the main road."

Eilidh's phone rang, and she excused herself. Her smile wide when she returned. "They got him on the cameras. Ladies, if I can answer any questions, please don't hesitate to ask."

"Can they identify him?" Hope beat in Bonny's heart.

"Not so far. The image is very grainy from the rain last night."

"I hope they can apprehend the guilty parties. I'm sorry about the delay of your placement. You're the sort of family we need." Isobel's voice remained calm. "Show us your albums for the birthmothers. We'll get out of your way whenever the police are available to escort us."

By the time the women looked through the albums, Hugh MacFadyen arrived to escort them to the A87.

Rhona waved with unmistakable eagerness. Isobel stopped and lowered her car window before they turned onto the single-track. "Thank you for your hospitality. I expect a raincheck on the complete tour. Please, don't worry. Keep in touch and stay safe."

"She's offering encouragement, love." Kieran held the door. "We can't change the circumstances, but we know the one who can."

A lump in her throat the size of a boulder stayed her tears until the door closed. "You're calm because an immediate placement would frighten you. If this attempt fails, we'll never have children. Are you ready to give up on any hope of family?"

"Let's go to our room where we can have some privacy."

A flood of tears loosed halfway up the stairs. Once they were alone, Kieran sat on the couch, patted the spot beside him, and offered his handkerchief. The scent of damp wool, sweat, and Kieran only increased the pain.

"Look at me, love. I desire your happiness and God's will. And I do want a family. Never think my hesitancy means I don't care. If God gives us a child through adoption, I'll be more excited than any time except the day you married me."

CHAPTER SEVENTEEN

The jewel-tones of autumn faded. Leaves had been trodden underfoot, and skeletal gray branches pointed skyward like fingers. The first powdered-sugar snow dusted the ground, yet still no progress by the detectives, unable to identify the person on the security video, and no news from the adoption agency. Helpless and windblown as a leaf with its glory gone, approaching holidays and life itself generated no enthusiasm in Bonny.

She and Kieran walked along the loch with Eilidh, Ross, and the dogs. The daily ritual brought a degree of relaxation to all of them. A year ago, Brennan Grant shot Kieran. Who could have guessed the fear of that day would linger and increase? In spite of their trials, the nearness of their first wedding anniversary marked a year of happiness and fulfillment greater than she ever imagined.

Along with joy came the bittersweet memory of stars in her husband's eyes at the news of her pregnancy and a Christmas marked by name selection and nursery planning. Now, their lives hung in limbo, controlled by fear and uncertainty.

Ross's cell phone jangled. "Inspector, what's up?"

Bonny grasped Kieran's arm with both hands.

"She what? Of course. We'll be waiting." He pocketed his phone and looked skyward. "Deirdre Adair turned herself in to the police a few hours ago. Her real last name is MacDonell and her brother, Gavin MacDonell is Gavin Gunn. He beat her, but she escaped. She's in protective custody at the hospital in Fort William."

The air left Bonny's lungs in a whoosh. "Brennan told the truth?"

Kieran pried her fingers from his arm. "Your nails are sharp, love."

"The detectives will be here soon." Ross motioned toward the house. "Let's get inside where you're safe. Maybe we'll have cause to celebrate before long."

She searched his eyes. "I'm afraid to hope."

"Eilidh and I aren't out of a job yet." Ross followed them inside and locked the door. "If Deirdre's escaped, there's no way to predict what Gavin might do."

Her knees gave way and she sank into a kitchen chair. "I've never understood why he waits such a long time between attacks, but her absence might instigate one."

"The chap's a *bampot.* He may not have the intelligence or means to carry out all the threats he's made. For that reason, he could be even more dangerous." Ross echoed her inclination as he closed and locked windows.

"He's managed to destroy a good portion of our sheep and steal an entire flock, which says something." Kieran stomped into the foyer and checked the front door.

"Let's not take chances." Eilidh helped empty the dishwasher while the men secured the rest of the house. Charlie and Flora jumped and barked in excitement when Alasdair and McLeod arrived.

"Deirdre's been tortured and beaten," DCI McLeod said. "I'm amazed she made it to Shiel Bridge from their hiding place near Glen Affric. Gavin beat her with the butt of a shotgun and kicked her. Her right arm's fractured in two places. She suffered a concussion, three broken ribs, a cut over one eye, and serious bruises. Officers are on the way now."

"Glen Affric?" Bonny quaked like an aspen leaf in the wind. "So close? No wonder you couldn't find him in Caithness."

"Did she shed any light on what her brother might do?" Kieran moved closer.

For once, Alasdair refused tea in favor of water. He couldn't tap his spoon on the saucer. "Aye, he doesn't give her information ahead of time, though he gloats after the fact. She's been a prisoner off and on for years, but in the past few weeks, he became more agitated and said the time had come to end the stand-off with Kieran."

Bonny gasped. "Does she know what he meant?"

"Aye, he plans to kill you both. He caught Deirdre when she attempted an escape to warn you. Says he forced her to participate. A psychologist took over when she claimed emotional abuse." McLeod's gentle voice reminded her more of a pastor than a police officer. "We'll have officers check around the house, bridge, chapel, and barns daily for a while."

Ross looked up from the notes he scribbled. "What about the cottage?"

"We have a team in the area now." Alasdair leaned forward in his chair. "We're very close to closing the case."

The fragrance from her balsam candles soothed Bonny, and she rotated her neck and shoulders to ease the tension. "Take him alive and make him pay for what he's done."

"I'd like nothing better." McLeod's lips slanted into the closest approximation of a smile he had ever shown.

Distrust swirled with unbelief and shock. She took a long drink of the warm chamomile Eilidh handed her.

"How do we know she can be trusted?" One glance at Kieran's gray-shadowed eyes set her nerves tingling. "One of her brothers shot me, and the other wants to. Their family isn't noted for favors."

Alasdair's phone vibrated. "Oh my." He excused himself, reentered a moment later, and sank into his chair. "I will take a cup of tea, Eilidh." When she pushed it across the table, he scooped in enough sugar to precipitate a trip to the dentist, stirring until the inspector cleared his throat. He swallowed half the cup and sloshed the remains into the saucer, his pasty complexion gone gray. "There's no good way to explain other than to say it straight out. Deirdre claims he raped her. She tried to escape and reach her mother in Aberdeen. When he left, she took off again."

Bonny rested her forehead on her hands to stop the room spinning. "How horrible!"

"It's gone on since she was a child." Alasdair's voice sounded a funeral dirge.

Her vision swam as her stomach flipped upside-down. "I feel sick to my stomach."

"I'm sorry, Bonny. I know it's hard to hear. Perhaps you should lie down." Kieran scooped her into his arms and headed for the library.

She shoved against his chest. "I'm not a child. Put me down so Alasdair can continue."

He settled her on the couch and the others drew chairs around. He sat close and rubbed her hands to warm them. Alasdair continued at Bonny's nod. "She's suffered lifelong abuse."

Kieran frowned. "Why didn't she stay with her mother?"

"Gavin abducted her whenever she tried. They found her mother too, a Brighde MacDonell."

Kieran let her hand fall. "My father's sister is alive?"

"Your father's sister?" McLeod's eyes mirrored Kieran's. "You're certain?"

"The mother confirmed it, and you know her." Alasdair nodded toward Kieran. "It's Isobel McGuinness from Forever Family."

Kieran dropped to his knees. "How did Brighde MacDonell become Isobel McGuinness? Why didn't she contact us in all these years?"

"It's complicated. Isobel's her middle name. She married a Robbie Adair, the father of Brennan Grant, about thirty years ago after Taran's death, and moved to Aberdeen. We don't know all the answers yet." He sat back and thumbed through his notes.

"You'd better fill me in." McLeod glanced from Alasdair to Kieran and back.

"Hold on." Kieran stood and headed for the foyer. "Isobel McGuinness asked a lot of questions about the family and farm. I sensed something familiar about her from the day we met—her eyes, her voice." He headed toward the foyer and re-entered with a portrait. "My grandmother, Isobel Grant MacDonell." He filled the gaps in the story while McLeod's expression changed from puzzled to impatient.

"Grant." The inspector scratched his head. "As in Brennan. And you never suspected the relationship?"

"Never. No one in the family mentioned them until Da told me after the attack. Why would I have put them together?" Kieran nodded. "Look at her face, Bonny. I remember her—smaller than you, with pure white hair and eyes blue as a Scottish sky."

"Like Isobel." Bonny wiped her cheeks. "Call your father. What a gift to find the beloved sister he believed was dead is alive."

ભ્ર

Dressed in a soft-blue business suit, short, white hair curled around her face, Isobel McGuinness sat wadding a tissue in her hands when they entered the conference room at the Fort William police station. Bonny held her breath. Hamish crossed the room, knelt before her, and cupped her face in his hands. "Brighde, my wee sister, all these years we thought you were dead along with your *bairn*." Tears poured down his cheeks like water over a spillway. "I never imagined I would see my Brighde again. *Tha gaol agam ort, mo phiuthar.*" My sister.

Her eyes were the twins of Hamish's, in a lovely, feminine face. Her interest in the farm, the family portraits, the sheep, her earliest memories, all made sense.

Maggie stepped forward, handkerchief in hand. "Dear Brighde, why did you not come to us? We would have helped you. We might have convinced your da to let us take your baby, given time."

Brighde leaned into her brother's embrace, their tears mingling. "Hamish, please forgive me. My strong will and fancied love for Taran led to nothing but shame and abuse. Now it endangers your family. Taran bred hate. To my shame, Gavin does the same. I'll try to help the police put Gavin behind bars, where his father belonged."

Hamish looked up. "Belonged? They executed him years ago."

"No, *mo bhrathair,* Taran escaped prison. I lived with his family in Caithness when he reappeared a few months before our son, Gavin, was born. I should have listened to Da. We married, but he beat me into obedience and filled our son's heart with hate. He seduced me and made my life miserable because I represented everything his family lost. He died in a pub fight when I was three months pregnant with Deirdre. I never gave them the satisfaction of crying except when Diarmid refused my request to return home. After Taran died, his father continued the cruel control I hoped to escape. He ruined any influence I might have had on Gavin with bitterness and lies about the land he signed over to you."

The man at her side placed a protective arm around her. "*Wheesht, mo chridhe,* you did your best." He extended one hand toward Hamish. "Robbie McGuinness Adair, Isobel's husband. My family owned the store where she shopped. I saw the signs of abuse and befriended her, offered my help. After Taran's death, we fell in love, escaped to Inverness, and married. We took my mother's maiden name, McGuinness, in an attempt to hide. We did our best for Gavin, but he stole Deirdre and Brennan when they were very young."

Kieran sank into the nearest chair. "My own cousins are out to destroy me? Your daughter, my own cousin, tried to seduce me?"

She crossed the room to Kieran, accompanied by a peaceful cloud of lavender scent. "Deirdre didn't know. Gavin took them back to Caithness when they were ten and twelve. He made their lives a nightmare and robbed the purity of his own sister with more cruelty than Taran stole mine. Please forgive all the pain I caused."

"Forgiveness comes from God. I can't deny it to you, Auntie Brighde, or do you prefer Isobel?" Kieran rested a hand on her shoulder.

"Auntie Brighde is more than I ever dreamed to hear. Isobel's a character I created to hide and to make amends for the pain my foolishness caused. Robbie's been my source of strength and help through these thirty years. He rescued me, though our children are lost to us. When I saw your name and the address of Loch Garry, I couldn't resist a chance to return to my old home."

"Isobel … Brighde. I don't believe Deirdre or Brennan are lost." Bonny's tears dripped on the hand she grasped. "Her notes, even what she said at a *ceilidh* in our home, indicate she's an unwilling participant. Go to her, and ask God to go before you."

"I have no doubt you believe it's true, but God turned his back on me years ago. If I owe anyone, it's Robbie." She smiled up at him. "We'll do what we can."

"The Lord never turns away from us, even when we turn from him." Hamish embraced his wee sister. "We may not understand, but he brought you home at last."

The sun shone high overhead when they left the police station. Hamish and Maggie walked alongside Brighde and Robbie to the police car waiting to drive them to the hospital. When Brighde seated herself in the car, Hamish leaned in to kiss her cheek. "Come home tonight, baby sister—to the farm. We have so much to catch up on, and you need to be near your daughter."

"You'd welcome us, after what I've put you through?"

"Forgiveness comes from the Lord. We can do no less. It's time we got reacquainted. I can't let you out of my sight. I'll never forgive myself for not helping you more."

Robbie nodded to her. "Thank you, we'll come."

"Who knew what a miracle God had in store," Bonny said, reaching for her mother-in-law's hand.

"My dear, doesn't he always?" Maggie kissed her cheek. "Warn Eleanor we have guests to prepare for."

"I don't think she'll be surprised from the way she looked at Brighde the day she visited the farm." Her cell phone rang before she could dial Eleanor. "Graeme, oh my goodness, do we have a story for you."

"Janet went into labor a few hours ago. Don't you check your messages?" Graeme's voice was high-pitched with excitement.

"It's been a peculiar day, to say the least. We'll be right there." She stuffed her phone in her purse. "Janet's in labor. They want us at the hospital."

Maggie took Hamish by the arm and headed for their car. "Give them our best. We'll go on to the farm."

Quiet through all the family drama, Ross held up his hand. "Wait, Mr. and Mrs. MacDonell. I want you to have a police escort."

Hamish beamed. "My wee Brighde—alive."

ים

Bonny's jittery nerves began to settle. She dozed in a chair until the nurse informed them they'd be allowed to see Janet and Graeme soon. "I'm such a mess of emotions I don't know what I feel." The curve of Kieran's arm formed a solid pillow while they waited to meet the newest member of the MacDholl family. "Our loss and my determination to pursue adoption led to your aunt. Between the miracle of Brighde and a new baby, we should feel only joy."

"We're certainly never bored protecting you two," Eilidh said. "I know it's been terrible, but you're due for some happiness."

The door to the waiting room opened, and a nurse appeared. "Mr. and Mrs. MacDonell, Dr. Moncrieffe says you may see the new baby. Your friends are allowed as well."

When they entered the room, Janet looked up from the bundle in her arms. Graeme motioned them close to see a tiny red face peeking out of the blankets. "Uncle Kieran and Aunt Bonny, meet Brody Kieran MacDholl."

Kieran's mouth dropped open. "You named him after me?"

"And Graeme's father." Janet smiled. "You're our best friends."

Bonny touched the soft cheek with one finger. Perhaps one day it would be their turn. For now, she rejoiced in a reunited family.

αβ

Gavin Gunn had disappeared into a black hole. None of Deirdre's tips led to success. Bonny stared out at the loch. He could be anywhere in the unpopulated wilds of the Scottish Highlands. Would their lives remain forever on hold?

Hamish and Maggie had a wonderful visit with Brighde and Robbie in Aberdeen. It would be a while before Deirdre became comfortable enough to see her and Kieran. In the meantime, they prayed for all of their new-found cousins. A definite act of obedience because her emotions lagged far behind.

Bonny closed her Bible and went downstairs where Eilidh stood at the Aga with Flora at her heels. "I decided mutton stew sounded good today. I'm a much better cook than before we came here."

"The aroma of stew on a fall day is perfect, and I'm sure it will be delicious. At home, it's time to prepare for Thanksgiving. Maybe we should order a turkey to pick up next time we're in Fort William. I still haven't convinced Kieran to raise a few." She reached for two mugs from the cabinet.

Eilidh accepted the tea with a smile and leaned against the granite island. "Are you having a hard day? Your eyes are red and swollen. Shall we take the horses and find our husbands?"

"I'm in a miserable mood again. So much has happened. You must be tired of my doldrums by now." Each leaf in the wind reminded her of another hope drifting away to be trampled and decayed. "I remember your comment about all our prayers, and I do believe God orchestrated everything. But we're blind to his timing and can't conceive of the marvelous ways he works."

Eilidh studied her over the rim of her mug. "I'll give it some thought. I don't mind your moods. The chance to stay in one place with people who've become good friends is by far the best assignment we've ever had."

She traced circles in the dust on the window. "It could turn into a lifelong job if there's no break soon." Her phone chimed Brahms Lullaby. She chose the ringtone for the adoption agency when hopes were high. "What could they possibly want? Hello, this is Bonny."

The world went into slow motion. Eilidh guided her into a chair, handing her a tablet, pen, and a tissue. Following questions and scribbled notes, Bonny lay the phone down, afraid to speak when her thoughts swirled in a rainbow, which threatened to explode and paint the room in color.

"Are you all right?" Eilidh's voice reached through the muddle, and she raised her head.

"It was Brighde. They have an emergency placement. In light of Inspector McLeod's reassurances, and their desperate need for families, the board wants us to consider a little girl who needs a home immediately." A chill shivered through her limbs, and she rubbed her arms.

Eilidh retrieved her phone from its holder on her belt. "I'll tell Ross to bring Kieran home now."

"It's so complicated. I only want to explain the details once when Kieran comes." She pushed the chair back toward the table and grabbed another tissue. "Eilidh, what if he says no?"

Her lips widened in a smile. "I'll handcuff him in the pantry until he comes to his senses."

Bonny's heart fluttered like a flock of ducks when breadcrumbs land in the water. "We could be parents tomorrow."

The men stopped just inside the door, faces red and huffing after their run from the barn.

"What's wrong?" Ross panted.

Bonny grasped Kieran's hands and bounced on the balls of her feet. "Your Auntie Brighde called. They need a family for an emergency placement tomorrow. They want us."

His face paled. "Slow down, hen. Tell me what she said."

"Sit. They need an answer before the end of today. A grandmother who's cared for an eighteen-month-old since birth received a diagnosis of terminal cancer. They need an immediate home for the little girl. The sixteen-year-old will deliver a son in two months but can't raise either of them. They want to keep the siblings together. The grandmother's scheduled for surgery in two days and wants to meet the new parents first. This is in preparation for a permanent placement. Kieran, we could have two children."

He closed his eyes. "What do they know about the birthmother? Can we call Brighde for some answers? I know what it means to you, love, but think of the wee lassie, taken from her grandmother and given to unprepared strangers? What do we know about an eighteen-month-old? And we're not out of danger yet."

"We don't know much about a newborn or an eighteen-month-old." One deep breath turned to two and then three. "She suggested we call when you got back."

"No. First, we pray." In the circle of his arms, she bowed her head. *Dear God, let him say yes.*

"Lord, we have no idea of your plans from one moment to the next. You know both our desire for a family and my own uncertainties. We need guidance to do what's best for the girl and her brother. Show us what we need to know."

"Amen, Lord." Bonny tiptoed to kiss his cheek, retrieved the phone from his shirt pocket, and dialed. Brighde answered on the second ring and he put the phone on speaker.

They could hear Brighde chuckle. "Kieran, you remind me of your father when it comes to minute details. You've asked more questions than most adoptive parents can even think of. I texted you a snap of the little girl. She's bi-racial, half-black with dark blonde hair and the bluest eyes. Other than the color of her skin, no one would believe she's adopted. Ainslie Blair's a wee lassie in the fifth percentile on the growth scale. If she takes after her mother and grandmother, she'll remain small. It's rare to see such an outgoing, adaptable child."

"Auntie, we're not ready. We have a crib along with toys for children at the chapel. I'm not sure I'm ready to adopt a child. Have you forgotten we're not out of danger?" His eyes widened and he mouthed, "Help."

"Listen." Bonny shrugged her shoulders and pointed to the phone.

"Excuses, Kieran. You can get whatever you can't find in Fort William when you arrive in Aberdeen. There's no history of drug use. The mother made some bad choices. The father's no longer in the picture. The grandmother's cared for Ainslie since birth, and the mother is completely unequipped. I think if you see the child, it will provide the answers you're searching for."

Bonny tried to keep up while he circled through the kitchen, hallway, library, and living room. "We don't even have time to discuss it. What will Mother say?"

"Your parents won't have a problem with the child. We had a long talk when they visited me. DCI McLeod assures me you're safer than most people." Bonny imagined the twinkle in Brighde's eyes resembled Kieran when he was one up on someone. "Call me tonight if necessary. Ainslie's a very bright little girl. The birthmother wants no contact. Our foster homes are above capacity. She needs a family. Now."

Though business-like, Brighde gave a clear picture of a child in need. Bonny opened the text and showed Kieran a smiling little girl dressed in bright pink who clutched a doll by one arm. The picture showed a cherubic child with a hint of mischief around her almost turquoise eyes and skin the color of a mocha latte.

He swallowed hard, clenching his jaw.

"Any more questions?"

She leaned close to the phone. "What do you know about the mother?"

Papers shuffled. "Petite. Blonde. Blue-eyed. From Aberdeen. Dropped out of school. Works in a market. The grandmother took Ainslie at a few weeks old because of an abusive father. The new baby's due in seven weeks. The doctor thinks he may come early because they estimate his weight at ten pounds already. Ainslie's father's parental rights were terminated by the court. The new baby's birthfather agrees to the adoption. His parents both teach at university. He's about your size, Kieran, blond hair, blue eyes, a footballer for Victoria United. They had a very brief relationship."

Kieran cleared his throat. "Auntie, we need to talk and pray. Can we meet the grandmother with the understanding we're not certain yet?"

"Of course." The hollowness in Brighde's voice echoed in the emptiness of Bonny's heart when momentary hope hit the rock wall of Kieran's hard-head.

"I appreciate it, Auntie. We'll see you in the morning."

Bonny sank into a chair at the dining room table, because he stopped there. Her chest burned as if she had run ten miles. "Kieran, I can't believe you'd consider stopping now. It's cruel to make a sick woman feel we're inspecting her granddaughter to see if she's good enough."

He pocketed his phone and lifted her to her feet. "Bonny, we're talking about a child's life. We need to be positive we're a good fit. Did you ever think the grandmother might have reservations about us?"

"These children are meant for us. Kieran, we'll never have a child with your eyes and my nose. We have to trust the God we've prayed to all these months."

He pulled her so close she heard pounding in his chest.

She had no words beyond the aching plea of her heart.

ೞ∞

The stark granite office building looked less formidable than before. Bonny shoved her own car door open and stepped out the second Ross stopped. Visions of a fluffy white comforter she'd seen in a catalog, covered with bunnies, ducks, and pigs with pink-and-blue bows around their necks danced through her mind laced with fears. Kieran might still refuse. Perhaps she'd never hear a child call her *Mama*.

The cold metal of the office door handle steamed when she touched it. Her breath disappeared in a puff of mist the way her dreams would if he allowed this door to close.

He reached for the handle and pulled it open. "I haven't said no."

Brighde, still Isobel at the office, stood behind the reception desk. A bright-red jacket and black skirt created the picture of efficiency and beauty. Her smile, coupled with Kieran's words made Bonny tingle from head to toe. She might soon embrace their child—the child they decided to call Ainslie *Grace* Blair during the long night. And she relied on God's grace now to convince Kieran.

"Come into my office, all four of you." Brighde opened the door and stood to one side, motioning them toward the circle of chairs. "Before we meet Ainslie and her grandmother, I want to discuss your situation. Would you consider hiring someone specifically to protect the baby?"

To Bonny's relief, Kieran nodded a yes. "Funds are tight but we'll find a way if Ainslie is the child for us."

"We know the perfect person." Eilidh looked at Ross. "Nanny and former police officer extraordinaire, Jess Poulson. You'll love her, and I happen to know she recently finished an assignment."

"A bodyguard who knows about children?" Bonny wondered if everyone heard her heart, it pounded so hard. Was it right to ask a grandmother to send a child into their nightmare?

"The best. Should I step out and call her?" Eilidh slid to the edge of her seat.

"No, I want these two to visit the playroom and meet Ainslie first." Brighde stood.

Kieran's hand engulfed Bonny's when the sound of little girl giggles issued from behind a door down the hall. Brighde opened it and ushered them into the room where a thin, gray-haired woman bent from her chair to stack blocks on the rug. She no sooner piled up three or four, when a beautiful child with tight, blonde curls and *café au lait* skin knocked them over with a deep, belly laugh.

The child turned when the door closed, and Bonny paused. Ainslie's eyes shone a brilliant aquamarine against dark skin and startling golden curls. She stared with curiosity at the newcomers.

"Hi!" Ainslie grinned and turned back to knock the blocks over again.

"Bonny, Kieran, I want you to meet Ainslie and her grandmother, Mary." Brighde seated herself next to the woman and motioned them to chairs. "How are you today, Mary?"

"If only I would wake up and discover I'm having a bad dream." She dabbed her cheeks with a tissue. Her eyes roved to the child, attempting to stack blocks herself.

Mary wore her hair drawn into a tight bun, her deep lined face the same shade of gray. Neat, but worn clothes hung on her frail frame like on a clothes hanger. The brilliant blue of her eyes matched her granddaughter's. "I'd be grateful if you could give Ainslie a home. My daughter, Bethan, won't raise her, and I'm not going to live long. She's a lovely child. Happy, obedient, and a good sleeper." Ainslie tugged at the woman's twisted pants leg, and she stooped to stack the blocks again.

"We're very sorry about your illness. May I call you Mary?" Bonny lowered herself to the floor next to the cherubic child.

"Of course. I appreciate you coming to meet us."

"You need to feel comfortable with us … for Ainslie's sake." Kieran's voice cracked with emotion, and compassion shone from his eyes.

"Mrs. McGuinness says you've had some trouble. She assured me it's well in hand and you have excellent protection. I don't have long, Mr. MacDonell." Mary's eyes teared, a desperate plea for help. "Your notebook gave me all the information I need. You're fine, Christian people who will raise my babies right. I want to die knowing my bairns are loved. You'll love my Ainslie and her baby brother?"

"Of course, but we have no way to know when trouble will strike."

Ainslie turned at the sound of his voice, one tiny hand still fisted around a block. She stood and toddled across the room toward Kieran, reaching out her hand.

He stared—mesmerized, then lowered himself to the floor. Bonny held her breath when Ainslie reached out a chubby hand and touched his cheek. "Hi." She stepped between his legs and wrapped her arms around his neck. "Wike you, man."

"Well, I like you too." Kieran's eyes widened. Cheeks wet with tears, he looked first at Bonny then Brighde. "It appears I've been adopted."

Bonny's heart lodged in her throat, a pulsating knot of emotion, love, and gratitude.

"I prayed for a sign. It couldn't get much clearer." He placed a tentative arm around the child, ready to pull back should she become frightened. Ainslie wiggled closer. He picked her up. When he buried his face in her curls a sob escaped.

"It's a miracle for certain." Mary's poignant exclamation ended on a note of surprise. "Having no da, she's not around many men. She hides behind my leg at church. I believe God intends you to raise my lassie and he will protect you."

"Take time to get acquainted." Brighde headed for the door, brushing tears away with her hand. "I'll be back to help you handle the formalities when you're ready."

Mary had planned everything out. Bonny listened attentively. She needed to remember every detail to relate to Ainslie when she was old enough.

The dear woman wanted them to take Ainslie's crib, toys, and clothes to provide her with familiarity. Gifts from her grandmother with love. In the short time since her diagnosis, she'd prepared a hand-written family history, a photo album, and letters for when both children were older. She asked them to visit her home the next day, take Ainslie out to a playground, and to spend the night at their hotel. They would stop to say goodbye on their way out of town.

Mary's daughter, Bethan, planned to sign the relinquishment papers when the new baby was born so they could take him home straight from the hospital.

The way Mary turned her eyes upward now and then, made Bonny believe she already saw the gates of heaven and needed this one detail in order before they opened on its glory.

⊰⊱

All the way to the hotel, Bonny fought the fluttering in her stomach and a non-stop need to pinch herself. A dream-like quality permeated the entire situation.

Alone in their room, she perched on the edge of the bed. "Kieran, in spite of Mary's generosity, we need to furnish two nurseries. I know we don't have a lot of extra money right now. How much can we do?"

He knelt in front of her. "God answered all of our prayers. How can I deny you the joy of decorating their rooms? Shop for anything you need. I'll call Angus and tell him to sell some of the cattle. We'll not scrimp where these babies are concerned. Mary was generous in giving us clothes and furniture. I've seen your list of baby items. Enjoy."

"You're sure?" He nodded, and she retrieved the paper from her purse. "While you and Ross make arrangements to move Ainslie's belongings, Eilidh and I will take a cab downtown. We can buy them right here in Aberdeen."

"Just bear in mind there are two of them." He tucked a strand of hair behind her ear.

"We'll also pick out paint. Your parents offered to buy it in Fort William and have Seumas and Jamie paint the room when I find the right color." When she hugged him, the sweet scent of little girl still mingled with his own. "Will you be da or daddy?"

"Mary told her she'd have a daddy and mummy. Do you sense God's control in the entire situation?" He grinned. "I can't wait to hear our daughter say it."

Our daughter. Exhausted with emotion and excitement, sleep refused to come. Tears alternated with laughter through a night cuddled in Kieran's arms dreaming about a pink bedroom, a nursery for the soon-to-be-born baby brother, and an eighteen-month-old who would miss her grandmother.

⊰⊱

"Tell her she was loved," Mary whispered when Kieran picked up Ainslie to carry her to the car.

"She will never doubt you loved her and did your best for her." Bonny accepted framed photographs Mary removed from the wall and a shelf in the corner, sacrificing her own memories for her grandchildren. The grandfather Ainslie never knew. Pictures of her mother showed a little girl, identical except for skin color. Mary holding her as a newborn. Legacy and love.

With the baby secure in the car seat, Kieran lifted Bonny and turned in a slow circle. "We have a family, love. She's the most beautiful child I've ever seen."

A thorny rose bloomed in Bonny's heart, beauty and pain together.

Chapter Eighteen

Their welcome committee consisted of Kieran's parents, Eleanor, Angus, and a young blonde in jeans and a blue sweater, their baby's protector. The bubble of joy he hadn't anticipated threatened to burst when Ainslie kept her face hidden against his shoulder until Bonny coaxed her with a biscuit. Even if her grip loosened, he felt no desire to let anyone else hold her. Even a child of his own blood couldn't feel more perfect—more their own.

"Ach, you've a real beauty on your hands, son. You'll have to fight off every wee lad in the church nursery." Hamish shifted from one foot to the other, anxious to pick up his granddaughter, sheltered in Kieran's arms, thumb in mouth.

Bonny shook her head. "I've only held her a couple of times. She chose him. I came along with the deal."

Jess Poulson laughed. "Nonsense, comfort grows over time."

His daughter's bodyguard already fit in. "Did they finish her room?"

"Late last night." Maggie laughed. "You should have seen Seumas and Jamie. You'd think those two had never seen a little girl's room in their lives. The baby furniture and crib arrived about two hours before you did. With Jess's help, it's all sorted out."

"I can't imagine Seumas and Jamie around a baby. I can learn a thing or two from you, Jess. You seem very comfortable with everything." Bonny fingered the plump hand Ainslie rested on her father's arm.

When he laid the sleeping baby in the crib, he reached for Bonny. She wrapped her arms around him. The answer to their prayers lay snuggled under a pink blanket, dolly clutched tight.

There were no words. A peaceful sensation settled around him with the warmth of a hug, unlike anything he'd ever experienced.

Bonny bent to kiss Ainslie's forehead. Kieran kissed a petal-soft cheek, inhaling the sweet, baby scent. Then they both stepped out, crossed the hall to their own room, and turned on the baby monitor.

"I think you're going to have to quit work and stay with your daughter all day. She wants no one but you."

"*My* daughter. Why do you think she wants me?"

"Children sense love. Your sweet, gentle manner communicates acceptance and security to everyone. I'm no longer the only girl in your life, and I don't mind one bit."

"I'm surprised she's not afraid since there's never been a father in her life." He headed for the closet. "We should go to bed. If she wakes up, we might have trouble getting her back to sleep."

Bonny reached for her gown. "She'd drop right back to sleep again in your arms. I suspect you'll spend lots of time in the comfy rocker I put in there. Give her a dolly and daddy, and she's a happy girl."

"Daddy. I like it."

"Jess says all of a sudden we'll know we're parents." She stuffed her feet into slippers and headed for the bathroom. "I still can't get over how fast everything happened."

"She came to me, love. I knew God had chosen this child for us the second Ainslie giggled."

Her arms wrapped around him from behind. "We have a lot to be thankful for, but I may fall asleep before we finish our prayers."

☙❧

"Nana!" The baby monitor amplified the screams from across the hall.

Kieran's eyes popped open. Daylight peeped around the edges of the blinds. Ainslie had slept through the night. "Bonny, you go." He stretched and rolled out of bed. "She needs to know you can comfort her."

She paused with her robe half on, hand on the doorknob, quivering. "But she wants Mary, not us."

"Pick her up and see what happens. Auntie Brighde warned us to be prepared for a tough time since the entire placement moved so fast." He grabbed his robe and followed her into the hall, stopping at the door.

Holding onto the crib rail, Ainslie stood with her dolly clutched close, eyes red, and nose dripping. "Nana!"

"Mummy's here, Ainslie." The tiny body stiffened when Bonny lifted her.

"No. Nana."

"Carry her and her dolly to the kitchen. I'll start the porridge." Kieran headed downstairs before the wailing little girl caught sight of him.

"It's under control, son." Maggie stood at the Aga with a pot of porridge ready. "You needed sleep, but babies always wake up hungry. The highchair and bib are ready."

Eilidh, Ross, Jess, and Hamish sat at the table with empty bowls and smiles.

Kieran stayed in the hallway while Bonny entered with the baby, who silenced like magic and pointed, feet kicking when she saw her bright-pink sippy cup, familiar bowl, and child-sized silverware with animal handles. He stayed out of sight while she fed the baby the entire bowl of porridge. Ainslie drank from the cup on her own while she looked around with eyes wide. He didn't realize how hungry he'd been to see Bonny mothering their child. Funny, he had no trouble believing Ainslie belonged to them.

She laid her cup on its side and looked around. "Nana?"

"Mummy and Daddy are here." When Bonny wiped her face clean, removed the bib, and lifted her from the chair, Kieran came out of hiding.

"Da?" Little arms reached toward him.

"So much for daddy. She'll call you what she wants." Maggie set the cup upright and retrieved the empty bowl. "Stick close for a few days until she feels more at home."

Ainslie leaped for him. Small arms circled his neck and legs wrapped around his middle. She held on with all her might, face hidden against him. He buried his lips in her sweet-smelling curls. "*Mo nighean.*"

Bonny stepped closer and hugged them both. Hamish snapped a picture.

"I never knew love could grow so strong so fast." Kieran attempted to clear the emotions clogging his throat. "My girls. You were right all along, Bonny. God created a family for us."

"Since the entire family's together, we have some news for you." Ross draped an arm around his wife's shoulders.

"All these months, we've watched you. No matter what the problem, you turned to God. After talking about it for weeks, we prayed the prayer you say at the end of the church service."

"You accepted Jesus as your Lord and Savior?" Bonny jumped out of her chair to hug Eilidh. "How wonderful."

"We never felt any pressure. You lived what you believe in front of us on a daily basis, no matter what went wrong." Ross accepted Kieran's handshake.

Eilidh's eyes shone. "The miracle of little Ainslie, the way God reunited you with Brighde, proved what you said about God having a plan. We believe."

"How perfect. Yes, now we're truly family. All along, I thought my moods, fear, and angry outbursts were detrimental to anyone learning from me." Bonny grabbed a napkin to wipe her eyes.

"You were honest and real in front of us. I can trust a God big enough to handle my doubts who doesn't expect me to be perfect. You've given us a gift more powerful than the protection we have to offer." There was a new glow in Ross's eyes too.

"Thank you, Lord." The four friends joined hands and Kieran offered a prayer of thanks, even though their struggle wasn't over. The two had seen them at their worst, yet God used them anyway. "All our problems are worth it. And I mean it. If God spoke through our trials, we wouldn't have it any other way."

"We're glad to stick around for a while and learn more from you two." Eilidh placed an arm around Bonny. "While we're sorry Gavin hasn't been found, we'll miss you when it's all over. Besides, your precious little girl has stolen our hearts."

"When we no longer need protection, you're welcome here any time." Kieran placed a hand over his heart. "Here's to finding my cousin. Soon. I'd much rather you were our friends than bodyguards."

03 80

Bonny covered her eyes with one hand when Kieran rolled over, turned on the light, and reached for the ringing phone. The grandfather clock downstairs struck two a.m., and she wished for more sleep while wondering what crisis necessitated the call.

"Already? Of course, we'll get on the road right away. I'll let you know what time we'll arrive."

Wide-awake now, she scooted across the sheets. "What's wrong?"

"We're going to have a son today, *mo chridhe*. They've put Mary in hospice with only days to live, and Bethan notified the social worker on call she's in labor. We're off to Aberdeen."

Bonny gave him a quick kiss, grabbed her robe as she leaped from the bed, and headed for the door. "It's good we finished the nursery over the weekend. I'll wake Jess. You tell Ross and Eilidh. At least we have a lot of helpers."

A few hours later, Ross pulled the Land Rover into the hospital parking lot. Kieran unloaded a bag stuffed with diapers and the blue outfit Bonny wanted to bring their son home in, along with the ice chest of milk donated by their nursing friends.

Brighde greeted them with hugs in the hospital lobby. "They wheeled Bethan into the delivery room a few minutes ago. Let's head upstairs."

Two hours later, a nurse escorted them to a room near the nursery, where Brighde cradled a blue bundle. "He's a big one. Eleven pounds two ounces. Cesarean birth. No complications, but too large."

Bonny reached for him. "Ainslie's chosen Da as her favorite. This one's mine." A daughter and son within one month. She held her breath and lifted the blanket from the tiny face. "Kieran, he's a redhead."

"The way God reveals a sense of humor in the circumstances he orchestrates removes all sense of doubt." One finger nudged the blankets away. "You'll need a wagon to cart him around."

Little eyes screwed tight, and the pink lips opened wide in a wail that almost made her drop him. "Andrew Hamish, you have a healthy set of lungs. Let's see about your appetite."

"Mother's milk, right?" She seated herself in the nearest chair, and the nurse handed her a bottle.

"Yes, we have several friends who offered to supply us, though they didn't plan on one who'd eat so much." The tiny mouth tugged on the nipple with astonishing strength, undisturbed while Kieran poked through blankets, seeking out fingers and toes. "Such a wee one."

"Kieran, he's huge."

Bonny thought Brighde might fall out of her chair laughing. "He's twice the size of Brennan. The other two … Well, let's just say MacDonell genes grow them large." She cleared her throat. "I want to check in on Bethan. Remember, she has to sign papers. She can still change her mind on both."

At seven p.m., Bonny curled into Kieran's arms. "Well, Da, we have our complete family. I never imagined she'd sign the papers today. Mary was right. She's not prepared to be a mom."

"Poor girl. Look at the mess she's made of her life at sixteen. I could never give those lovely babies to anyone."

A wave of emotion swelled in her throat and set her heart pounding. "And you once said you could never love someone else's children."

"God does have a way of communicating his intentions. I can't swim against such a strong tide of love. No matter how many times the waves overflow, I have more to give. Thank you for pushing me."

The intensity of Kieran's embrace formed a life preserver in a life filled with uncertainty. Happiness and the excitement about the future flooded her with a passion equal to his and swept her away.

❧

Pressed close to Kieran's side, Bonny grew aware of the gentle strains of "The Rosebud of Allenvale" playing in the background of her dream.

"Wake up." Kieran nudged her. Where were they?

Her eyes snapped open. The Marcliffe Hotel. Aberdeen. Andrew Hamish MacDonell, of course.

"Honey, your alarm. We're taking our son home today."

She silenced her phone and rubbed the sleep from her eyes.

"I dreamed of you all night long, *mo gràdh*. The last I remember you were running across the pasture with a baby on each arm."

"Running? With those two? Not likely. Do you realize if Drew's birthweight is any prediction of how big he's going to grow he'll pass Ainslie's weight in no time?"

"It was a beautiful picture." He pulled her tight against him and kissed her. "I suspect our morning cuddles are at an end for a few years."

His sleepy scent of soap and sweat would have made her linger on any other day. "Kieran, it's 5:30. We promised to meet Brighde at 7:30 to pick up the baby."

He rolled over and sat up. "We need to stop at the Land Rover dealer before we head home. Ross made some phone calls yesterday."

"Two babies aren't enough? We need a new car?"

"Two babies with all their gear and a third bodyguard. We can't take two vehicles everywhere. They had a slightly used seven-passenger for a good trade."

Morning traffic, a forgotten inconvenience after life on the farm, slowed their progress toward the hospital. They signed the papers, changed a diaper, and headed for the farm.

When they stopped in front of the house, Hamish came out first with Ainslie in his arms and a grin as wide as Loch Garry. "Look who's taken to her Grandda. All it took was getting you two out of the way."

Maggie passed him on the way down the steps. "I let Hamish hold her so Granny gets first look at your wee laddie." Lifting him from the car seat, Kieran held the baby toward her. She stopped, hand over mouth. "You never said he was a ginger baby. Give him to me."

"We kept him wrapped up for the picture on purpose."

"Oh, Kieran, I never imagined he would be big like you with hair so close to the same color. Bonny, I was wrong to criticize your plans. They're lovely children."

Along with Eleanor, Angus, and Jess, Janet and Graeme came through the door, bringing their little Brody to meet his future playmate. All afternoon, friends arrived nonstop with gifts and food. God's blessings more than made up for their trials.

ͣȢ

Bonny loaded more baby clothes into the dryer, shoved the next batch into the washing machine, then headed to the kitchen. The time when both babies slept each afternoon had become precious over the last two months. Though she had far more help than most mothers ever dreamed of—thanks to their protectors' assimilation into the household—the women prized their time of silence. Eilidh was in the shower after their walk. With Jess out for a run, Bonny had few moments alone.

She smiled at the thought of Jess whose gift with children was a godsend. The baby's protector fit well into their odd family group. She enjoyed farm life and offered countless hints for how to help Ainslie adjust.

Lifting the laundry basket filled with warm towels, Bonny glanced out the window in time to see Jess head up the hill by the barn, nearing the bridge. Walking alone and carefree outdoors was a distant memory. She grimaced at the realization of how long it had been.

"Mum-mum." Ainslie's cry sounded through the baby monitor.

"There goes our easy afternoon. It's her tooth coming in." She set the basket down and headed for the stairs before her crying daughter could awaken Drew.

The front doorbell rang, and she detoured to the entry hall to look through the peephole. She never answered the door these days, but at the sight of Brighde, she swung it wide. "Auntie, what are you doing all the way out here? Come in."

Puddles formed in the MacDonell-blue eyes. "Bonny … Gavin—"

"Shut yer gob, old woman, and get inside." With the thump of large boots on the stone porch, the hulk of a man stepped into sight, shoving Brighde to the floor. Black hair reached to massive shoulders and stood up in a greasy rooster's comb, a few tangled braids around his face sported feathers. Amber eyes radiated hate like heat from an open flame. If not for the kilt of faded MacDonell tartan, which hung almost to his ankles in back, he reminded Bonny of Native American warriors in old Westerns. They were under attack.

She stooped to help Brighde up, but the sneering giant jerked her away so hard she stumbled against the wall. A strong scent of body odor and peat smoke assailed her nostrils, and she peered into eyes of a mountain lion ready to pounce.

Ainslie had succeeded in waking Drew and both screamed for attention. Bonny's arm burned from his grip, and he thrust her toward the stairs. "Mongrels will never inherit MacDonell land and deny me my heritage. Hang the courts. You and those brats are comin' with me."

"No." The rage of a mother grizzly erupted from Bonny's throat. "I'll go anywhere. Do anything. Kill me if you like, but my babies stay here. Kieran will give you whatever you want."

He stopped her protest with duct tape over her mouth and did the same to Brighde, binding her hands and feet. Opening the door to the hall closet, he tossed his mother on the floor, and slammed the door.

Bonny kicked with her right foot, hoping to catch him unaware. Her blow had no more effect than a fly caught in a spider's web. Gavin matched her husband's height but surpassed him in bulk, muscles bulging larger than Kieran's when he competed in the Highland Games. She attempted to wriggle free the way a fish squirms against a hook but he dragged her to the top of the stairs. Strangled cries erupted from her throat in hopes of alerting Eilidh but resulted in a blow to her windpipe. She gasped in pain.

When he neared Ainslie's door, a gunshot boomed from across the hall and entered the wall beside him. With a snarl, Gavin pushed Bonny to the floor and lunged. Eilidh's second round went wild. He pounced and squeezed the gun from her grasp. She bit the hand over her mouth. He roared. Knocking her head against the wall, he yanked the tape from his pocket and plastered it across her lips. Hands and feet secured, he propelled her back into the room and slammed the door.

In the moments he grappled with Eilidh, Bonny grabbed Ainslie and slipped into Drew's room. If only she had time to make it to the back stairs. She seized her son when one massive arm lifted around her waist, almost cutting off her breath. Dropping her, he snatched Ainslie away. "I'll take her. That should stop your tricks. Make a sound and I'll strangle them both."

She stumbled down the stairs before him, her arm grasped tight. Babies wailing, he flung the front door open. An ancient Land Rover, riddled with rust and so many colors of paint it appeared to have resurrected from a junkyard sat at the foot of the steps, back door open.

Dragging her toward the truck, he froze. She followed his gaze toward the bridge where Jess ran full speed toward the house. Her yells brought Ross and Kieran from the barn at a run.

Gavin snarled an expletive in Gaelic. "Too many people. Drop the screaming brats and get in the truck." He flung Ainslie to the ground, wrenched Drew from her arms, and pitched him where his head almost collided with the porch steps. With brutal force, he thrust her into the truck and slammed the door.

Gunn climbed in and the engine sputtered to life. Bonny toppled onto her side when he gunned it and roared out of the drive onto the single-track, cylinders knocking. An explosion rocked the truck. Swerving wildly, he aimed a shot out the window.

A scream stopped at her tape-bound lips.

The madman revved the engine and continued down the road, metal grating on dirt. "Your *eejit* husband shot my tire. There's a bloody army around here. I'll get those brats yet. I'm done waitin' for what's mine."

∞

Time was interminable on a dark, Scottish, winter afternoon. With the truck windows tinted brown, Bonny lost all sense of direction. Once away from the farm, Gavin stopped in some rutted, uneven spot, bound her wrists and feet, and changed the tire Kieran shot. He kept to dirt roads. The vehicle bumped and groaned, gears grinding in protest of their rugged path.

It was late when they screeched to a stop, pausing Bonny's continuous prayer for her babies, Kieran, and the police. Rusty door hinges protested as Gavin climbed out. About the time she feared he might leave her in the frigid cold, the back door whined open. Rough hands jerked her upright in the mud. He slid a huge knife from his belt and cut the tape binding her legs.

Bonny squinted through the dark at an old *bothy*, visible by the faintest light flickering through two small windows. He dragged her through the creaky door where an inadequate peat fire smoldered in a small fireplace. A large person, she assumed a woman, stood at a stove, back to the door.

Gavin forced her into the other room where a single oil lamp sputtered on a crooked table. Shoving her into a rickety chair, he cut the tape from her wrists, rebound them behind the chair, and taped her legs again. He stomped from the room and slammed the door.

Voices sounded in low tones from the other room. Once, she heard a slap and sharp cry. Heavy boots tramped across the dirt floor before the door slammed, and the muffler thundered into the distance. A woman's sobs sounded from the other room. The only other sound was the drip of rain on the metal roof. Could it be Deirdre out there?

With Gavin gone, danger seemed less imminent. The knowledge of Ainslie and Drew's safety gave Bonny hope. An occasional sound drifted through the door. A drink of water and the bathroom would be welcome.

She resumed her prayers, begging for the police to come and the courage to stand strong. Surely God wouldn't give them a family only to allow her to die.

ଔ ଓ

Kieran cradled Drew against his chest and paced the floor. The children, bruised and scraped, had cried themselves to sleep. Jess perched on a straight-backed chair in the corner on full alert, eyes roving from window to door to Kieran.

Downstairs, the library, with its huge map of Stonehaven Farm, served as a command center where DS Alasdair Kavanaugh and DCI McLeod took charge.

Kieran's emotions swung from relief for the children's safety to white-hot anger at Bonny's capture. He needed to do something. Now.

From the moment Jess ran past the barn yelling about a strange truck at the house, he knew he alone could stop the madness. Bonny was the means, but he and the farm were the targets.

He laid Drew in the middle of the big four-poster bed, tucked the blanket around him, and motioned Jess out the door. "I have to talk some sense into McLeod and Alasdair."

Did she let him pass because a hungry wolf stared from his eyes?

The library buzzed with voices, phones, computers, and radios. Bedlam filled his home because of a maniac, a cousin, but a fiend nevertheless. McLeod looked up from the map. "Kieran, I was on my way to break some news."

"I can't sit still while Gavin uses Bonny for bait. It's me he wants. My children won't grow up in fear. Find Bonny and send me in alone. Hang the farm."

The inspector rested a hand on his shoulder. "First, you need to listen. We know how Gunn poisoned so many sheep during the *ceilidh* and stole an entire flock without attracting attention. Right now, officers are headed to your barn to arrest accomplices we never knew existed. Your aunt informed us that Seumas and Jamie Matheson are cousins to Gavin and Deirdre. They've been involved since the beginning. The dogs didn't bark because they knew the intruders."

Outside the window, he saw four armed police head into the barn. Kieran's knees buckled and he dropped into a chair. "I can't watch. Friends who painted Ainslie's bedroom. Men I trusted to protect my family conspired against me?"

"It will be over soon, and you can rest in the knowledge we caught them all."

"It must have taken years to get all the players in place. I never had a clue." He covered his eyes. "I have to get to Bonny. Draw Gavin into the open."

"We're sending in a team. Wait until they're in place. Eat something. If necessary, we'll take you." The inspector nodded toward the kitchen and grabbed the phone.

Auntie Brighde sat at the kitchen table, head down, tears dropping onto her hands.

He downed one sandwich in four bites and gulped a large glass of water. The smoldering anger grew to a fire of determination. He headed upstairs for hunting camo, then back to the kitchen. He tugged on hunting boots and crammed his pockets with food and water.

"Kieran," Brighde reached her hand toward him. "I'm sorry. I knew Gavin was angry and mean. I had no idea he'd go so far. Let me talk to him."

"No, Auntie. It's me he wants. It's not your fault. Only God can stop him. Even the hardest heart isn't immune to the workings of the Lord. I'll do my part or die trying."

"I don't know. Maybe if I had clung to my faith, my family wouldn't have come to this. It's my fault for refusing to listen to my parents. If I accepted the truth about Taran, things would have been so different. I only hope Gavin someday knows he is loved."

"God's forgiveness is only limited by our failure to seek it. He's always waiting with open arms." Kieran cleared his throat. Perhaps in time, Auntie Brighde and her family would discover the God who understood their tragedy and wanted to heal their hearts.

She shook her head. "I don't know what I believe anymore."

"Trust me then. I'll do my best to see that he lives." His boots dropped chunks of dry mud between the kitchen and library.

Several officers bent over a large topographical map spread across a table in the center of the library. Alasdair waved him over and pointed to a tiny speck on the map. "Brennan claims Gavin sometimes used a *bothy* to the southwest on the lower slopes of *Beinn Tee*. Are you familiar with the area?"

"Aye, I've hunted deer there. The *bothy's* rough, but still used."

"We have a plane headed there now. We need eyes on it, and a chopper would alert them. It's risky, but you know that." McLeod's voice was low and gravelly. "How long does it take to get there from here?"

Kieran breathed a prayer of gratitude. He was headed into familiar territory. "Half an hour if you move slow and cautious. Would he keep her so close?"

"Don't think about going alone. Let our team get there." Alasdair grabbed the radio when it squawked.

The radio crackled. "We've got smoke from the chimney. No vehicles."

"Kieran." McLeod gripped his arm. "It's a little over a mile from the A82 at Laggan Locks, and they're coming from Fort William. Go upstairs and wait."

"Aye, if you say so." He turned and walked out of the room. A daylight kidnapping proved Gavin was desperate. He detoured through the kitchen where Eleanor consoled Brighde and ran to the barn for his old truck. Only he could end Gavin's insanity.

⚜

Low four-wheel drive gears growling, the truck jolted up a rutted road toward *Beinn Tee*. So far, no one followed him. Kieran steered carefully up the rock-strewn hillside, barren except for a few isolated trees. He breathed a prayer of gratitude because one of the few forested areas lay near the old *bothy*. Resolve solidified, he prepared to sacrifice the farm, his life, everything, to save Bonny and the children.

His mobile rang. "Kieran, it's Alasdair. Get back here now."

"I have the power to bargain with Gavin and end it with no loss of life."

Alasdair groaned. "An old, rusted Rover just turned off the A82. It's about ten minutes behind you, in the other direction. The team will be at Laggan Locks in thirty minutes. Wait for them." Alasdair's concern was clear, though phone reception wasn't.

"Right. I'm speeding up. I prefer to beat him, hide my vehicle, and walk in."

"You have no idea who's there. We're not even positive Bonny's inside. Don't go in alone. Wait for the team."

He tossed the phone across the seat and pressed down the accelerator. If Gavin got there first, he might kill Bonny before the police arrived. A couple of miles further, and the trees closest to the cottage loomed on his right. He backed in among some tall firs, dragged broken branches over the truck, and studied the cottage.

Tugging on a camo ski cap, he headed into the open at a dead run, stopping at the corner of the cottage. He crouched below the small window, then ran for the door and shoved inside.

"I surrender!"

He looked into the fear-glazed eyes of a woman with hands raised. The air, pungent with mold, wood rot, and hazy with peat smoke, burned his eyes.

"My brother forced me. It's not my fault."

"Deirdre?" He pulled the cap off.

"Kieran. Thank God you came."

He crossed the small room in two strides. "Gavin's not far behind."

"Bonny's in the other room. Don't worry about me. Save her." She unlocked the door and shoved past him. She looked up, tiny and wide-eyed in the dark room. A muffled sound issued from her throat. Pulling out his pocket knife, he cut the tape binding her hands and feet and tugged it gently from her mouth.

"Kieran!" Bonny lunged for him and he held her close. "Oh, Kieran, I prayed you'd come."

"Now, pray we get out of here safe. Gavin's almost to the cottage." He loosened his grip on her and turned. "Deirdre, do you have a gun? I won't leave you to him."

She shook her head and looked around. "Just kitchen utensils and the bar for the door. Please, stop him."

"Bonny, behind the bed. Deirdre, help me?"

The corners of her mouth quirked into an evil grin. "Aye, with pleasure." Stepping into the other room, she grabbed the heavy wooden bar.

"Hit him hard when he enters. I'll come out and subdue him." He stepped behind the door.

Without warning, the door screeched open. A shotgun barrel entered first. *Bang! Bang!* Both barrels fired.

Kieran leaped from behind the door and knocked the gun from Gavin's hands. The big man roared with anger and lunged.

Deirdre brought the bar down hard, opening a wound on the back of his head.

Gunn roared a curse in Gaelic and crumpled to the dirt. When Kieran knelt on his back, Gavin bellowed like an angry bull and reared, knocking him off. It was inhuman what the man could do with a bleeding head. Gavin staggered and dragged Kieran to his feet. With maniacal strength, he tightened his grip around Kieran's neck.

Bonny screamed.

Spurred by her outrage, Kieran grasped Gavin's forearms and shoved until the vise-like grip loosened.

"Thief." Gunn's voice was a muted growl. "You'll never imprison me like my weakling brother."

Kieran backed him into the wall and punched him in the face. He slumped, blood dripping from his misshapen nose.

"You animal! I'll see you rot in jail." Deirdre aimed the shotgun at her brother. "You raped me. Abused our brother. Kidnapped us from our parents. You deserve worse than prison."

Gavin moaned while Kieran tied his hands behind him.

"Deirdre, no. The police will be here any minute."

Bonny ran from the other room and stopped at Deirdre's side. "Don't sink to his level. Your mother needs you and so does Brennan."

"He stole our lives. Forced us to hurt you. Killed your flocks." Deirdre's amber eyes, so like her brother's, filled with tears, and she lowered the gun. "I hate him."

"You're doing the right thing. The law will punish him." Bonny eased the gun from her hands.

Kieran bound the big man hands and feet before he yanked him to a sitting position and dumped a basin of water over his head. "Tell me why. Why do you want to destroy me and my family?"

The wounded man looked up and snarled like a rabid wolf. "Your father stole our land and left us to starve."

Deirdre grabbed her brother by the hair and peered into his eyes. "We starved because you, Da, and Grandda were lazy and no good. Ma and Robbie loved us. They tried to give us a better life but you were too full of anger to accept it."

Kieran knelt in front of him. "Why didn't you come and talk to me like a man? We could have worked something out."

"I want you dead. But first, I'll kill your wife and children while you watch. You marry an American and call mongrel brats MacDonell. They'll never own MacDonell land. I hate you. We groveled and scraped while you grew rich. Enjoyed fancy schools, a big house, and fine flocks. We froze. Starved. My mother, always findin' fault—sayin' my father and uncle were lazy and mean. Tellin' me to be different. I'll see you dead. I'll see you all dead."

Kieran pulled a handkerchief from his pocket and gagged him. "That's enough, 'cousin.'"

The doorway darkened and he looked up to see a policeman. A heavy sigh of relief escaped. He was so tired. "Thank you for coming. Take him out of here."

"I'll tell you what he did." Deirdre twisted her hands. "He should never go free."

When two large officers took Gavin under the arms and jerked him to his feet, Kieran let himself go to Bonny. "Guard him well. I want my family safe."

She wrapped her arms around him. "I love you, Kieran MacDonell," she murmured against his chest. "I knew you'd come. Now take me home to our babies and Deirdre to her mother."

Her soft, warm lips quivered. He closed his eyes, almost unable to breathe from the joy of holding her again. "Let's go home, love. It's over at last."

The police shoved Gavin into the back of a Land Rover as Kieran led the women outside.

Heavy, wet snowflakes drifted down and Bonny shivered. He pulled off his jacket and wrapped it around her shoulders. "The truck's over there. Can you walk?"

"Walking sounds good. I sat long enough. Are the babies alright? What about Eilidh and Brighde?"

"All fine. Deirdre," Kieran met her eyes over Bonny's head. "Don't blame yourself for what he forced you into. You're family now. We'll help you."

She tucked her head. "Thank you. It's more than I deserve."

"You're wrong. You have our forgiveness. If you want it, you have a job at Stonehaven Farm. We'll help you overcome the abuse you've suffered."

She turned to Bonny. "I'm sorry for everything. I never knew until recently that Kieran was my cousin."

"I forgive you, cousin."

Deirdre looked at the ground. "I never believed in God. But I watched you. No matter what Gavin did, you built your chapel, loved each other, helped people. I don't understand."

Bonny reached for her hand. "We'll help you, and someday you'll understand."

Kieran looked toward the clouds and heaved the first deep breath in a long time. With Bonny safe, his heart could beat again. Their family was reunited. Two beautiful babies waited at home. In spite of the clouds above, the sun shone because his wife walked alongside him, free.

☙❧

Maggie and Hamish stood in the yard holding the babies when they drove up. Bonny's breath caught at the sight of Ainslie and Drew. Their bodyguards and the detectives were all there. Family. She brushed her cheeks with her hand, jumped out of the truck, and ran to her children.

"Da." Ainslie held out her arms to Kieran while Bonny reached for Drew. Her husband's solid arm wrapped around her, pulling their little family close. His tears mingled with hers, lips pressing into her hair.

She breathed the sweet smell of her babies. "We're safe."

"I came so close to losing you." Kieran choked on the words. "But God protected us."

"It could have been so much worse." She looked deep into his eyes. "I had a lot of time to think and pray. Kieran, I've behaved badly at times. I acted out of fear, not faith, and failed to trust you or God."

He chewed his lip. "I wanted to kill Gavin. When he called our children mongrel brats, I realized, to my shame, that my attitude about adoption was no different than what he said about mongrels. I was so wrong."

"You're not like him. You were afraid. Our baby's death will always hurt, as will Liam's. But these two—how could our family be more perfect? I haven't learned all the lessons I need to either. But we're going to be fine because God never leaves us alone, even when life seems the darkest. His bars of iron and bronze protected us."

The End